THE MARRIAGE CLUB

KATE LEGGE is an award-winning journalist who has covered politics and social affairs in Australia and the United States. She edited *The Australian's Review of Books* in 1997 and now writes for the *Weekend Australian Magazine*. She is married with two children and lives in Melbourne. Her first novel, *The Unexpected Elements of Love*, was longlisted for the Miles Franklin Literary Award.

PENGUIN BOOKS

KATE LEGGE THE MARRIAGE CLUB

PENGUIN BOOKS

Published by the Penguin Group
Penguin Group (Australia)
250 Camberwell Road, Camberwell, Victoria 3124, Australia
(a division of Pearson Australia Group Pty Ltd)
Penguin Group (USA) Inc.
375 Hudson Street, New York, New York 10014, USA
Penguin Group (Canada)
90 Eglinton Avenue East, Suite 700, Toronto, Canada ON M4P 2Y3
(a division of Pearson Penguin Canada Inc.)
Penguin Books Ltd
80 Strand, London WC2R 0RL, England
Penguin Ireland
25 St Stephen's Green, Dublin 2, Ireland
(a division of Penguin Books Ltd)
Penguin Books India Pvt Ltd
11 Community Centre, Panchsheel Park, New Delhi – 110 017, India
Penguin Group (NZ)
67 Apollo Drive, Rosedale, North Shore 0632, New Zealand
(a division of Pearson New Zealand Ltd)
Penguin Books (South Africa) (Pty) Ltd
24 Sturdee Avenue, Rosebank, Johannesburg 2196, South Africa

Penguin Books Ltd, Registered Offices: 80 Strand, London, WC2R 0RL, England

First published by Penguin Group (Australia), 2009
This edition published by Penguin Group (Australia), 2010

10 9 8 7 6 5 4 3 2 1

Cover design by Allison Colpoys © Penguin Group (Australia)
Text design by Anne-Marie Reeves © Penguin Group (Australia)
Cover photograph © Dana Hoff/Beateworks/Corbis (door) and © Image Source/Getty Images (hand)
Typeset in Fairfield Light by Sunset Digital Pty Ltd, Brisbane, Queensland
Printed and bound in Australia by McPherson's Printing Group, Maryborough, Victoria

National Library of Australia
Cataloguing-in-Publication data:

Legge, Kate, 1957–
The marriage club / Kate Legge.
ISBN 9780143202806 (pbk.)
Marriage – Fiction.
Man–woman relationships – Fiction.

A823.4

penguin.com.au

Mixed Sources
Product group from well-managed
forests and other controlled sources
www.fsc.org Cert no. SGS-COC-004121
© 1996 Forest Stewardship Council

FSC

For J.D.L.

When Leith Kremmer was growing up there were things that she learnt to lock away in air-tight compartments.

Once, arriving home early from school, she came upon her mother in the arms of a stranger. That night, when she was setting the table for dinner, her mother drew Leith's gaze and held it, as if daring her daughter to blink. The stranger was never mentioned although he continued to call.

Leith had sensed remorse at least in her father's glassy eyes when she came upon him raiding her piggy bank for the dollar bills she'd saved judiciously over the sum of her short life. He'd held his nicotine-stained finger to his lips. 'I'll pay it back, with interest,' he'd whispered, always sure his luck was turning.

The family sat on her brother Cameron's secret until he left for a place where he could skip free.

Leith had never suspected their grandmother's artful concealment. Then one morning she took a sip from the matriarch's cup of tea and spat out a mouthful of whisky. The old woman leant close to recover her cup and saucer. 'The trick to secrets is where you stow them,' she'd confided.

SUNDAY

Ensconced in her comfortably cushioned chair, supplements from the paper strewn around her feet, Leith listens to her husband George descend the staircase, the clip of his shoes on the tiled hallway as he swings through the kitchen to loom at her side. He waits for her attention. She hooks her liquorice-black hair behind her ears and adjusts her frameless glasses – small swift movements. Not once lifting her eyes from the columns of print, she notices in the periphery George's dark-brown corduroy pants and his two-tone golf shoes, white leather, heeled and fringed in tan, dapper.

'I'm going out for a hit,' he says.

'You sound like one of the junkies in this article I'm reading,' she leavens the tension.

'I'll visit Margaret after I'm done.'

'Thank you,' Leith's grateful at being relieved of a Sunday duty that she dislikes as much as Margaret, George's 92-year-old mother, who's pricklier and sourer for the indignity of outliving her husband and her friends.

'I've made her some biscuits,' Leith says, getting up to fetch a blue tin decorated with lilies. 'Her favourites, ginger shortbread.' She opens the lid and offers him a golden-coloured square, the sweet, buttery aroma rich in the thin air between them. 'I hope you don't get a blast from her about the niggers on the night shift.' She hands him the tin. 'Tolerance seems to be the only faculty Margaret's lost. If she ever had it.'

George fences Margaret off, letting her opinions and judgements – on manners, euthanasia, the human condition – go unchallenged. His mother restricts Leith's influence to the realm of toiletries, as if lanoline and soap are the sum of Margaret's faith in her daughter-in-law's capacity.

'I'll be back around six,' George says as he bends down to pick up the papers at Leith's feet, putting them in a neat pile on the table. 'What've you got planned?'

'Shopping with Eva. I thought I might get Jesse a few things. He needs a Polartec vest and a pair of gloves.'

George warms at this mention of their youngest son. 'Tasmania's an ice box in winter. He's got no idea what he's in for.'

'I think I'll go and see him. Cook him some soups to fuel him up. Fill the freezer.' She cherishes her mothering all the more in these lean years.

'Good idea,' George approves. 'I'm jealous. I miss him.' Protectiveness towards their adult sons, Jesse and Art, solders he and Leith together.

'You can go when it snows. You like the cold.' He smiles at her observation as he leaves the room. She hears him pause in front of the hall mirror as he always does, to straighten kinks in his appearance. The front door shuts. She's not far behind him, catching every red light, on her way to pick up Eva, convincing herself this is not some portent.

Eva's waiting, as promised, on the corner of her street, her full lips tightly set, hands deep in the pockets of her quilted knee-length coat, stooped a little against the wind and the brunt of mid-life disappointments. Leith wishes her a second chance, a surprise, a boon, something to bounce her step. Their friendship was one forged in youth and reinforced by the weathering years of consequence. They'd met on the tram, rattling their way to university, noticing each other the moment Eva hopped on in the city. Out of breath and flushed from running in heavy black clogs, she'd plonked down opposite Leith, who was calmly collected after her long commute from the suburbs. They didn't exchange names until they fell into step walking across the forecourt. Eva wore a tight T-shirt with an anti-war slogan, its red letters enlarged by her generous chest. Leith held a new leather briefcase, initials stamped in gold above the catch. Eva was to discover that Leith Davies had inherited her mother's fondness for accessorising. A clutch purse, a pair of tortoiseshell spectacles, a detachable fox-fur collar, plucked from a drawer granting either woman instant membership of whichever club or coterie they needed to impress. Eva's parents were clever Polish migrants and just as creative at stretching whatever they possessed; but their nous was a necessary survival instinct whereas the Davies' lives were never at risk, merely their ambitious goals.

Leith and Eva drive to a nearby shopping mall, circling for a park, every space taken on this Sunday morning. 'Well,' Leith says, 'there's obviously no one at church!' She peals with laughter. Eva loves Leith's laugh, which always begins with a high-pitched honk, warming the air, priming her audience for amusement. The car slows to a crawl, stalking a man with keys in his hand. While they wait for him to leave, Eva picks out a tawny-streaked seashell from amongst loose coins in the tray between their seats.

'Jesse found it on his travels,' Leith says, watching Eva turn it in her hand, curiously. 'He spent a few days photographing a bay where they used to gut whales. He said the sea would be stained crimson with blood and carcasses.' She wraps her falsehood in fabulous detail as Eva tries to remember where she's come across a shell just like this one, just the other day. She worries at her wooliness, but thoughts of the shell's twin are swept aside as she reaches for her bag, listening to Leith chat about the ferry she'll ride across Bass Strait so that she can drive her car in Tasmania.

'I'm going to get some things for Jesse so you might want to browse for a bit,' Leith says.

'I can't browse!' Eva shrieks. 'You know that.' She tags behind Leith, who's quick and sure in a shop, making straight for the outdoor section of menswear, flicking through the racks as if she works here. Picking a bright aquamarine vest, she holds it at arm's length, feeling the pockets, the finish, the thickness. She doesn't ask for Eva's opinion, simply checks the label for size and takes it to the cashier. 'Gloves?' she asks him and he points across the way to a tabletop. Leith sniffs at the small selection. She tries on large fur-lined leather gloves that fit like baseball mitts on her bird-claw hands. 'Soft,' she purrs, 'but he needs to be a hundred per cent waterproof, so perhaps I'll get these,' and she fingers a black pair, lightweight, expensive.

'Scientifically tested,' Eva snorts as she reads the manufacturer's tag. Leith's extravagance, her brand loyalties, feed Eva's superiority. It's a small niggle in the scheme of their lifelong friendship.

'I can't bear to think of him freezing down there. I have these nightmares that he's gone missing, outdoors, in the biting rain,' Leith's voice wrings.

'You worry too much,' Eva shrugs. Her only daughter lives overseas, fiercely independent. Leith envied Eva her girl for the dresses and indulgences and intimacies of special outings.

They take the escalator down to the bridal registry. Eva's niece is marrying next month. Guests have been furnished with a wish list. Together they peruse the couple's tastes in manchester, silverware, saucepans.

'Sheepskin mattress protector,' Eva scoffs. 'Waffle toaster. Romantic!'

'Practical,' Leith says, alternating roles as they've done for decades, taking turns at rebellion. 'Get the stemless wine glasses.'

'I guess you can never have too many,' Eva says dryly. 'What did I give you and George? Honestly, my memory's kaput.'

Leith laughs. '*The Kamasutra*. How could you forget?'

'Guests got to choose in those days,' Eva defends herself. 'It's outrageous being told what to buy as if you can't be trusted. I've still got the cookbooks you gave me. Elizabeth David. Vince taught himself to cook the perfect omelette.'

'How's his new job?'

'There's an internal review, so he feels vulnerable and I'm not sympathetic enough. We've hardened to each other. When I left today I realised, when I was halfway down the street, that I'd forgotten to say goodbye to him.'

'The hardening,' Leith says. 'I know exactly what you mean.' She thinks of the small courtesies, small civilities, discarded unwittingly.

'It doesn't have to be that way. I mean, look at Bernadette and Monty.'

'There's always an exception,' Leith sighs, steering Eva into a café, lucky to find a spare booth. She pushes the dirty plates to one side then picks up the menu. She can't stop herself – even in

9

a cheap food court like this – from studying inventories of meals and snacks compulsively, open to inspiration.

A teenage girl stands awkwardly, bulging in her tight jeans and T-shirt, ready to take their order.

'Peppermint tea, please,' Leith decides.

'For two, thanks,' Eva follows her lead. Outsiders might think she's boss, with her career and strong opinions, but she's impressionable in Leith's company, falling sway to mannerisms or accents that infiltrate her lexicon for days afterwards. A streak of white hair stripes the right side of her thick brown curls. She gets sick of telling people it's natural.

'It's your birthday next month,' Leith says. 'We should go away for a weekend, all of us, somewhere nice. Why don't I plan something?'

Eva's stuck for an answer. Everything before her seems flat, rolling on unrelentingly. Death has nothing to rob her of any more. That, at least, is a novel sensation. 'I think I'm catching Rosie's disease.'

'You're not an alcoholic!'

'No. Melancholia.'

'We've all got that. It's an epidemic,' Leith laughs and Eva grins. The waitress interrupts with their beverages. 'I was thinking today,' she continues, 'of how the boys used to surf off the rocks in summer, how they'd wait for the wave to wash over before they'd launch their boards. If you waited a moment too long, you'd have to hang about until the next one. Jesse was too cautious. He used to get stuck waiting to jump.'

'That's me.'

'Me, too,' Leith offers her support.

'Particularly at the moment,' Eva says. 'I'm so low on confidence.'

'I know.'

'Does it show?'

'No, I mean I understand.' She reaches out and grasps Eva's hand.

'God, we're a pair.'

'I don't think we're alone. Over there,' Leith diverts Eva's gaze to a middle-aged couple at a table by the window, silently staring off in different directions. 'Look at those two. They're dying before each others' eyes.'

'They could be madly in love. You just don't know. You never do.'

Leith takes a sip of tea. 'You're absolutely right. You never do.'

MONDAY

Glancing up at the Roman numerals on his grandfather clock, George Kremmer selects a putter from the rack he keeps in his Family Court chambers for practising his short game whenever he can snare a moment for himself. He chooses a Scotty Cameron Newport 2, the model Tiger Woods made famous when he won the 1997 Masters. As soon as his fingers connect with the grip a lightness pulses through him. From the windows of his corner suite on the tenth floor he can see the mauve and turquoise folds of Mount Macedon to the far north-west of the city.

He shoots a glance up at the overcast sky then down upon the swill of humanity streaming across the forecourt into the belly of the steel and glass tower. The austerity of its sharp angles and clean lines foils the messy domestic tangles that preoccupy those who come here.

The black shirts are protesting out front again. From where he stands behind the double glazing, George can't hear a word these

disgruntled fathers shout, but he admires their zeal. The compunc-
tion to shake things up, to set things right, once stirred his own
heart. But his head steered him along a conventional path, sub-
scribing to the values of a conservative profession, with his eyes
on the prize he now holds.

Family law, with its gable of respectability on the frontier of
social change, offered him a halfway house. His choice of special-
ity was a limp slap at his father, Sir Arthur Kremmer, a High Court
judge, who thought the new jurisdiction soft and squishy beside the
ramrod discipline of commercial or constitutional practice. If he'd
been truer about what he'd really felt, if he'd been encouraged to
express himself, if he'd only imagined how the ground would shift
so spectacularly . . . If.

Last week he'd drawn a diagram with a child at the centre
to remind him who was who in the line-up of adults claiming a
relationship. There was the mother who provided an egg, the woman
who carried the foetus inside her womb, and the one married to the
man whose sperm fertilised the ovum – a complexity inconceivable
when George joined the bar. Then, adultery was as exotic as it
got: private detectives, cameras strung around their necks, sniffing
out grounds for divorce. These days, marriages are dissolved in a
snap. You can get out of jail easily. But the freedom to leave hasn't
altered the hazards of falling in love. Broken hearts, broken homes,
broken promises hobble before George, starring all the deadliest
sins and their relatives. Occasionally he's surprised by a novel twist

of vengeance, a smash-and-grab abduction of children overseas. The stubbornest cases are reserved for a court where the buzz word is mediation. These people can't even share the same elevator but let's get them together around a table and fire the starting gun. Terrific idea! George smirks into the cuff of his billowing robe whenever he's cornered by its greatest advocate, the Chief Justice, a man ten years his junior who in his inaugural address bragged about being an agent of change. George was beaten for the top job by this brash symbol of tolerance: the son of Lebanese migrants; twice married; a former magistrate who's even admitted to inhaling, passively, in a magazine profile flattering his appointment.

For years, professional success sweetened George's personal blight. He blanches at this euphemism for his hell. Didn't some well-known psychologist once say that naming the problem is the first step towards its resolution? By that measure he should have remade himself. He smiles as he composes a salacious footnote to his 600-word entry in *Who's Who*. During lighter moments he likens himself to Germany during the Cold War, divided: on one side the heavily regulated eastern state, on the other a wild, unconquered western land beckoning him over the border.

He positions his hands precisely and firmly around the top of the shaft of his club and places his feet at ten to two on the green baize cloth. His wife, Leith, was the one who nudged him into golf to sedate the demon disfiguring his personality because she couldn't conceive of him doing yoga. She knows him intimately and yet they've become strangers in the confined space of their lives, together apart. Golf saved him. The crunch came when his personal assistant resigned, bringing the turnover of staff in his office that year to a total of three. Fluent in human resources babble, the Chief Justice asked him to attend anger-management classes. George blamed the tension on external events. The murder of a brother judge had triggered a spate of copycat death threats against him and two other judges of the court. Security was ramped up with precautions George finds suffocating.

Nothing soothes him as miraculously as a swing of the club. Every other second his mind ticks over his game, rehearsing his strokes or unravelling his grip or reflecting on the stance of his feet as he begins to address the ball – which he does now, blotting out the sound of office peak hour: the peck of his PA's fingernails on her keyboard, the elevator's ping as its doors glide open, good-natured greetings sprinkling congeniality into the air.

His father's unforgiving minutes haunted his childhood. Arthur's infrequent visits to the nursery were spent drilling young George in the value of scholarship and worship. He was barely five when he realised his father wasn't omnipotent and hadn't any idea of the subversive thoughts entertaining his son. So long as the boy had a book in his hand or a pencil poised above a sheet of a paper, Arthur felt comforted by a purposeful sense of order and took his leave. Whenever his father was held up by people who couldn't reveal something interesting or useful, George heard the stopwatch clocking wasted seconds. The meter must be genetically hard-wired; George is just as impatient in the company of ignorance. He's driven spare by the rise of litigants in person, idiots running their own cases without a counsel to steer them.

The lusty baritone of Justice Lewis alerts George to his colleague's approach before his stupendous girth barricades the door.

'You'll kill someone with that thing one day.' Lewis isn't a golfer. Singing's his passion. 'I've got two spare tickets to the opera tonight. We can't go – June's twisted her ankle.'

'Leith's got her book club at our place tonight, but thank you for thinking of us. Give June my regards. I hope you're waiting on her with a suitably exaggerated degree of servility.'

'Of course,' the judge smiles at George. 'She'd make a fine colonel. All she needs is a pith helmet and a rifle!' He exits as swiftly as he came, humming a libretto, fainter as he disappears down the corridor. George returns to the dimpled ball at his feet.

A gentle knock from the plump hand of his new associate interrupts him. 'Your honour?' she says softly as he squares his body to the target line and repeats silently to himself the advice he read last night for improved putting. Was it knees springy, shoulders level and slightly open? She waits until he strokes the ball into a plastic socket with a clunk that triggers a mechanical flag of congratulation. She refuses to praise his aim. She didn't come here to caddie.

'You're on in five minutes,' she prompts. 'Dunlop S J & Emory G C, hearing room 17B.'

The judge leans his club against the bookshelves that line the wall and picks from its foam stand a wig that he arranges on his thick silver hair, tucking a stray curl under the cap as he regards himself in the full-length mirror inside the door of a slim, built-in wardrobe. Dunlop, he thinks. He dusts a fleck of lint from the collar of the black gown before adjusting the woollen cloth over his broad frame. The details of this case elude him. 'Dunlop?'

'Dunlop S J is the father. The child is living with the mother. She's refusing him contact. They've been to mediation. The mother didn't attend the final session. He's unemployed at present.' She pauses and hands him the file, relieved by his mild demeanour.

'By the way . . .'

'What?' he stops.

'The dad's representing himself.'

'Glasses?' he hisses suddenly. 'Where are they?' His blue eyes dart over the tidy surface of his large mahogany desk where the elbows of a former Victorian governor once rested. She grabs a pair of steel-rimmed magnifiers from a small box on the shelf beside the door which her predecessor suggested she keep well stocked with cheap spectacles: the justices are at an age when sight and memory are not to be counted upon.

This is no way to start today, Leith muses, on her knees in her pale-blue satin nightie. Mop in hand, she cleans up a broken bottle that she dropped while removing George's Belgian beer from the bar fridge in the laundry to make room for the champagne she wants to chill. The phone rings and she searches for the cordless receiver vibrating under a damp towel on the bench.

'Only me.' Rosie's husky voice is instantly familiar. 'Are we on tonight, and if so, where? Whatever I've written in my diary has been crossed out. Totally illegible.'

Leith laughs. 'Everyone's muddled.' She'd arranged to host tonight's book club midway through a good red and a loud argument at last month's meeting. 'I've just had Marion on the phone.' She had rung to check whether they were expected at the big house where Leith lives on one side of the Yarra or the crowded house, as they call Bernadette's renovated cottage, on the other side of Melbourne's tea-coloured river. 'My place,' Leith tells Rosie. 'Usual time.'

'Shall I bring anything?'

'How about a few insights as proof you've read the book,' Leith laughs, stirring. Rosie is renowned for wandering off on tangents or else subjecting the group to a long-winded summary of a film she's seen because she couldn't track down the novel for discussion, or she lost it, or she lent it, or any number of excuses. 'I'm serving the most expensive champagne you can buy.'

'What's the occasion?'

'Wait and see.'

'Oh go on, tell me!'

'It's nothing,' Leith reassures her. 'I'm teasing.'

Rosie promises herself not to get half-rotten on cheap plonk beforehand.

Leith and her friends have been gathering once a month for almost twenty years and while attendance fluctuates, there's a hard core of stalwarts whose very closeness discourages newcomers. Every now and then one of them brings a stray but the visitors rarely return.

The phone rings again as Leith squeezes the mop. She dries her hands and takes the call. 'It's Bernadette.' Leith had a feeling she'd be next. 'Please tell me . . .'

'Yes,' Leith butts in.

'Thank God. I thought it might be my turn. I'm working late today and there isn't a cracker of food in the cupboard.'

Leith is known for her lavish table and Bernadette for spreading goodwill into corners of the community. She teaches English as a second language to new arrivals and lazier old comers nervous at the tightening of citizenship tests. The back of her station wagon is crammed with boxes of things for other people, hand-me-down clothes from her large brood, now scattered, plus extension cords and tools belonging to her husband Monty, a Mr Fix-it. Leith admires them, the only married couple she knows who'd happily renew their vows.

Her champagne on ice, she swishes a dry cloth over the floor and order is restored. Next door is her sweatshop, as George calls her study opposite the kitchen, big enough for her antique desk, bookshelves, and walls chock-full of photographs – the boys' bodies entwined on a swing together; standing knee-deep in surf; school portraits, braces straightening their teeth. She collects the one of them swinging, heads conked, giggles on their faces, their hilarity fresh in her memory, and puts it together with her passport and an address book from the drawer. Then she picks up a pen, holding the tip to her lips as she smiles at the calendar above her desk and composes an entry which she inscribes beneath tomorrow's date.

She pads bare-footed down the black-and-white tiled hallway, dappled with swatches of crimson, green and blue light from the stained-glass panels on either side of the front door. Her tiny figure's swamped by the cathedral spaces of a house that complements her husband's height. She turns into the master bedroom, once a ballroom – big enough to dance cheek to cheek with a rose in your teeth, although Leith and George have never dared. On the bed there's a black suitcase neatly packed with folded clothes. Between each layer is a treasured object: her father's leather-jacketed hip flask; her mother's set of babushka dolls, one inside another; the wooden box that Jesse made for her at school, tiny brass hinges on its lid; her journals; the self-portrait Art did when he was twelve. She presses her latest additions into a zippered compartment before sliding the bag beneath the bed until it is concealed by a patchwork quilt that kisses the pewter-coloured carpet. She's incredulous when she thinks now of the many hours she must have spent sewing each octagonal piece into place. She'd begun the quilt when she was pregnant with Art, setting it aside as he started to wake for longer periods, and putting it away altogether for almost a decade until she needed something therapeutic to absorb her. In these middle years the needle's jabbing was often angry, forceful, as her frustration grew. It amuses her to notice that the left-hand side warps slightly with the tightness of her stitch.

In the ensuite she washes briskly, her mind busy with all she must accomplish today. In the mirror, her face is a medley of excitement and sadness. Tears brim in her hazel eyes. She blinks them back, telling herself she's no time for second thoughts. Unscrewing the lid from a teeny frosted-glass tub on her dressing table, she takes a scoop of face cream. 'Must be made from the sweat of a very rare South American sea snail,' George had joked when he'd borrowed a dab for a dry spot on his chin the other day and seen the price tag.

They'd both laughed, a burp of gaiety that dislodged whatever was stuck between them for the briefest of moments.

The preservation of Leith's porcelain skin is a tribute to her mother, who thought beauty worthier of cultivation than an intelligence of incalculable return. She'd christened Leith her second-born while under the hair dryer admiring a British actress, Leith Hammond, on the arm of royalty in a *Women's Weekly*. To her, matches were a means of advancement, a view sharpened

23

by the mess she'd made of her own. As for Cameron, Leith's only sibling, their father had lobbied to call him Jack but their mother liked the look of an American soldier, Cameron Reeves III, whom she'd spotted in a *Reader's Digest*.

Leith had always regarded Cameron as a brother and sister rolled into one. 'Not because you're gay,' she'd once told him, because long before Cameron had announced this to the world – a shock their parents never acknowledged publicly – she'd known he was special. As children, they'd acted out the charade of family life in a two-storey doll's house, her brother's mimicry of their grandmother snoring or their mother spouting wisdoms from the pages of her glossy bibles pitch-perfect. Their father blamed himself for Cameron's difference. He scoured their childhoods as if searching for the black box at the site of a plane crash, certain that mechanical malfunction had corrupted his son's masculinity. Cameron left for America before finishing his Dip. Ed., yet another demerit their father chalked up against his son and reaffirming their estrangement. Leith's marriage to George had been all the more celebrated by her father in the forlorn hope an excess of organza could stand as proof that not all his progeny were damaged.

Dressing in a lightweight fawn sweater and charcoal trousers, Leith brushes her straight hair from crown to shoulder-length tip. With each stroke she ticks off her shopping list: red peppers; goat's cheese; calamari; olives; artichokes. They're having tapas tonight. The Spanish theme occurred to her after reading one of the poems in this month's book, Ted Hughes' public response to the death of his first wife, Sylvia Plath. He'd kept quiet for almost forty years while others filled the void. Leith had devoured Hughes' poetry then dipped into a collection of Plath's letters, stunned by the discrepancy between her chirpy recounting of events the British laureate describes from a distant vantage point through a darker lens. 'You Hated Spain,' Hughes begins his ode to their sojourn in the market village of Benidorm. They'd shared a small, pink-washed room with a balcony overlooking the blazing blue Mediterranean. Plath had sat here describing the scene to her mother in a letter dated July 7, 1956: 'I have never felt so native to a country as I do to Spain.'

Are first words truer because they spring pure, unpolluted by the mellowing of age? Or do later observations gain the authority of distance because they take consequence into account? Leith thinks of herself and George when they started out, of who she was when she first took George's arm compared to who she is now. It's the last words, she decides, that carry clout: Hughes' ink, blackened by guilt and anger, while Plath's light-hearted scribble is deaf to her destiny. These last words come weighted with insider knowledge you can't possibly glean as you stand at a fork in the road, flooded by the flimsiest of impressions. *What if?* is a game they all play, the women who belong to the book club.

Abandoned by her philandering husband, Rosie now drinks too much. Eva's job, or the lack of one, is more important than the health of her relationships. The quarterly journal she co-edited went under five months ago. 'Nobody wants to hire old women,' she'd griped to Leith yesterday after being pipped for a public relations job 'by a young girl with a fake tan and a Master's degree in bull-shit'. Prosperity's been kinder to Marion, who's grown her father's party-hire firm into an event-management business, recently add-ing funerals to the menu of functions that require planning and style. But Marion's restless, bored with her husband, cranky at becoming a grandmother. 'I just can't imagine answering to Nanna,' she'd scowled, running her hand through her bottle-blonde clip. Bernadette's youngest moved out of home a month ago, the last of her lot to lift off. Long envious of her empty nester friends, she's unsettled now by the stillness of a house that has always overflowed. 'As if you stop being a mother just like *that*,' said Eva, snapping her fingers for effect when they'd mulled over Bernadette's mixed feelings.

Leith understands the emotional lurch. When her sons were young she often woke at night scared she'd left them at the shops or forgotten to pick them up from school. Once they'd gone for good it was as though she'd misplaced her self. Growing up, she'd dreamed of mothering five children, though her maternal longing was unfashionable for an educated woman. George had prom-ised her as many babies as she desired, confident of his prowess as the provider on every front. They'd started out so grandly, tak-ing a punt on the dilapidated mansion beside the river – a house where the downstairs walls blistered with bubbles of damp plaster while, up above, brown stains from a leaky roof mapped a trail across the pressed tin ceilings. She'd restored each room, joyfully, bountifully. He was making good at the bar practising family law while she taught at a girls' school. Blissfully happy to fall pregnant with Art, she'd resigned from her job. It had taken them another four years to conceive Jesse.

The harder she'd connived to bear a third child, the less George had complied, uncomfortable at having to perform on cue. The lace lingerie she'd purchased – a lone female shopper amongst a lunchtime queue of ruddy-nosed men – doused his flickering of desire. Rosie, who'd experienced her share of miscarriages, lent Leith books on fertility.

After two years of prayers, thermometers, and the inexact science of seducing George, Leith was ecstatic at the telltale signs of nausea. But she miscarried one evening, cramps doubling her up as she fought through to the happy ending of the boys' bedtime story.

She'd thought of leaving George then. If he'd beaten her or bored her or cruelly exacted his conjugal rights she would've gone, but not wanting her enough seemed scant reason to sabotage her family. His ambition had promised her a destination: judge's wife. She blushes, hating the shallowness of her simple arithmetic, still unsure where she figured in his. Why did he choose her? She doesn't know the answer. While he built his reputation she lavished her attention on their two sons, who sometimes left her wondering how she'd have energy for another.

She's closest to Jesse, the youngest, a shy boy, small like his mother. Once she'd spied him in the playground at lunchtime, sitting alone watching other children play. She'd mistaken his diffidence for insecurity. It was George who'd put a camera in his hands on his fourteenth birthday, giving purpose to the boy's preferred place on the perimeter of gatherings. As soon as he'd sold his first photographs – green shoots in a charred landscape – Jesse had abandoned his law degree. Last year he settled in the south-west of Tasmania, disappearing for weeks on end from the crumbling stone farmhouse that he inhabits like a monk, tiptoeing through old-growth forests and peeking over the ridges of mist-filled valleys, out of mobile range for days at a time. She writes to him every week, hiding her unhappiness in fictionalised versions of her life.

Art shook loose straight after school, exhibiting the confidence Jesse lacked, following his father's path to college, studying commerce instead of law. They never worried for him. 'So like his father,' was the compliment offered by admirers who didn't have a clue what a curse this could be. George and Leith keep their fears to themselves of how this frailty might warp him. Wired into phones, Art directs money electronically around the globe. They never have trouble reaching him, yet he seems to switch off when they talk, distracted by the keyboard or television they can hear in the background of his Sydney office. He rarely contacts them when he flies to Melbourne for meetings, down and back in a day. Just a phase, she tells herself, certain that once the boys have children of their own they'll restore connections. She's done some growing up herself during their absence. About time, she smiles.

Once the boys left home George colonised the rumpus room upstairs. He's had cable TV installed, and a cinema-size plasma screen so he can watch the international tours whenever he wants. The sofa bed's been upgraded for his comfort. Leith never visits. Club members only, she jokes to her friends, but even she was taken aback the night he rang her on the mobile to ask if she was making tea downstairs and could he trouble her for a cup. The next day she'd bought him an electric kettle and sachets of tea, coffee, sugar and long-life milk, just as you might find in roadside motels.

'When he retires you'll never get him down from there,' Bernadette had laughed, assuming his seclusion will be accommodated in some kind of shared future, together. *As if*, Leith scoffs now, bolshie at the preposterous idea of them continuing side by side, here in her private domain.

The horseraces spirited her out of the house into a world of seedy characters and ripe smells. Her father's passion's hooked her. Slicking back his hair in front of the bathroom mirror every Saturday morning, he'd catch her staring. 'Kiss me twice for luck,' he'd say to Leith who wondered why their mother was spared this ritual. He promised he'd take Leith and Cameron with him one day, but he promised them lots of things if he won, which he seldom did. Bernadette's husband Monty is a punter and Leith's been accompanying him to the track for the better part of a year.

She's on a streak right now, her family's hex broken – lucky after all. The confidence she's gained in backing her judgement has bigger dividends in store.

She walks into a kitchen splashed by the morning sun. The cosy clutter that once drew warmth from comings and goings presses in on her. Homemaking's a craft she's plied as devotedly as any artisan. The hearth was the womb of this house. Rich red Middle Eastern rugs soften the floorboards. Cookbooks and gourmet magazines fill shelves lining the nook where cane chairs cushioned in pinks, an ottoman with soft throw rugs and small tables for cups or glasses lend the feel of a Bedouin tent. The boys would plonk here after school to scoff scones or muffins, hogging the oven's heat in winter. They'd do homework at the table while she prepared dinner, peeling vegetables, sautéing onions. Now she sometimes feels as if she's on a country station where the city express train no longer stops.

Taking a pad of writing paper and a pen from a drawer in the pine dresser, she sets the white china cups swinging from their hooks as she pushes the drawer closed. A tennis game starts next door and the bounce and thwack against the strings produces a hypnotic rhythm. She pulls up a chair and clears a space amongst the newspapers on the table to write a letter to her brother.

Leith has her reasons for avoiding electronic transfer of her news. Airmail will slow the domino effect of one drama triggering another. She writes in her jaunty, circular script, straightening the sequence that led her here; turning points once obscured from view are now brought as testimony in the case against George and, by default, herself. They are custodians of their respective deceits. Pausing, she unfolds a thin, yellowing sheet of stationery with a tightly worded paragraph addressed to Cameron penned in George's militaristic hand. The letter had fluttered loose from an old college journal as she'd sorted through boxes three months ago. Her discovery revises history just as foreign coins found in a hulk off the coast enrich the patina of a country's past. Why not leave be, let bygones, etc? Well, because candour's moon is in the ascendant here, though she can't quite believe she's daring to ask her brother for enlightenment. Her pen marches on, stopping before her tears smudge the ink as she describes the wasteland of a marriage she's cultivated.

Years ago, when Jesse first left home, she and George had gone to the opera in the city. George had wanted to leave early. She'd consented, cheerfully. Arriving home, she'd led him into their bedroom, her silk skirt rustling – she still remembers the sound.

'Is this an ambush?' he'd asked. 'You know I don't like it.'

'Like what?' she'd laughed dumbly, licking his ear as they sat on the foot of the bed. George rose to tip his cufflinks into their velvet box. She'd watched him as he undid his laces and slipped off his shoes, his socks, his pants, his shirt, hanging his jacket and smoothing his trousers to keep the crease. From the bathroom she heard him washing his face with soap, cleaning his teeth, rinsing and spitting, aiming a steady stream of piss into the bowl.

He dressed in his pyjamas – pure cotton boxer shorts with matching top. Then, without kissing her goodnight, he'd turned over a triangle of sheet and got into bed, facing the long sashed windows draped in Florence Broadhurst fabric (egrets picked out in deep crimson on a grey silk). She lay there for hours, her heart racing as she stared at the ceiling rose, withered by George's disdain.

Even now she's hot with shame at his rejection and her paralysis. But she spares Cameron from minutia that labours her point. Rereading her handiwork, she wonders whether tonight's conversation with George should be had on paper – civil, cautious, without the timbre of disgust or anger. If only she could just leave him a note.

The future, tantalisingly close, averts her concentration. She reaches her conclusion, signing off affectionately, proposing they holiday together at Christmas for the mother of all debriefings. She lifts her gaze to the collection of antique tins stacked on the top shelf of the dresser. Standing on a milkmaid's stool that she keeps in the kitchen, she reaches up and brushes aside a cobweb abandoned by its occupant and takes down a small flat tin that long ago held Three Nuns pipe tobacco smoked by her great-grandfather on the battlefields of France. The tin saved his life: stuffed in his top left pocket, it had shielded him from shrapnel.

She opens the back door and steps outside into her sunken garden, the worse for drought and neglect because she's given up on the place that once absorbed her as gardener, cook and nurturer.

A hedge of rosemary bush borders the crazy paving that wends through the garden; bending down, Leith snaps a spiky twig from the robust plant that has scented countless lamb roasts. Before she puts the dark-green stalk inside the tin, she inhales the memories. Something old, something new, something borrowed, something blue – she was careful to observe the superstition on her wedding day. When she leaves here other talismans will line her pockets.

Returning to the table she adds George's letter to the six sheets of cream stationery, pressing firmly on the fold with her fist to flatten the bulk. As she licks the seal of the envelope she sees the law list in today's paper and – not so much out of habit because she doesn't look for him any more, but to commemorate the significance of the day – she reads through the Family Court list. There's His Honour, her husband, with his first case, Dunlop S J & Emory G C, entombed in bold type.

Cameron logs on to his computer. All of the friends who are coming to tonight's birthday celebration have sent electronic cards, high alert, well aware of how much he loves a fuss being made of him. He returns these favours, conscious of reaping what you sow. Scrolling through the messages, he can't see any from his sister, or his nephews, which peeves him. Jesse can usually be counted upon. Leith always remembers his birthday. He checks her last email in case he had skated over news that she's away, although she's like Frank – a stay-at-home.

Hi Gorgeous

Hope you two are not freezing to death. There were pictures of the ice storm in Massachusetts on the news last night and I wondered whether you and Frank got the day off work because it said schools have been closed across the northeast. I hope for your sake there were some fringe benefits because I know how much you hate the cold! We are praying for rain here. Everything in our garden's doing it hard, except for the rosemary which I replanted from Mum's front yard. That bush could survive a nuclear attack.

Today I found a box of furniture from my old doll's house. Remember! I kept everything for the little girls that I expected to raise. Perhaps one of the boys will deliver me a grand-daughter. I'm in the middle of a big spring clean, discovering things I'd forgotten, memories that set me wandering, and I get completely distracted. George is upstairs. Plus ca change. Pity we don't have an intercom. These days we communicate by eyebrow semaphore and monosyllables. Tea, toast, lights, thanks, night, have you seen my glasses. I want to ask you a question which has been nagging at me for the longest time but I've drunk too much wine around at Rosie's.

Love to Frank and love to you.

L

He'd forgotten this teaser.

Cameron had introduced Leith to George never imagining they'd make a match. He'd known Kremmer from the university law revue. The stage was Cameron's safe house, a place where he could be everyone but himself, and he wasn't picky who. Macbeth's witches, Bottom the weaver, the arse end of a donkey. His favourite character was Cynthia, associate to a High Court justice, Herbert Picklewick, a sozzled, lecherous, pompous old bastard. George hadn't auditioned but the director had coaxed him to join the cast because he'd been bred for the part.

Clad in fishnet stockings, a blonde wig, false eyelashes and a miniskirt, Cameron became Cynthia, a promiscuous femme fatale in the highest heels he could find. He queened it up, bending at every opportunity to flourish his firm arse as he retrieved His Honour's hip flask or brown paper bags of money stashed in the bottom drawers of a desk, their only prop. Queues had snaked outside the Union Theatre as praise for this rollicking lewdness made Cameron and George the toast of campus. There was talk, briefly, of touring. For several weeks they became inseparable, able to decipher each other on stage through a twitch of the mouth, a narrowing of the eyes or the furrows on a forehead. Their sketch lengthened, taking up almost the entire second half of the show as they departed from the script in impromptu flourishes that audiences loved for the derailment. Rumours of their relationship were feverish.

One night, very late, weeks after the revue's sell-out finale, George was walking back to college after a binge at the library to compensate for the hours frittered away on theatrical endeavour.

Months shy of graduating, he couldn't allow himself to fall for the siren song of dressing rooms delirious with adrenalin and the thrill of applause, so he'd knuckled down in the race for a Rhodes Scholarship like his father. He was weighing up his competition when Cameron stumbled out of the mirror bushes, giving him such a fright that his relief on discovering friend not foe made a drink mandatory. Cameron had a bottle of vodka in his coat pocket – he'd been helping himself to it over the course of his less successful evening writing an essay, long overdue, on Henry James.

'Your place or mine?' Cameron minced with the lisp that was Cynthia's trademark.

Well over the limit, he didn't detect the trace of irritability in George, who was sober as the judge he would become and whose ambition meant he hadn't time to loiter with the likes of Cameron.

'Come on,' George cuffed him over the head. Cameron tingled at the physical contact and the shoulder-rubbing closeness of their bodies as they barrelled down the path in the frosty air towards the Gothic brownstone tower of George's college.

'You've been hiding,' Cameron said. 'Nobody's seen you for dust.'

'It's all right for you,' George prickled, sledging the soft education of an arts degree. Cameron didn't register the slight. 'Torts, contract law . . . I've got exams in two weeks. Our learned friend Picklewick didn't get to the bench entirely because of the size of his cock,' he lightened up.

Cameron felt his own hot and hardening as he gripped the cool metal rail of the iron banister on the stairs to George's room. The corridor was deserted. Simon and Garfunkel's *Sounds of Silence* played in a room nearby where the clink of bottles and voices created another kind of music. Male laughter floated through the hallway as George fumbled for the key to his room.

Inside, Cameron hid his erection under a copy of the student newspaper, which he flicked through casually even though he'd read it from cover to cover procrastinating over his essay. George went to the bathroom to rinse his only tumbler for them to share. The building's central heating was broken and Cameron glanced around for a blanket. The walls were dotted with tack marks and chipped paint where prior occupants had stuck posters, or traffic signs procured on drunken rampages through the streets of Carlton. A framed photograph of a bronzed man face-down on the sand in the sun leant against the wall, waiting to be hung. Cameron drew warmth from the bather's skin, his shoulders patterned with drop-lets of water glistening in the sun.

When George returned, he sat in the vinyl swivel-chair beside the desk laid out like a table setting: pencils and pens, tidy, on either side of the square blotter with its corners enveloped in dark-green leather and edged by a garland of gold. A poster for the law revue was pinned to the corkboard, skew-whiff amongst the grid of lecture timetables and ticket stubs for the Law School ball. Cameron lolled on the bed and willed George to lie beside him, propping himself up on an elbow to make room. He admired George's handsome masculinity. Every aspect of his friend's appearance was generously proportioned, from his thick waves of brown hair to his black eyebrows drawn like hurried brushstrokes, full lips and eyes bluer than the lapis lazuli stones on a monarch's crown. George took several swigs of vodka and leaned towards Cameron to give him a turn. Their hands touched. As Cameron's slender fingers stroked George's knuckles, lust surged through him and he reached out to encourage George gently towards him. Instead, he was jerked upwards by George's fist, the mug smashing his front tooth and cutting his lip. Tasting blood, he lifted his hand to his face instinctively.

'Get out,' George shuddered as Cameron stood shakily, dazed by the kind of aggression he'd encountered once outside a toilet block but had never anticipated meeting here. A violent headache laid him low the next day. His lip required three stitches. He blamed the drink for misreading George's intent but he never sent an apology because by then he'd decided George was the one who should be riddled with shame. They'd avoided each other thereafter. Cameron fell in with the thespians while George renewed his vows to the lonelier course of academic glory.

After Leith arrived on campus, Cameron kept a proprietorial eye on her, recruiting her friends to promote his plays. A year later, when he left for America, she'd accompanied him to the airport. As he hugged her tight George Kremmer glided into view, farewelling an older man and taking his leave with a firm hand-shake. Their eyes met and George hesitated for an instant then strode towards Cameron, spurred by second thoughts.

'Cynthia?' George's voice boomed at him across the departure lounge.

Struggling for control, Cameron found his character's falsetto register. 'Your Honour, His Very Special Person, Grand Poo Bah of the legal profession, fancy meeting you here.'

'Where are you travelling to?' George asked.

'America.' Cameron kept his destination open the breadth of the continent.

'Well . . . good luck and goodbye, I guess.' George offered his hand. Then, turning to Leith, 'I don't think we've met.'

'I'm Cameron's sister, Leith,' she sweetened the air. 'And we have met, or at least I saw you in the revue. You were hilarious. The two of you,' she said glancing back at her brother.

'Do you do any acting?' George asked her.

'Cameron's the showman,' she said. 'I sing. Very badly,' she'd added.

'That's not true,' Cameron had countered her modesty, his loyalty and admiration for her talents overriding his desire to brush George aside and be gone.

'I'm going to miss you,' Leith said suddenly, flinging her arms around Cameron's neck. He was grateful that her crush cold-shouldered George from their circle.

When he turned around at the gate for one last wave, George had disappeared and he blew kisses to his sister before vanishing too.

Frank was the official reason why Cameron had never returned to Australia, not even for his sister's wedding.

Mack the dog – his and Frank's surrogate son – nudges him impatiently.

'All right, all right.' He swirls around and scoops the West Highland Terrier, a coarse white scruff ball, on to his lap. He begins typing Leith's email address to send her a cheeky prompt reminding her that he's 58 today. As his hands pause over the keyboard, he decides to wait at least until the morning's post has arrived and the UPS van has been given every opportunity to deliver a parcel of birthday wishes to his door.

Sam Dunlop weaves his way between the cars banked behind the red light at the intersection. 'Hey!' he shirt-fronts the shiny grille of a four-wheel-drive that's creeping forward. Jaywalkers have no rights but there is the biblical wrong of crushing a man to death. He hammers the bonnet with his fist. The driver blasts his horn. Sam gives him the finger, at home amongst the bumper bars – but he's not letting on to the Family Court that he once captained a concrete atoll, cleaning windscreens for a gold coin, a plastic bucket of grey suds beside him and a bandana tied around his dark locks.

His ex-wife, Gabe, loved his street-urchin antics until she got pregnant. The prospect of a baby piloted her into the fold of her prosperous parents, who'd tried to procure a late-term abortion behind his back, as if Mags could be pumped out like the contents of Gabe's stomach after a teenage episode of binge drinking. He'd never have forgiven her for deleting Mags. And he's never going to tell Mags that her life hung in the balance. There are some things you're better off not knowing.

Since he began fighting to see his three-year-old daughter, he's been schooled by his sister, Angie, working at the kitchen table in her shoe-box apartment, assembling his case. They're twins, although you wouldn't know it to look at them. Angie's plumper and her dark-brown hair falls in thick waves halfway down her back. She's organised, punctual, neat: a turtle to his hare.

They were raised by their mother's older sister, Jo, who'd no choice, as she used to tell them whenever they ground her down. 'Your father didn't want you, believe me I begged him to take you,' she'd lashed out at them once without thinking, convinced that in this makeshift family, she clutched the shorter straw. Aged three-and-a-half the night their mother died, they were unreliable witnesses, awoken by the sirens of emergency vehicles scream-ing outside the house. They've built on biographical fragments to satisfy their yearnings. Angie's coped better than Sam. Her tidi-ness, her cool temperament, her thick ankles lifted from their mother's template – the provenance of her character annotated beyond doubt. And this belonging spared Angie from the angriness that Sam carries. Whatever possessions their father left behind were incinerated by their mother, apart from a birth certificate with this stranger's name assigned to a role that hasn't progressed beyond a signature fancily done.

The shadow of this man has shaped Sam, the absence influencing him just as powerfully as a father's presence moulds a son. To be unloved, a crippling thing. Accidents happen, he knows that now, mistakes are made. He and Gabe were too young, too loosely knitted together to cradle a child in their midst. He fingers the charm in his pocket.

For all her prepping, Angie couldn't ready Sam for emotional whiplash. The last-minute instructions she issued on the phone this morning churn in his head as he checks that his shirt's tucked in and the grey synthetic leather shoes he bought from Target yesterday are clean. His op-shop suit swims on his slender body; the jacket was missing two buttons so he'd yanked off the third. He joins the throng of people neatly dressed, some of them wigged and gowned, a step ahead of younger barristers towing briefcases on wheels like golfers with their buggies.

He hears the shouting before he sees the bald head of the tall bloke on an upturned plastic milk crate rousing a small crowd of men with black armbands outside the entrance to the court. Two of the men hand out fliers demanding changes to child support. Sam went to one of their meetings once, but he's not a joiner. He'd hoped to learn a few tips, share in the tricks up their sleeves so he didn't fall victim too, but the mood in the stuffy room where they congregated was too angry for trading advice. The quiet bearded man who hadn't seen his son since his ex-wife bolted interstate was speechless with rage. Every time Sam tried to talk through the chronology of his own story with one of the other men, the saga took such turns and backtracks and twists that he got tangled in thickets of blame. He didn't confess to half admiring the acne-scarred father who confessed he'd mailed death threats to a judge, express post. Angie's started him thinking twice before he opens his trap.

He scouts the forecourt for Gabe, twiggy thin and swanky in her tight, hip-hugging jeans and low-cut gypsy tops. She hangs her streaked blonde hair loose, constantly gathering it up and sweeping it extravagantly from her face. It broke him up when he first saw Mags, with barely enough hair to bunch in her fist, copy her mother's stroke and flick. Gabe won't take his calls. Six months, three weeks and two days it's been since he held Mags, drinking in her pure smell, her inquisitiveness, her jolting speech, the way she sucks her breath in when she's excited.

Inside the glass doors a queue builds where security personnel herd visitors through metal detectors. Sam forgets to empty his pockets and the uniformed lady's wand beeps as it glides over the bullet shell that he carries with him for good luck. 'Back you go,' she waves a circle in the air and he drops the slim brass casing in a blue plastic tray. The guard gives him a once-over that beats the wand and the x-ray machine for spotting trouble. Sam collects Angie's folder as it washes up against legal files, laptops, pagers and palm pilots. The crush disperses through the white marbled foyer, where people pair off along unmarked pathways. He pauses to look for directions to hearing room 17B.

'He who hesitates is lost,' a curt female voice behind him says and he swings around to see the tailored curves of a stranger disappear up the staircase. Sam approaches the reception desk, where a woman in a grey blazer sits behind a computer, her face puffy and bronzed with make-up. 'Of course I'll pay,' she says into her telephone headset. 'Hello . . . Hello . . . *Hello*,' urgent now, her large brown eyes darting from side to side. 'Damn it,' she swears. 'I'm sorry,' she apologises to Sam. 'I got cut off. The switch said she had a reverse-charge call from my daughter. She's 15. She's run away from home. We're crazy with worry.'

He's amazed how calmly she swings from the lost connection with her child to his pedestrian enquiry. As his legs follow her instructions along the corridor, turning left and then up the stairs towards the first room on the right, his mind returns to her plight. For a moment his fear of losing contact with Mags is flattened by the fact that even families who stay together can be blown apart. He wonders if the Family Court is like one of those sick buildings he's seen on the telly, only instead of brain tumours or breast cancer those who work here get poisoned by the conflict that leaches into their kin.

*　　*　　*

George dips his chin and lifts his eyes over the steel frame of his ill-fitting spectacles to study the character of the young man before him: his callused hands, the suit and tie. Cleanly shaven, he's free of piercings and doesn't fidget like the addicts who can't stay still. No appearance by the wife who's briefed one of the best female barristers around. George likes to compare what he reads in the demeanour of those who come before him with the wealth of often contradictory information set out in affidavits and reports submitted by psychiatrists, psychologists, relatives, employers, friends. Most candid are the children when they open up during interviews with court consultants.

George sometimes imagines the petitioners in his court sizing him up by deportment and dress, just as he scrutinises each of them at the outset of every case. Starting with his shoes (Italian leather, polished in accordance with his mother's immutable belief that footwear is the measure of a person), they might note the judge's preference for silk socks and expensive suits; they would see silver hair, full for his age, parted on the right side and framing an attractive face buttoned by a pair of eyes so blue that anyone who looks into them wonders whether they're artificially coloured. He still turns heads in the street, where he likes to catch his reflection in shop windows. Just as his father could be fooled by appearances, the world misinterprets George's sure-footed dash.

He looks up at the rows of empty seats that are sometimes filled on each side by supporters, much as families divide on either side of the church on the day now damned by them all. Then he nods at the wife's barrister, a middle-aged veteran with a colourful marital history that is said to have honed her dexterity in this court. She consults her notes and continues her plea that the man seated to her left can't be trusted with contact visits: 'Your Honour can see from the first hearing into this matter that Mr Dunlop's drug use was one of the reasons for the breakdown of the marriage.'

Sam closes his eyes as his sins are revisited and tinted in shades that corrupt his entitlement to Mags, until Gabe's lawyer starts on about him violating court orders.

'On the 21st of September, Your Honour, Mr Dunlop visited the community childcare centre attended by my client's daughter. There was no agreement for this contact. No prior warning. The staff member on duty, in her confusion, allowed Mr Dunlop to leave the premises with the child. He failed to contact my client until later that evening, by which time she was hysterical.'

This feat still staggered Sam himself, who hadn't considered such a thing possible until the young girl watching over nap time in the Possum's Corner had inadvertently popped the idea into his head. She was new, unsure of procedures, so he'd exploited her ineptitude. All he'd intended was to quench his thirst for his daughter in the couple of minutes he assumed he'd be able to haggle; instead, she'd let him sign Mags out.

'Gabe was the one who broke the order,' he snaps. 'She didn't bring Mags around when it was my turn.' He remembers to stand, like Angie said, fracturing the proceedings with his unsolicited interjection.

The judge motions him to sit, patting the air with a downward gesture. He observes irritability rippling Sam's threadbare composure.

After a sideways glance skewering her opponent, the wife's counsel picks up her thread. 'Your Honour, the childcare worker told my client that Mr Dunlop appeared to slur his words. She said that she was afraid of him.'

Sam's on his feet again.

'Take your seat,' George tells him.

He stays where he is. 'Your Honour,' – he's learnt quickly – 'it's Gabe . . . my wife . . . my ex-wife, if she . . . she won't stick to the deal. That's the problem. That's why I've come . . . It's not fair, it's not fair to Mags, my girl, our daughter. She needs me. She doesn't know the other side to this. She'll pick up words and paste them together so that she's got some picture in her head that's not me, but she . . .'

'Be seated, please,' sharply this time. Put-downs from the bench can incite volatile temperaments as easily as subdue them. It's the men who implode. They thrash around, banging fistfuls of frustration. Women are mistresses of containment, sweet-lipped in their violence, artfully manipulating allegations of sexual abuse to salve their wounds. George sits here, god-like, assessing the risk of damage done through parental contact versus the risk of damage caused by alienation. How can he possibly know for certain the calibration of days and nights that will benefit a child? He can make an educated guess but he can't see inside the houses or the hearts of those who come before him. The algebra does him in, which is why he envies his barrister friends.

'Twice the money and half the responsibility,' he tells Daniel Forrester, his closest ally, whose family law firm briefs the scrupulously prepared woman now on her feet.

Sam Dunlop loves his daughter – today's appearance testifies to that – but on paper he's a mess. Something about him catches George's sympathy. Close in age to their younger son Jesse, whom Leith and George would bail out with love, money, shelter, whatever support he needed, this kid's a scrapper because he's alone. George notes the vacant seats behind Sam. There's probably no one to keep him together. Whatever he and Leith lack, they had given their sons security of tenure. George looks at the boy with his head cast down, tracing grains in the wood with his thumbnail, deepening a groove begun by others who have sat where he sweats now. How much access will benefit his daughter? Is she safe in his custody? He's impulsive. George's thoughts hurdle every jump and trench. Curbing visits could destroy him or strengthen him.

The room falls quiet. The wife's barrister leafs through one of her large black ring folders, bookmarked with hot-pink post-it notes, searching for a psychologist's report on her client's daughter.

George motions for her to continue.

'Your Honour, the child was found to be withdrawn after contact with Mr Dunlop and it appears the little girl has been becoming more anxious, particularly . . .'

'Who says so?' George interrupts because he knows where she's leading.

'My client, Your Honour, has drawn this behaviour to the psychologist's attention. It's in the report, Your Honour, on page 156.' She pauses while George flips through his copy of the documents. 'Section 6 (a), in the middle of the page,' she assists him. 'You can see there the reference to more frequent nightmares and episodes of bedwetting . . . and my client believes this reflects her daughter's fear of being taken by her father.'

'How would *she* know?' Fury ejects Sam from the chair before he can invoke Angie's commandments and this time his arms are raised, riding his jacket up around him like a scarecrow's coat. 'Mags always had trouble sleeping,' he shouts. 'I was the one who got up to her so Gabe could rest. It was me who rocked her for hours, watching the sun come up, too scared to put her down in case she woke . . .'

George lets him uncoil.

'She needs me. She needs to know who I am. It's about feeling loved, being wanted. This is about Mags. It's not about Gabe or me,' he insists, pounding his chest, emotion thickening his throat. Then, ashamed by his wrong turn, he floods with anger at his father, his mother, the judge, Gabe, the lot of them.

'Sit down, Mr Dunlop, or this case will be adjourned,' George warns.

Sam steps back awkwardly, knocking his chair over. Sheets of paper spill on to the royal-blue carpet. He scoops them up and turns one way then the other like a bewildered bird that has flown inside. A court official who had ducked out to the toilet opens the heavy panelled door. Sam bolts, charging down the stairs without slowing until he's outside, caught in a shower of rain, slipping between oncoming cars as he crosses the streets against the lights to get away.

The morning's summery winks of sun have gone by the time Leith's ready to leave the house; the crisp gusts of wind and overcast sky announce the arrival of a new season. On the cusp of change herself, meanings harbour everywhere for Leith as she packs the last of her cardboard boxes into the boot of her car. Deciding what she couldn't live without was a peculiar exercise for a woman who's drawn comfort from material possessions. One of her spinster aunts held to the creed that a good cook requires just three staples in her kitchen: lemon, parsley and onion. Leith has organised her possessions around the same principle of bare necessity, leaving – for now, at least – paintings, kitchenware, a wardrobe of summer clothes, jewellery, books, albums of photographs. For months she's been combing through thirty years of stuff, cleansing, archiving, discarding the trappings of a past age, another life – like a character leaving medieval England for mid–twentieth century New York, from thatched rooves in boggy fields of peat to skyscrapers and martinis. Here amongst the scraps of her life she's uncovered her self, brushing dust gently from a fragment, a face in a photograph, her first love, a teenage boy . . .

She and Cameron had spent languorous summers with an aunt, their father's sister, who lived in the main street of a country town. The boy's grandmother lived next door and the three children had whiled away hours together, playing endless games of Monopoly. On hot days when the pavement burnt their feet they climbed the giant mulberry tree in the backyard for the coolness of the leaves and the chance of a breeze. Reading the boy's slim pile of letters again had set Leith pining, leap-frogging to other rivals for her affection, each one preferable to the one she eventually chose. In her loneliness, she married them instead, guessing at the shape of alternative lives. The dreaming has sustained her.

She became obsessed with how they'd fared as men, searching for their whereabouts, unsuccessfully. This drew a line finally through girlish fantasies so embarrassing she'd kept them from her friends, even Rosie. But the wondering awoke parts of herself that she'd written off as dead, spawning the affair she also hides. Delinquency is how she rationalised this roguishness, her age, her disappointment with how life's turned out. But the idiocy's been fruitful, freeing her to start over, here at the point of departure, steadying for a step thousands take every day, sometimes without warning, suitcase in hand, door slammed, no place to go.

Leith has planned her exit, choosing her timing, renting an apartment, smoothing the transition.

'It's ridiculous to be opening your first cheque account at my age,' she'd told the Indian-born bank manager, in her fifties like Leith, but worldly, financially literate, enjoying her customer's apologetic gush. Leith, guilty as a criminal laundering ill-gotten gains, began depositing her winnings. Over the year she's made up for her father's losses, the piggy bank out of his reach, securing enough after last Saturday's splurge to pay a deposit on a place of her own: modern, pristine, nothing to fix except picture hooks, close to the market where she's always shopped. She'll cling to this familiar ground – the comfort of bantering with stall holders she knows by name, aware of their ailments, their children – as she resettles. That's where she's going now, her wicker basket on the back seat, to buy tonight's supper.

Hers might be shorter than most migratory flights but she's just as torn departing familiar landmarks and rituals. Not that the neighbourhood with its high fences and houses set back from the street encourages friendships. Rosie will miss her terribly but Leith's decided they both need a seismic jolt. She'll talk to Art tomorrow and Jesse can wait until she visits him next week. This morning she booked her passage on the Spirit of Tasmania. Then, on a whim, she ran her finger through the classified job advertisements, pausing at the one seeking a chef for 'our young funky team . . . sharp, enthusiastic with a sense of HUMOUR' before circling a smaller bar of print asking for a cook in a city bistro – 'must be passionate about food'. Well, she's overqualified on that criterion.

The traffic is mercifully light and she finds a park easily as she arrives at the market. The air is pungent with cabbage, oranges, buckets of basil and coriander as she walks through aisles where fruiterers shout to one another over the noise. She heads for the post office on the corner, her basket on one arm, the plump envelope in the pocket of her grey trench coat. The young man behind the counter is camp. She can tell by his upward palm held midair while he reads the scale, from the way he folds and tears three stamps from loose-leaf sheets and wets his finger to pick up a blue airmail sticker from the jar, which he licks and hammers nimbly into place. 'This is a fat letter,' he says to her. 'Someone sure has a lot of news.' His flamboyance gives the lie to secrets – a good omen, she's sure. As she steps out on to the street, raindrops spot the pavement, quickening until they pelt down and force her under the veranda of a greasy takeaway. The sudden wet reminds her of the cloudburst on her wedding day as she floated beside her father in the white Rolls.

'A shower is bad luck,' she worried.

'You make your own luck, sweetheart,' he'd offered to calm her nerves, and she invokes his mantra now to soothe her jitters, because she's leaving for herself, not for anyone else. But if her father was here she'd make him kiss her twice all the same.

*　*　*

George came to golf late, unprepared for imprisonment on its greens. His moods, his thoughts, his capacity to endure unhappiness are contingent on how close he comes to choreographing a perfect swing. Sleep is often disturbed by questions of anatomy, shoulder lift, hip swivel, eye line, the grip of his iron. Lately, he's turned too often from the task of writing judgements to test new tips and pointers that trumpet revelation. He met Anthony Pringle by chance, as members of a group of four playing 18 holes at the club early one Saturday morning, sprinklers chugging in the distance as they teed off. A curator for Sotheby's auction house, Pringle shared with George more than an uncommon absorption in golf. By the tenth hole they had confirmed a mutual interest in early Australian photography, dropping the titles of their favourite works by Laurie Le Guay, Max Dupain, Athol Shmith and Lewis Morley over neat whiskies in the club lounge after the game (now a weekly tradition). In between times they hunt down first-edition golf books, old clubs, quirky gadgets invented by masters of the game.

Returning to his chambers this morning after the abrupt adjournment of proceedings in room 17B, George's mood had lifted upon discovery of a yellow slip on his desk notifying him of a call from Mr Pringle. 'You won't believe what I've bagged for you,' Anthony boasted when George called him back.

'Animal, vegetable or mineral?'

'It's a surprise. Come over this afternoon, as soon as you can get away,' Anthony said, stoking George's anticipation. 'But just to confound you completely, I'll confirm that it's vegetable, at least in origin.'

George leaves court at 5.30. As he drives through the afternoon traffic, busier for the shower of rain that swept through town, the hasty exit of Sam Dunlop bobs into his mind. Some characters, some faces, get a hold on him for some peculiar reason of psychology, just as certain cases are intrinsically more interesting than others for the legal precedent they set. George guesses this kid, barely a man, doesn't have the wherewithal to make things work – lacking opportunities, singed by the flames of impatience. At times he wishes he had a temperament that answers to a rush of blood. He and Leith stand on a bald hillside, rooted in a patch of earth that no longer nourishes them, waiting for a storm or some other act of God to knock them asunder.

They'd spent their first afternoon together in a Carlton pub discussing authors, poets, novels that changed their lives. He'd never relaxed so much in a woman's company. I could marry her, was the thought that limbo-ed under his guard – a thought he'd unpicked since, a trillion times. Their courtship was interrupted by his scholarship to Oxford. This sabbatical gave them a breather, although George barely made time for socialising. He chummed up with a South African physicist who was called home when his father died. Then Leith had arrived for the summer, travelling with Eva, and he never really found another opportunity for self-discovery. Marriage was expected of him so he proposed to Leith on his return, busy with finding chambers and establishing his practice. It wasn't until after Jesse was born that the fights flared over sex. Leith wanted a bigger family. He avoided coming home after work. One evening when he came in the door, late, she was crying; Jesse was on her hip, too big for carrying, his face covered in measles.

'I was in a conference with clients,' he'd pleaded, reaching out for Jesse, but the boy had screamed for his mother's arms. Later she'd served George dinner, interrogating him between mouthfuls for details of the clients – stupid questions, personal details that he couldn't invent as easily as the twists of a case – barking up the wrong alley in her suspicion. He didn't want to go to bed with her, but he couldn't tell her, so he kindled disagreements, snubbing her with a meagre offence that he could stoke until the bickering kept them apart. These rows were a necessary friction. 'Why do you always reject me?' she'd begged him once. Gradually the intervals between his surrender lengthened. For years he's faltered, fearful of the other admissions that must flow from divorce. Another day together won't make a jot of difference so the years tick by.

He spots a jackpot of a parking space right outside Sotheby's, its impressive architectural façade flanked by bridal boutiques and antique galleries, where customers make appointments in the spirit of a consultation and price isn't discussed. George reverses his car using the reflection in a shop window to navigate a tight wedge. Inside, a girl gowned in cream silk studies herself in the mirror;

an older woman with pearl-tipped pins protruding from her pursed lips kneels on the carpet, adjusting the hem.

Pushing open the brass door, George helps himself to a catalogue from a small pile on the reception desk. He passes through the empty foyer lit by the jabs of yellow, green and blue on a sprawling canvas that covers the entire back wall, the work of an indigenous artist who gets around in a striped woollen beanie and bare feet.

Anthony stands to welcome him into his office, furnished with a honey-coloured leather chesterfield sofa. Above his desk hangs Max Dupain's photograph of women queuing at the butcher's, all wearing hats and coats, waiting their turn. George always sees his mother, Margaret, in the narrowing eyes of one customer sizing up a cut of meat; this was a look she often spent on her only child.

On a round oak table in the centre of the room sits a small wooden box, no bigger than an egg carton. Anthony reaches for the white gloves on his desk and pulls them on with a firm tug. George feels the same tickle that turned his stomach in his early days as a junior barrister, prosecuting the divorce of a society matron before a room crowded with scribblers and newspaper artists rubbing charcoal-smudged fingers to secure a likeness on their sketch pads. He leans towards the box. Anthony lifts the lid with the tips of his index fingers, one on either side. George circles the table slowly before placing his bet. 'This is "The Gate", isn't it?' He looks at Anthony expectantly because his whole life has been a series of calculated guesses.

Anthony nods, impressed.

'It was dreamt up by that American fellow, I'll get his name in a minute . . . Edgar. James Edgar.'

'James Douglas Edgar,' Anthony corrects him, everything a contest between them. 'The set was part of a deceased estate. A pro in the Druid Hills Golf Club in Atlanta rang me last week but I didn't want to get your hopes up.' He shakes out a square of oilcloth. 'This was to protect the floor if you were swinging indoors,' he says, flattening the cloth onto the table. Brandishing gold tweezers from his trouser pocket he removes the dried shell of a beetle from inside a crease of the sepia-stained fabric.

'Edgar died in 1920. He was just a boy. Twenty-five years old.'

'What happened?'

'He was murdered.'

'Really?'

George knows about the gadget, and the theory behind its application, next to nothing of its architect's fate.

'Do you want the official version or the conspiracy theory?'

'Just give me the truth,' George laughs, itching to be done with the foreplay, but these spiels are what distinguish Anthony's curatorial edge. George relaxes into the ride, letting himself be taken.

'No one knows for sure what happened,' Anthony continues. 'Edgar's roommate found him unconscious outside the boarding house where he lived, with blood gushing from a half-inch wound in his thigh. He died before he got to hospital. Cause of death was a severed femoral artery. The police wrote it off as a hit-and-run to begin with, because neighbours reported hearing a car accelerate like a rocket from the scene. But the strange thing was Edgar's body didn't have a single bruise. The ladies at the Druid Hills Golf Club had flocked to his lessons because he was incredibly handsome and extremely eligible. So the local gossips pinned it on a jealous husband. You'd know all about them.'

George grins as Anthony assembles the two pieces of dark India rubber on the oilcloth. 'Find me a golf ball,' he orders, waving at a glass bowl on the sideboard behind him where dimpled white spheres are stacked in a pyramid. George takes the pinnacle and Anthony sets the ball gingerly on the tip of a two-inch arm jutting out at right angles from a thicker twelve-inch strip. Using a pocket-sized tape measure, he marks out a four-inch gap for the head of the club to pass through and places a second, smaller strip parallel to the longer axis for disciplining its path through the impact zone on completion of the swing.

George can't contain a competitive desire to display the fruits of his own research into J. Douglas Edgar. He borrows a sharpened pencil from a tray on Anthony's desk to describe the golfer's breakthrough theory of the masterstroke.

'Edgar called it "The Movement". He realised that in order to hit a straight shot, the club head must not travel in a straight line towards the target but instead must cross that line in a curved arc on an inside-to-outside path.' With the pencil he demonstrates Edgar's revolutionary tack by drawing an imaginary curve in the air.

They stare at the Gate as if beholding the first split atom. Anthony wouldn't dare puncture the moment by repeating the Atlanta golf pro's sacrilegious claim that you could create the same effect with two ordinary tees. You don't rise to become Sotheby's king hitter by slicing the shot.

'The box comes with Edgar's book.' Anthony hands him a faded green cloth-bound edition of *The Gate to Golf*. George opens it, tilting his nose towards the spine because he's always loved the woody smell of bound paper. He turns back to the frontispiece and reads the inscription written in fountain pen across the top of the page. 'To Iris. My star pupil. My one true love.'

Surprised by her husband's early arrival home, Leith emerges from their bedroom to greet him. He doesn't register her presence as he glances at the letters on the hall table and drops his keys in a brass bowl, guiding his briefcase under the table with the toe of his black leather brogue.

'I'm sorry I'm late,' he says, looking up. 'I went to High Street, to Anthony's.'

'Dinner will be ready soon,' she says. 'You know I've got book club here tonight.'

He nods.

'What've you got there?' she asks of the distinctive green-and-gold Harrods shopping bag that Anthony had given him to convey his purchase home.

'Just a couple of golf books.' He dampens her interest, knowing his devotion to golf only invites ridicule or contempt and without another word heads upstairs.

Leith bites her tongue, happy to humour him. Last Saturday she'd told Monty that the golf thing's gone too far.

'I guess we've all got our crutches,' she'd said. 'I mean, Rosie drinks, I gamble, Eva smokes. What does Bernadette do?' 'She prays,' he'd laughed. 'She reckons it's relaxing, like meditation.'

Leith ties the apron strings twice around her waist. Cooking's always been her therapy. She'd toyed with going back to teaching. Eva nagged her for ages. 'You'll like it when you get there. Schools are different these days,' she'd counselled. That's what scares Leith. Electronic whiteboards, memory sticks, PowerPoint presentations. 'You should never have given up,' Eva told her. Leith had wanted to be home for the boys. They'd argued this toss so many times, her indecision a luxury, as Eva pointed out, suggesting that perhaps a sudden plunge into poverty might cure Leith's dithering. Indolence handicapped her, sapped her confidence. She's started to clamber back. Her call earlier today to the city café brought a rush of pleasure. She's kept her phone by her ever since but they haven't rung back. She's not giving up, determined now that everything she does from here on will be for love.

She hears George upstairs moving furniture. Panic flutters against the bones of her rib cage. Pouring olive oil into a black skillet, she slops it over the stove. 'Slow down,' she tells herself, fetching the fish from the fridge. She tosses two fillets into the pan, focusing on the bite-sized tasks of a meal's preparation. The table's been set. She throws salad leaves into a bowl and seasons the fish with sea salt. Hunger draws George down from his den. She can't eat a thing.

'Candles?' he blinks, noticing but not remarking on the silverware they'd been given as a wedding present by Leith's parents, who'd held George in awe, allowing him to cruise above their altitude.

'And I got the good cutlery out.' Leith spoke his mind's thought. 'It just sits in the credenza like bones in a coffin and as I was setting the table I thought, why do people put all the special things they own away in cupboards? I mean, what are we saving them for? We could be dead tomorrow.'

He helps himself to the salad garnished with pears and walnuts and served in a bright blue and yellow ceramic bowl. Leith had bought it from a crowded market in Perugia while backpacking with Eva through Europe when they were students. She'd carried it home wrapped in clothes to survive the rickety buses, sardine trains, once even a horse-drawn dray.

'I guess people are afraid of breaking family heirlooms,' Leith continues to think aloud, ignoring the noise George makes when he chews, thirty-seven times before swallowing a mouthful, as his mother taught him to do. 'Perhaps if we used things that are precious all the time we'd get better at looking after them. Then every day would be special,' she concludes.

George draws a small translucent fishbone from the side of his mouth and sets it on the lip of his white china plate, aware that some response to her musings on crockery and domestic life is due.

'You're right,' he begins as he always does when he hasn't been paying close attention, and switches the subject. 'Which book are you discussing tonight?'

'Ted Hughes's *Birthday Letters*.' Once she would have dazed him with her readings out loud. She might have lent him her copy, keen for his comments, because he'd written poetry to woo her in the early days, often quoting Frost, Whitman, Owen from verses that he'd learnt by heart – a task set by his father, who'd wanted the boy to savour language. The poems would be recited after dinner to celebrate Arthur's return from High Court sittings interstate.

'Have you ever read the poem Hughes wrote about the fox cub on Chalk Farm Bridge?'

'No,' she blinks, amazed by George's mind.

'It's about them. Hughes and Plath. He's on his way to the tube one evening and he meets a man with a fox cub in his jacket. He dices with the dare of buying it, bringing it home, but – wisely, I think – decides not to. They've got a newborn baby of their own . . .'

'Go on,' she says for old time's sake, challenging him to spout the opening lines, a game they used to play when they first met.

'I can only remember bits of the last verse.'

'That'll do,' she smiles encouragingly.

He focuses intently for a moment, testing his memory, his lips moving soundlessly towards the poet's epiphany that the young father's failure of nerve as he faced the wild foundling signified a grander failure of heart.

The inescapable comparison with George's own struggle censors him. 'I've forgotten how it goes,' he lies. She sips from her glass to smooth her unease at the silence that shrouds them. His eyes are on his plate as he forks another mouthful, the clink of silver on china, orchestral as they retreat from an uncommon convergence. They haven't kissed for the longest time or touched each other intimately. George has never liked exploring the surfaces of her body. She's done her best to lead him, encouraging him to open his lips with her tongue, but he refuses as if he's discovered all he wants to know.

'Who was in court today?' she enquires nonchalantly, as she's done most evenings since his elevation to the bench.

'A young man, a fox cub.' His face softens. 'Rangy, he couldn't sit still. No lawyer, no money, unemployed, mad for his daughter. I didn't handle him well,' George sighs, critical of himself, so that Leith feels a tickle of sympathy.

'What was his name?' she quizzes him.

'I can't remember,' he says, irritated by her questions, one after the other, a poor substitute for conversation.

Uncomfortable in her stare, he pushed his chair back from the table and makes for the cellar, returning with a bottle of Grange, suddenly game to be done with the confession he's rehearsed a million times. But Leith has scraped the plates, stacked the dishwasher and tossed their cream linen napkins into the laundry basket.

'The girls will be here any minute,' she says to justify her efficiency, opening drawers to choose platters for tonight's supper.

Upstairs, George opens his very expensive vintage drop; to hell with letting it breathe. From the sideboard that once sat in his father's study he takes the soft cloth he uses to clean his spectacles and polishes a crystal glass until it shines. He fills it up then sets the bottle on a cork coaster, finicky here in his domain, overcome by sadness at the distance he and Leith put between them, each accommodating the other – for how much longer? He sinks into his leather chair with Edgar's book on his knees. Only a gifted imagination could describe a swing as The Movement, an almost mystical culmination of intent, aptitude and athleticism that eludes most players most of the time. For those who have acquired the masterstroke, Edgar writes, 'golf is intoxicating. It has the exhilarating effect of champagne, without the after-effects.' Quite, George concurs, hearing a cork pop downstairs. He savours a mouthful of Grange while devouring Edgar's instruction for gaining entry into heaven.

Typically, the steps are like a dance which looks simple enough until you mentally try to throw the club around the right hip, letting the body go well round on the backward swing, not too cramped, picturing the curved line of the club head on an inside-to-outside path so that it clears the gate and sends the ball towards your target. 'The Gate,' according to Edgar, 'should be a strong and potent enough attraction to completely fill the player's mind, and all the cells of his brain.'

'We'll see,' George decides, downing the dregs of his second glass, hopelessly hostage to Edgar's challenge before he has even lifted one of the heavier irons from his arsenal, arranged like rifle barrels in the clasps of an antique wooden rack from Scotland's Royal Dornoch clubhouse, the first curio Anthony had procured for his single-minded connoisseur.

Rosie's the first to arrive at the Kremmers' although she'd delayed her departure from home so as not to appear conspicuously eager for social intercourse. 'I thought it'd be you,' greets Leith, diminutive beside the solid oak door, in a purple silk blouse and flowing black pants, a strand of pearls around her fine white neck that is collared by shoulder-length black hair.

'You look just like a black-eyed pansy,' Rosie teases. She thinks of herself as a pine-cone, wooden and heavy. Towering over Leith, she spends her life trying to shrink her height, an effect assisted by flat heels and low self-esteem.

'What did you think of the poems?' Leith asks her as she leads her down the hallway into the kitchen.

'Creepy. I had to keep coming up for air.' She helps herself to a chorizo sausage from a platter on the bench where Leith resumes her preparations, crumbling goat's cheese on toasted triangles of cornbread. Voices and the crunch of heels along the gravel drive-way announce other guests. 'I'll get the door,' Rosie offers.

Bernadette has come straight from a board meeting of a Catholic charity that she chairs, her reading glasses perched on top of her auburn frizz, a wilful mop of hair that adds to the impression of an energetic woman who doesn't care for pampering. Eva's in high heels and a suit, her professional garb worn even between jobs. The tailoring jars with Leith's memories of her at university, strung with slogans, denim clad, passion reddening her cheeks. Her complexion has toughened up, her voice gravelly from years of smoking.

They talk over each other, their laughter echoing around the high ceilings as they make themselves at home, spreading around a circle of comfortable chairs in the front room. Rosie can't stop herself bending down to stroke the blue suede of Eva's high-heeled shoes.

'Try them on,' Eva says, popping one off. Rosie removes her leather loafer but her foot's too broad for the narrow fit.

'Ugly sister, that's me. I'm not bred for glass slippers,' she frowns.

'Well, my feet are the only part of me that's not getting bigger,' Eva consoles Rosie, who laughs with recognition because she'd sprung the top button of her skirt getting dressed for tonight, the flummery of her stomach triumphant. After that every article of clothing she tried on seemed to showcase her ungainliness.

Another rap on the door draws Bernadette up from the couch as Leith swings in carrying a tray of champagne flutes. Marion, younger than the others, has arrived. Her short fair hair is tousled and wispy; she's snazzy in a mustard-yellow V-necked top and a black skirt tight on her trim hips. 'Business Woman of the Year,' Bernadette cheers as Marion enters the room.

'*Small* Business Woman of the Year,' Marion qualifies the honour. 'It's only a local council award.'

'We're impressed. Any publicity's good publicity.' Bernadette gives her a hug.

'What did you win?' Rosie asks.

'A new car, a $20,000 Tiffany's voucher and a return trip to Paris,' she laughs as their gullible eyes turn towards her. 'As if! All you get is a certificate signed by the Mayoress.' She moves around the room kissing cheeks, almost tripping over Eva's loose shoe. 'Wow,' she says. 'Fuck-me shoes! Isn't that what Germaine Greer calls heels that high?'

'Well, they don't seem to have had that effect on any of the men who've interviewed me for a job,' Eva grumbles. Marion holds out a bottle of wine to Leith, who tells her to keep it: 'We're having champagne.'

'What for?' Marion asks, but her query wafts upwards in the

hubbub and the pistol pop of a cork that Rosie fires towards the ceiling-rose, narrowly missing a glass pendant on the chandelier. Flutes are filled and passed from hand to hand and the women hold out glasses to clink, their arms spoking a wheel of friendship.

'To new beginnings,' Leith proposes.

'You're in a dangerous mood,' Eva ribs her as she sips the chilled wine, its fizz prickling her palate. The effervescence is infectious. Light bounces off Leith's silk blouse, her hair shiny clean, flighty as she hovers around her guests.

'I'm starving,' says Bernadette, making for a low glass coffee table in the centre laid for a feast. Baby tortillas, red pimentos flecked with black pepper, sausage, grilled calamari and cornbread. 'Delicious,' she mumbles to Leith through a mouthful of food as she piles her plate high and sits next to Rosie, always conscious of the underdog.

'I can't stay late,' Marion announces. 'Phillip and I are flying to Broome in the morning. We're going to a resort two hours north of there for a couple of days – it's a bonding session for partners, and their . . . partners,' she smiles. 'One of them has just come out.'

'Lucky you!' Eva smiles a grimace.

Marion snickers in consensus. Her phone beeps and she winks at Eva as she taps a reply fast.

'You're going to get caught, you know,' Eva goads, sure this thrill ramps up the allure.

'It's out of control.' Marion slides the phone into her hip pocket.

She locks eyes with Eva in a conspiratorial admission. Leith arrives at her elbow, pouring champagne into Marion's glass.

'You're worse than a sixteen-year-old,' Leith marvels. 'Phillip must suspect something by now, surely.'

Marion sniggers as though she can't quite believe he hasn't.

'When was the last time you and George had a weekend away?' Eva asks.

'In January, remember? We went to stay with Jesse.'

'That doesn't count,' Eva teases.

Leith doesn't return the question because she knows Vince and Eva haven't had sex with each other for two years. 'Don't forget to ride the camels at Cable Beach,' Leith tells Marion.

'I don't think a camel could hold Phillip's weight!'

'Take a jumper,' Eva suggests. 'It gets cold at night.' She's anxious to be relevant. Envious of Marion's escapades and Leith's high-sheen gloss, her own aura seems dull by comparison. But whatever undercurrents of disaffection taint individual friendships, there is no acrimony to spoil the collegiate atmosphere of the women who enjoy belonging to this club. Light on procedural rules, the only tradition they honour gives the host bossing rights. Leith calls them to order as the conversation becomes raucous. She's been antsy all day, moving at a clip through her engagements, every passing moment another step towards freedom. 'Ted Hughes,' she begins holding up her copy of *Birthday Letters*.

'You know his second wife also committed suicide,' Rosie

interrupts because she'd only just discovered this on the web an hour ago.

'Her name was Assia Wevill and she wasn't his wife. They never actually married. And she took their daughter with her,' Leith elaborates. A shudder of horror scathes the women, their necks extended by the scale of the tragedy.

'He must have been cursed,' Rosie says, 'Like the Kennedy clan. Some people are. I know a woman who's lost three of her four children. One drowned, one was killed in a car accident, and one got meningococcal. She said to me once that she was an expert on every size of coffin.'

'The poems are extraordinary,' Leith dives in before they take this sidetrack. 'It's no wonder he couldn't publish them until he was dying.'

'I can't believe both women topped themselves!' Marion's stuck on the symmetry of their deaths.

'And they both did it with gas,' Rosie says.

'A sort of copycat thing? How malevolent is that.'

'I don't think you're capable of rational thought when you suicide,' Leith suggests. 'There's actually a poem in the book about him falling in love with Assia.'

'Wasn't she also a poet?' Eva asks.

Leith nods. 'I don't know how good she was but apparently she was beautiful.'

'Well, death didn't deliver her posthumous fame,' Eva says.

'And Sylvia Plath was already bankable. Am I being too cynical thinking that Ted Hughes was out to get a fat royalty cheque for his estate?'

'Yes,' Leith answers, playing tag with Eva as they've done through years of friendship. 'You're so a-romantic. It's not some rushed job lot to make a quick buck. This is his side of their love story.'

'Why shouldn't he tell his side of things?' Marion agrees. 'He kept silent for such a long time. Their children are adults. As he says in one of the poems, this is his story.' She flicks through her copy of the book, looking for the page she's marked. 'He actually says, 'your story, my story', and his story is that she was mentally unstable, tortured by her Daddy complex, a deeply flawed character, fated to die – in other words, not his fault.'

Off they go, gliding over the poetic meter, to pick at the bones that Hughes lays bare. Rosie refills their glasses. Bernadette has second helpings. Marion's phone beeps. She peers at the screen, smiling as her thumb dances a double-jointed can-can across the keyboard, up, down, up down. Eva glances at Rosie talking earnestly to Bernadette, who's nodding, one hand raised to cover her mouth as she eats from the plate balanced on her knees. Leith has her glasses on, flicking through pages purposefully. She looks up at Eva.

'They were so in love,' Leith says.

'It didn't last.' Eva axes her dewy-eyed sentiment with the blade of cynicism.

'Better to flame for a . . . what's that quote?' Leith cocks her head.

'Better to flame and burn than never to catch fire,' Eva giggles, and Leith joins in, shaking her head at this implausible rendition of an adage neither of them can remember.

'Well, Plath burned all right,' Leith concedes. 'I've read her letters and . . .'

'You're such a swot,' Eva razzes, familiar with Leith in a way they haven't enjoyed for a while.

'Here, have a browse.' Leith passes her a heavy volume.

'What about his letters?' Eva asks.

'Trust you,' Leith grins. 'I've got them on order. Anyway, read the letters she wrote to her mother just before she died. I've marked the page.' Eva finds a strip of red ribbon. 'You'll see how frantic she sounds, exhausted. She's stuck in a bleak London flat, it's the middle of winter, struggling with her babies, depression, her muse and her diminishing energy. She was desperate.'

'How could she have abandoned the children?' Rosie pleads.

'I know.' Leith cowers at a crime she's sure that she couldn't commit. 'I've always been haunted by her leaving milk and cookies beside their bed for them to eat when they woke up, as if that could placate them.'

'Do you think her children remember it?' Marion wonders. 'I read somewhere that she taped up their room and stuffed towels under the door to stop the gas from suffocating them too.'

The women are shocked by the numbness required to perform these macabre precautions, a mother keeping little ones safe from noxious vapour as she prepared to steal the breath of their life.

'What about the poem where he describes buttoning his daughter's jacket and feeding the baby boy in his high chair? It's the one where he apologises to her for the children's betrayal because they allow him to fill their mother's shoes . . . Life rolls on. I felt so sad for her.'

'For once you've read the book,' Eva says and there is a communal chuckle, which Rosie joins in, happy to be the punching bag.

'Well, the first ten pages anyway,' she parries

'A woman who I went to school with packed her children off to play at a friend's then went home and drank a glass of Draino. I know you said before, Leith, that people this depressed aren't thinking straight, but I just don't understand how you can snuff out maternal instinct,' Rosie says.

'Her love for him was stronger than her love for the children,' Bernadette ventures, a thought they fancy for its novelty. 'Lust, desire – there's no stronger urge, it overpowers everything else.'

Marion's phone beeps again and she hunches over its screen, working the keyboard, lifting her eyes to a circle of disapproval at this breach of etiquette. 'If Sylvia and Ted had owned mobile phones we'd be reading their SMS's, haiku poems.'

'Brilliant segue!' Eva applauds.

'I never message anyone,' Rosie says, pinning another short-coming to her chest.

'Mobile phones are a necessary evil,' Bernadette reassures her friend, patting her arm.

'I thought this was just a game of electronic footsies,' Eva whispers in Marion's ear.

Leith reaches for the champagne in a silver ice bucket by her tiny feet. 'I'd have to say that I don't think I've ever experienced a love as strong as the love I feel for the boys. I'd die for them, happily.'

'But not for George,' Eva goads her.

'No, of course not,' she laughs and they echo her.

'We've got a few more kilometres on the odometer than young Sylvia,' Eva says drolly. 'If she'd lived with Ted for as long as I've been with Vince she'd have been glad to see him go.'

'No question,' says Marion.

'But was it ever like this for you,' Leith asks, perplexed, 'pushed to the brink of madness by love?'

They are silenced by the paler spectrum of their passion. Another electronic beep interrupts. Marion ignores it. Like children searching for a lost ball in an overgrown paddock, they've lost sight of the game's rhythm.

'Why did we idolise Sylvia Plath?' Eva asks.

'She was beautiful, talented, cut down in youth,' says Bernadette, who's stopped eating for long enough to speak.

'By her own hand!' Eva argues. 'She wasn't shot dead fighting for democracy. I've been thinking about this a lot lately. I'm confused as to why we canonised her.'

'For the tragedy of —' Leith starts, but Eva talks over the top of her. 'But then, of course, we did deify Princess Di.'

'I'm going to burst I've eaten so much,' Bernadette sighs. 'You've outdone yourself with the food, Leith.'

'It's Spanish,' Leith explains, 'because of the poem, "You Hated Spain".' She turns to a dog-eared page that she smooths open with the heel of her hand, telling them of the chasm between Hughes's description of his wife recoiling from the country's exotic primitivism, and Sylvia's joyful letters to her mother, giddy with discovery. She's about to read them the poem when Rosie interrupts.

'I had my bag stolen in Spain. In Barcelona, actually, and it's all I remember now. It's your experience of a place that defines it more than the tourist attractions.'

They descend from the slopes of literature to trade anecdotes drawn from their lives so that eventually Leith puts the poem aside to get dessert.

'And what are you up to, Madame?' Bernadette asks as she follows her into the kitchen carrying dirty plates, which she places carefully on the marble-top bench.

'Nothing, why?' Leith laughs.

'The champagne, the food . . .' she sucks in her breath. 'Don't tell me it's your birthday and we've forgotten.'

'No.'

Bernadette's unconvinced. Leith hands her an orange-and-almond cake, moist and heavy on its antique silver platter. 'Here, carry this in for me, will you?' She scoops up five small forks, each handle engraved with a capital 'L', elegantly looped as if drawn with a feathered quill. Into a small polished silver jug she pours a thick ribbon of cream, smiling at the merry hell erupting from the living room. She arrives in the doorway to find them in uproar. Rosie has her hands between her legs as if she might wet her pants. Tears run down Marion's cheeks as Eva smothers her snorts in a napkin. Bernadette is doubled over beside the coffee table where she has managed to slide the cake clean off its perch on to the frosted glass top. Rosie gains enough composure to point up at the ceiling. Leith looks, quizzically, and as the laughter ebbs in anticipation a heavy thud of solid metal swiping the floor is louder for their hush. 'Someone's being murdered upstairs,' Rosie sets them off again.

'It's George,' Leith's muscles tense. 'He can't help himself. I wear these,' she says, spinning out of the room and returning with two bright orange rubber earplugs and a set of industrial-strength protectors. 'It drives me nuts,' she complains, her face taut with the nuisance of it. Marion's phone beeps and there's another almighty thump as if George is answering his wife's scorn. Eva tries on the headset, liberated by a sense of the absurd.

'Sounds like he's slaying an elk!' Bernadette's joke restores the shambolic mood of the evening. Just as they pull themselves together another elk bites the dust. Eva threatens to drive to the nearest 7-Eleven for cigarettes, egged on by Rosie who wrestles the cork out of the last bottle of bubbly as Leith taps the side of her glass with a cake fork. There's a pout in the direction of the spoil-sport.

'I think we should have a toast,' she says.

Rosie tops up their glasses. 'S'okay then,' she slurs. 'So long as you're not making us read another poem by the wife-killer . . .' The others laugh at her unsteadiness.

Now that she has the floor Leith almost regrets her intervention. She looks around at the faces wearing shades of surprise. 'Life's a fragile thing,' she starts. 'We take it for granted and I've been thinking lately of how much we leave unsaid – not the least because of reading these poems, thinking of what you'd undo, as Hughes does – resonances that are clear to him now, but were unspoken then.' She's rehearsed this speech, Eva thinks. 'And I had this urge to consecrate tonight. I read somewhere that close friendships are the secret to longevity and I wanted you all to know that I count myself lucky to be among you.'

'Here's to us,' they clink. Leith's burst of sentimentality unsettles them. Silently, each of them contemplates various scenarios. Bernadette wonders if Leith's found a lump on her breast. Eva diagnoses a post-menopausal flush of emotion. Rosie verges on tears without a clue why. Marion consults her watch. 'It's after midnight,' she yawns punctually, reeling them back to the lateness of the hour. They take a compulsory sip of their last drinks, which Rosie has poured flush with the top of the glass. She skols hers, unchecked by the discipline of jobs and spouses, her internal alarm clock on snooze since she's been living alone. The others leave theirs otherwise untouched, mindful of hangovers and a sneaking sense of the damage already done.

'S'what are we reading next?' Rosie asks, burrowing in her handbag for car keys which Leith would confiscate if her friend's house wasn't just around the corner. Eva's on her hands and knees searching for her right shoe, which is under the couch. Marion can't find her copy of the book. The mood is muted as they gather their belongings. A sudden loud bang from upstairs as George resumes his practice shots is no longer funny. The women totter out the front door where Leith stands waving goodbye until the last car, Rosie's of course, starts, then stops while she fumbles with the headlights, before roaring away into the darkness.

Leith turns inside and walks slowly towards the staircase. She clasps the smooth wooden balustrade and lifts herself towards a conversation she's been dreading. Halfway up she stops to catch her courage and wonders whether she should wait in the kitchen where she feels more confident – clean up the dishes and down a last glass of champagne. But another whack, louder than before, urges her up another few steps. She's careful to avoid the boards that creak just in case she crumbles, until she finds herself on the landing, reaching out for the door handle, choosing the moment of her arrival. She waits for the thud of his swing to pass just as the boys used to pause for the waves to break before skimming their boards safely into the sea, and then there's no going back.

Sam can't sleep. He'd gone back to court this afternoon and waited by the entrance to the underground car park. Dumb idea. A stunt you could pull off in the movies, not here in this screwed-up place, unless he'd brought his rag and bucket and offered to do a deluxe job on the judge's windscreen in return for a minute of his time. In his dreams he conveys the trueness of his love for Mags so convincingly his wish is granted, orders reversed. Instead a security guard wearing a holster had told him to move away or face arrest. He can't bear that a stranger can stop him seeing his daughter. He's kept his distance, done as Angie's bid apart from one harmless breach. Now Gabe's saying he upsets Mags, that he scares her, that she's been wetting her bed. Next she'll accuse him of abuse and they'll believe her. He heard men at that meeting talk about some list for sexual offence cases and once you're on that you're gone. He lies back on his unmade bed, the possibility that there's worse ahead pestering him in the darkness.

Gabe threatened suicide when the doctors refused her an abortion. Now she won't let her baby go. Wasn't he the one who'd whooped at the news of her pregnancy, who'd promised to look after this baby, who'd found the bones of Mag's body in the grainy ultrasound photo, telling Gabe how the radiologist had reckoned their daughter was perfectly proportioned, giving a face to the foetus, binding mother and child together?

Vermont, Maine, Rhode Island . . . He begins naming the states of America, working around the continent in a clockwise direction, invoking the quiz he and Angie used to play together, imagining one day they might tour the world.

'You have your father's itchy feet,' his aunt used to scold. 'You never finish anything.' Sam likes imagining his father as a traveller. During childhood, he'd thought of him as an adventurer, dressed in a snakeskin vest with an eye patch and a dagger in a sheath strapped to his calf. Only as he grew older did his disappointment recast this stranger as a shifty nomad without purpose or direction. Desperate to know the alchemy of his identity, Sam sometimes thinks he sees his dad emerging from a throng of commuters. Alerted by a likeness in a face, he searches their eyes for a sign of loss, fantasising about the moment of recognition, inventing a haphazard meeting on a street corner. Angie thought she saw him in town once, grey hair sticking out from under a grimy cap, but when she pushed her way through to the door of a crowded tram he'd gone.

A tram rumbles past outside. Even if it's the last one for the night he reckons on his sister being up, and if she's not, well, he's woken her later than this plenty of times before. She answers on the first ring.

'Where've you been? Your phone's been switched off. You

promised you'd call. I've been waiting all day to hear how it went.' She's cross. 'Did you remember to do everything I said?'

He hangs up. He can't tell her. His phone vibrates and he answers it, his temples throbbing.

'Sam,' she is crying already. 'You've done yourself in, haven't you?' Angie traces the groove of her brother's self-destruction so that he hates himself.

'What's going to happen to Mags?' she worries for the brown-eyed mop-haired little girl with the lilting voice who was becoming a part of Angie's life before the troubles took her away. Mags is the only perfect creation Sam could claim any credit for in a past littered with pledges solemnly made and lightly broken.

He didn't have the words, even with a clear head, to explain how busted up he felt. He's got to fix things, but his sister doesn't want to hear plan three thousand one hundred and twenty four. 'I'm sorry, sis,' he croaked. 'The judge kept telling me to sit, like his damn dog. Gabe's got a lawyer. Your Honour this, Your Honour that. When she said Mags didn't want to see me, I cracked.'

Angie's silent, the receiver cupped on her shoulder, as their conversation dwindles. She watches car headlights pass by below her kitchen window in a relentless stream of traffic that never ceases. Sam takes his wallet from his back pocket, slipping his finger under the plastic film to slide out the photograph of his daughter, smiling. He wants to sob so he pushes the heels of his hands against the lids of his eyes to hold himself in.

An ambulance in the distance disturbs the peace, and Angie searches for the flashing light as the wail of panic intensifies in her ear; both of them are silenced by a sound that has spooked them forever. On the night their mother died they were woken by a bang. They lay there listening, neither speaking, waiting for voices or footsteps or a light switched on or for the stillness to continue long enough for them to settle back to sleep. Then the sirens began screaming, getting closer and closer until they were outside, terrifying, coloured lights dancing in the shadows on the wall of their bedroom. A policeman came and took them to a neighbour's. Their aunt collected them days later. The next time they saw their mother she was in a box with shiny silver handles.

'Is that at your end?' Angie asks Sam. He leans far enough forward to see a red-and-blue streak fly past on a life-saving mission and he wishes he could swap places with the person on the stretcher 'cause that way he might survive.

'Seat belt!' Curly Johnston barks at the female paramedic beside him on the front seat as the ambulance careers around the corner into Punt Road, slowing down on approach to the red lights at the first intersection in case some junked up idiot P-plater with a doof-doof and a head full of speed hasn't heard the siren.

'Move it, Mister,' Curly urges a dirty white clapped-out van taking forever to clear out of the centre lane as they turn sharp right into Toorak Road. He snatches a look at the driver's profile, scoffing audibly for the benefit of Gina, his offsider, because his prejudices have been confirmed. 'Probably don't have ambos where he comes from,' he snorts.

'I didn't see a single one in the Solomon Islands.'

'Was that where you went on your honeymoon?' he asks, hanging left down a side street towards the avenue that hugs the river bank. Gina had told him ten, possibly twenty, times where she was going, how much it was costing, what she was wearing. He'd even advised her on the colour of the roses in her wedding bouquet (burnt orange, crimson-tinged petals). There were times over the past year when Curly felt as though he knew more about last month's nuptials than the groom, but he'd never been any good with geography beyond the border of Australia. Bali's as far as he's gone offshore.

'What's the house number?' He readies himself for entry into an orbit of crisis where every second counts. Gina consults a screen on the dash. 'Twenty-five. House's on the right-hand side of the street, driveway entry.' This was her first shift back and she'd have preferred a non–life threatening emergency to ease her gently into the routine instead of an ice-cold plunge into the deep of a Priority 0. She feels nauseous for the second time since coming home. 'Patient's female. 55 years of age. Suspected head injury from a violent blow to the neck. She's in the first room on the left at the top of the stairs. Says here that the patient was hit by a golf club.'

'A domestic, for sure,' Curly says.

Gina can cut people out of twisted car wrecks but she hates

walking into neat and tidy houses where hatred ferments. In suburbs like this one families soundproof their disturbances, she thinks, sizing up the mansions set back on blocks three times the size of the land where she lives. The last domestic she'd attended, the week before her wedding, half the bloody neighbourhood had come out to watch what was left to stitch up after the screaming that'd been going on in a street where there weren't any buffer zones – no circular driveways or hundred-year-old hedges to screen a couple's loathing.

If there'd been arguments tonight the voices hadn't woken next door. The street's asleep. Lights are glowing upstairs and down at number twenty-five. The ambulance turns sharply into the driveway, spraying gravel as the tyres brake behind a black Audi. Gina leaps out before the engine cuts, flinging open the back doors to kit up with baseline drugs, cardiac monitor, blood-pressure cuffs, intubation equipment and IV gear. They make for the stately veranda where a tall, silver-haired gentleman beckons them inside a doorway flanked by stained-glass panels. Gina takes in the high ceilings and ornate plaster cornices above the black-and-white tessellated tiles. The man's been drinking. A claret stain crusts the corners of his tightly drawn mouth. As they turn up the carpeted stairs she sees empty champagne bottles, three or four of them, on the coffee table in the front room, where red cushions from a couch are strewn on the floor. They take the steps two at a time. The man, whom she guesses to be sixtyish, is calm and contained. Shock is an expression with a million guises and Gina's learnt not to interpret emotional lockdown as a lack of distress. He ushers them inside a dimly lit room adorned with golfing memorabilia. Tiger Woods is the only player she recognises in the framed and signed posters on the wall. They kneel on either side of the woman, who lies flat on her back just inside the door, to the left, where she was flung from the force of the club, hitting her head as she fell onto the wooden floor and complicating the injury already sustained to her neck at the point of impact. The man says he was instructed not to lift her. His carriage and coolness exude authority and control, although Gina can see from the woman's pupils, which are fixed and non-reactive, that the situation has passed into a realm where hope thins like the air at inhospitable heights. She is petite, dressed in evening wear – black slacks and a purple silk blouse with a Chinese collar not high enough to have offered any protection from the whack she copped. Loose pearls from the woman's broken necklace slide on to the floor in a flurry of hailstones as Curly performs an endotracheal intubation to pump oxygen around her rapidly deteriorating body. Gina hooks up the cardiac monitor and begins CPR. She inserts an IV tube into the patient's soft skin, fair like Gina's mother who is not much younger than the woman dying in her arms.

'It was an accident,' the man explains to them in a steady voice as he bends to pick up the pearls before someone slips on one. Gina parts the woman's dyed black hair for a cervical collar to address spinal injury. She notices that one of the woman's pearl drop earrings has been ripped from its fine gold anchor but other-wise her body seems deceptively intact with only faint bruising evident on the right side of the neck. 'It was an accident.' The man repeats the phrase plaintively, as if explaining it to himself. Curly and Gina slide the woman, light as a child, onto the stretcher, and the man pursues them out of the room. 'She walked into my swing. I didn't hear her. She didn't make a sound.'

That's your story, Gina thinks as they exit the house, their haste amplified by the crushed stones spinning underfoot and the silence of the street. The dog next door barks in a token protest.

'Are you coming with us?' she asks the man and for the first time she sees fear and uncertainty in his blue eyes. He weighs up his options amidst the spit and crackle of radio communications in the front cabin as Curly alerts the trauma team at emergency to the woman's condition. The man glances back towards the house.

'I'll come with Leith,' he decides, his voice quavering at her name. He pulls himself up, athletic for his age, and shrinks himself into the confined space. There amidst the oxygen units, stabilising drugs and cardiac monitors he capitulates to the terror of losing Leith and as he freefalls from grace he focuses on the stretcher, his seatbelt, staying calm as he begs and bribes the devil or who-ever might deal in miracles.

'Everybody right?' Curly demands as he starts the engine and the ambulance glides backwards before it shrieks forward into the night.

*   *   *

The command to escort a judge from hospital emergency to the scene of a possible crime saves Detective Inspector Dan Sinclair from attending a fatal stabbing in Sunshine. He knows George Kremmer from a corner of his past but he's had trouble locating where and when since the chief commissioner's call ten minutes ago, brusque, sharp.

'Tragic,' the commissioner had said with the flatness of a man whose nose has been pressed up against the despicable and unspeakable for so long he's lost the emotional range to sound as though he truly means the clichés he trots out. 'Treat it as a possible reckless injury charge. Take him home, interview him, check out the house. The paramedics have reported drinking – there are empties upstairs and down, apparently. His story is that this was a horrendous accident. He says his wife walked in while he was swinging a practice shot. Be gentle. He's a mess.'

Dan turns to the chubby copper of Asian extraction who's sitting a metre away at the next terminal, hunched over his screen. 'You ever play golf?' he asks, reckoning on a 'No', unless there was a card game by that name because the only clubs he's seen in the palm of Ken Nguyen's hand come in packs of fifty-two. Ken grunts a negative without swivelling his chair an inch off-course. 'Me neither,' Dan says.

He taps the words 'George Kremmer' into the computer's search engine, which tells him in a flash what would have taken much longer to dredge from a brain muddled with a myriad criminal investigations and a telephone book of witnesses, villains and their victims.

'Of course.' He scrolls through the data on file, which he nut-shells for Ken. 'Family Court. He got a death threat four years ago. We never found out who did it. Too many suspects. Single fathers who reckoned they'd been done over in court. It does them in, the ones who care.' Ken grunts again and logs off his computer to pay Dan some attention.

'I went to Kremmer's house, huge place with a front yard as big as a race track. His wife made us sandwiches and coffee.'

'Trust you to remember the refreshments,' Ken smiles, because Dan's diet, now that he has a girlfriend, is obsessive.

'She was small, smiley,' he says, ignoring the dig. 'Well preserved.' He doesn't reveal how Leith Kremmer got him talking when the judge was called away to the phone and how he told her more than he meant to about his separation, which had left him skinned, raw and tender. Wasn't she the one who said she knew of only one couple still in love after twenty-five years of marriage? It was her, he was sure of it. But then he remembers being sad for her because when he looked for a twinkle in her eyes to confirm she was the lucky one, there was none.

In the wide, tree-lined boulevard outside police headquarters, darkness loiters, questioning the purpose of pedestrians and a trickle of cars in the limbo hours before dawn. The police vehicle cruises along the centre lane; the metal tramlines glinting in the headlights x-ray the city's spinal cord. Above, thick electric cables cobweb the sky. Not a word passes between Ken or Dan as they make the short trip to the inner-city hospital where Leith Kremmer was pronounced dead on arrival at 1 a.m.

TUESDAY

Frank strokes Cameron's back, willing the birthday boy to find a third wind after a night's carousing with friends at the club where they'd danced up a sweat, stripping off their shirts, numbed by gulps of absinthe until, stumbling outside in the early hours, the bitter cold air had stung them sober.

'You're showing your age,' Frank says, nuzzling into Cameron's warm body under the doona. Cameron smiles consent but doesn't budge from his light-headed saunter towards sleep.

They live high up above the city that Cameron's always liked because Boston reminds him of home, with its broad river bridged by elegant architectural arches and its reliance on the clean industry of scholarship. Frank lies awake listening to Cameron's breathing and the intestinal gurgle of the building's central heating. Their dog, Mack, is dreaming: high-pitched whinnying then a snort as he floats off again. Frank hears the fridge's hum. He relives Cameron's delight upon opening the David Mamet biography, and wishes now he'd chosen a less predictable gift – the bakelite cigarette box he'd seen in a retro thrift store. But Cameron's own pleasure at the evening's celebrations was marred only by Leith's uncharacteristic silence. Cameron had gone to the screen in their study to check his email the moment they arrived home, disappointedly logging off before retiring to bed, leaving his clothes in a pile on the floor which Frank picked up obligingly and hung in the closet because in their house birthday boys are kings for a day. Frank closes his eyes, drifting into sleep.

Cameron hears the phone first. He lifts his head off the pillow and listens, then jumps up and skids across the polished boards to the landline on the table in the hallway. Mack barks at the excitement, waking Frank, who thinks immediately of his mother, alone in her eighties.

'Is that you, Cameron?' George's voice is timid.

'Yes. It's me. Is Leith okay?' He's filled with panic by the untimely call.

'She's had an accident,' George swallows, afraid for Cameron's sake. 'She died this morning.'

He means to expand, to explain as well as he can, but he hears the phone tumble to the floor and the sound of another man's voice asking questions and then the terrible avalanche of sobs.

'It's Frank Levin here, Cameron's partner. Is that George?'

'Yes it is.' George has never spoken to Frank before. 'Leith's been in an accident. She's dead.' He's shivering as though he's going to be sick.

'What happened?' Frank's soft voice takes control, his free hand massaging Cameron's back, hearing George's turmoil, needing to elicit information, thinking she's been in a car smash or a random shooting, killed by an intruder, a stroke or a brain haemorrhage, no warning, a sudden irreversible switch flicked off, gone from here, there, no chance for goodbye. That's how it was when he got the call about his sister. Ungodly hours bring horror, bloodied and dark, wet.

'It was a mistake.' George's voice is barely audible. 'I hit her by mistake. I was taking the head of the club inside-to-out. I just didn't see her.' George is crying.

'Where was she hit?' Frank must tell Cameron something.

'On the right side of her neck, severing an artery. Before we got to hospital she'd bled to death. She died at 1 a.m. Melbourne time.' The lateness of the hour is a mystifying detail that dangles, seeming to doubt him. In the background, the police investigations unit secures the crime scene – the noisy, business end of death at one end of the world and the silent agony of its theft at the other.

George hears a knock at his door. A detective enters the bedroom, motioning to him with a nod, and he stands as if preparing to follow. 'The police are here. They need to see me. I'll have to go. I wanted Cameron to know. I'm sorry.' He pockets his phone, shaken by what he's done to Leith and now her brother, twice victim of his brutality.

Frank wraps his arms around Cameron, who refuses every

attempt to move him from his huddle on the floor where he keens, gently rocking, calling his sister's name.

Rosie's awakened by bright sunlight, chastening her like a rooster's crow. She didn't draw the curtains last night before falling into bed. Her head pounds in lockstep with the prodding paws of Pugsley, an obese tortoiseshell cat, who's poised to reposition himself inside the crook of her knees, his purr full throttle. She squints at the time on her digital clock. Groping for her spectacles on the bedside table, she gives up as she remembers, groggily, that she left her glasses at Leith's place. Sight, like water, is a resource she's taken for granted up until now. How she steered the car safely home in an alcoholic haze she doesn't know. I'm becoming like a cockroach, she sniffs miserably, aware of her capacity for survival.

Perhaps that's what turned Alistair off, she thinks, me losing my vulnerability. Her husband, father to their three girls, crosses her mind daily. He walked out on her one Sunday last winter, a bitterly cold day. They'd been to a brunch party for one of Alistair's brothers in the morning. She'd drunk too much champagne and orange juice. Alistair had proposed the birthday toast – a rollicking speech, extracting tears of laughter from the guests, and she'd admired him up there on the shoe-cleaning box that someone had shoved forward to use as a podium. The afternoon at home had passed in a languid fashion. She'd dozed off on the couch in front of the Sunday arts program. He'd got busy cleaning out leaves from the gutters. Anything involving a ladder was his business. She'd been nagging him for months so the sight of his bottom half through the den window didn't surprise her although she puzzled over what had stirred his sense of obligation. When he'd raked up the mulch of decaying foliage and spread it over the garden beds at the back of the house he'd come inside and stood nervously by the door.

She knew as soon as he took off his thick gardening gloves and then his glasses that life was being rearranged around her. He made his admissions one after another in a cascading order of magnitude: years of unhappiness; a longstanding girlfriend, pregnant; he'd no choice, he was sorry, truly sorry. 'Aren't we all?' she'd managed sourly, before he resumed his valediction. She'd keep the house, the lot. He'd be starting afresh. Then he'd rushed from the house in the same breathless haste, Rosie struck dumb in her chair, the cat on her lap, absorbing her tears. The ladder still leans against the eaves where he left it that day. She couldn't be bothered putting it back in the garage where it belongs. Susie, their eldest daughter, says he has an apartment in town. No more gutters to clean. He drinks coffee instead of tea and rides a motorcycle to work, eager to trim his carbon footprint.

'Let him go,' Leith had advised her. Rosie had turned to Leith because she trusted her judgement in everything from where to keep coffee beans (in the fridge) to hormone replacement therapy (it all depends). Leith is measured. Her opinion matters. She'd responded admirably. Movies together every Wednesday; Italian lessons on Friday mornings; a six-week course of Thai cooking classes; serving breakfast at the city mission once a fortnight. 'You can't let yourself get bitter,' Leith insisted. She rang constantly, cheering Rosie up, almost as if she knew what it was like to be abandoned. Rosie was her personal project.

'You're not going to meet anyone here,' she'd remarked one evening, allowing her arm a laconic sweep around Rosie's kitchen as they shared a chilled white wine before fixing their respective dinners.

'I'm too old. I can't imagine taking my clothes off in front of a stranger. Could you?'

Leith had paused to consider the idea, tilting forward as if she was about to disclose that she had, but then she'd just smiled. 'You could always wear blindfolds. It might be sexier.'

Rosie had frowned. 'I think I'm getting ahead of myself. Besides, I don't even know if another man's what I'm looking for.'

Leith registered Rosie with an online dating site and they scrolled through the database of available men together. 'It's like going through the remainder table,' Rosie tittered. They crafted her profile, selecting music, films, books to attract a certain kind of intelligence, workshopping a pseudonym to badge her details. Leith came up with 'second coming', 'lifesaver' and 'new venture', which is the one Rosie adopted. During the past year she's been on four dates. Two of the men came back for a second nibble. The last candidate, an economist, had gloated at the 95 electronic kisses he'd received within 24 hours of posting his availability. 'You have to be quick,' Leith prodded her, and the next morning had woken Rosie with a phone call to notify her of a find. 'He's 62, over six feet tall, he's only been on for a day so hurry up, otherwise he'll be inundated. He's an engineer, runs his own business, likes bushwalking . . .' Rosie could hear Leith's keyboard clacking.

'What does he look like?' she asked.

'He's got glasses.'

'Hair?'

'Thinning.'

'Fat?'

'Full around the face but it's difficult to tell from this photo what's down below. He's sitting at a table.'

'He's probably in a wheelchair.'

Leith's interest in Rosie's fortunes petered out. She stopped emailing her electronic prospects. They still attend Italian classes but Leith's been promoted to a higher level. Rosie's in a funk. She's sleeping later. Drink numbs her loneliness so that self-sufficiency becomes self-fulfilling. She's slid into serious depression, giving up her part-time job managing rentals for the real-estate firm where she once sold dress-circle houses, unable to pretend any more that four bedrooms and a pool can deliver 'family perfection', as she'd once headlined an ad for a solid Edwardian residence. Her local GP regards her empathetically; since his suburban practice was taken over by a corporate health provider he's been reduced to writing referrals for specialists, his jowls a road map of capillaries. Rosie's an expert at picking the sozzlers. You get by on pride, caring what other people think, then even this shred of snobbery fades. After swearing that she'd never go down the street in a tracksuit, she'd worn a pair of pyjama bottoms because they looked like sweat-pants. Jumping back into her car that day, she'd checked her face in the mirror to find sleep in the corner of one eye. At least she'd brushed her teeth.

'I'm worried about you,' Leith said last week, frowning as she tallied the empty bottles in Rosie's pantry.

'I missed the recycling.'

Leith's lips tightened disapprovingly and tears welled in her eyes. 'You told me to leave you be and look what happens.'

'I need to hit rock bottom,' Rosie stated, flooring them both.

'Well,' Leith paused, 'are we there yet?' And they both managed a weak smile at this reference to whines from the back seat dur-ing family car trips.

'Just about,' Rosie answered duplicitously.

'Around the next corner,' Leith had said, hugging her, saddened because Rosie was losing this battle.

'I'll be all right.' Leith's pity was her lowest point, cutting her deep through the flab of denial. She moves through the house, her thoughts rambling, relieved the newsagent has managed to fling the paper within reach of her terrazzo porch and not on the nature strip or up on the roof where last Wednesday's paper is waiting for someone to climb the ladder. The other day she noticed a 'Hire-A-Hubby' van in the traffic and jotted down the number to book him for odd jobs. She rips the plastic sheath off today's edition and deciphers the headline. 'Terrorist cell in eastern suburbs.'

'Let's hope they're not next door,' she says to Pugsley, under her feet.

'No breakfast for you,' she scowls at the cat. 'You're too fat.' Pugsley mews sharply. 'Speak for yourself, is that what you said?'

She pours a glass of orange juice from the fridge and punches two headache capsules from the blister pack in the fruit bowl, empty except for two lemons and a small green apple with crinkled skin. 'Now,' she tells the cat, 'let's ring Leith so I can get my glasses, otherwise I just might have to trade you in for a seeing-eye-dog.' Her fingers read the keypad, pressing the buttons in an order she knows by heart. Nobody answers. The tone rings through to the message bank. Leith's mellifluous voice apologises for being otherwise engaged and promises to call back as soon as she's able. 'Oh,' Rosie fluffs, 'I hope you've pulled up better than me.' She pauses. 'Thanks for the hangover. I can't find my glasses and I'm sure I've left them at your place, somewhere. I thought I might pop by to collect them if that's okay with you. I'm cactus without them.'

She turns the radio on, almost tripping over the cat, who glares at her indignantly. Rosie relents. 'It's not as if you've been on a 40-hour famine,' she chides him gently as he sits on his considerable haunch, determined that she will open the cupboard.

'Okay. You win,' she relents, scooping the contents of a gourmet chicken meal into his Peter Rabbit bowl, once treasured by all three of her daughters. The youngest left home soon after Alistair's departure, as if the gate had been marked with the black cross of the bubonic plague. Not a thought for their mother's welfare. The girls told her that if it'd been them they would have kicked him out years ago. This hurt Rosie more than Alistair's sin because of the years she'd wasted holding things together on their behalf. She hadn't wanted them shunting back and forth between two households, splitting holidays down the middle, dividing affection evenly or, worse still, empowering them to express a preference for one parent over the other.

The façade of togetherness Rosie had stencilled with comforting motifs of domesticity was too easily pierced. 'Get yourself a new life,' her daughter had recommended, as if you could choose one from a rack out the front of a boutique at the nearest mall. Rosie was attached to her old life, thank you very much, and still in love with the man she'd married over twenty-five years ago, the youngest son of her parents' oldest friends. None of her girls have serious boyfriends. 'You're too fussy,' she tells them and they look at her as if to say, 'We've got higher standards.'

She decides to walk over to Leith's place right away. Pulling on a pair of cotton calf-length pants and the smock top she wore last night, she brushes her thinning brown hair. 'Come on, Rosie,' she gees herself, conscious of her resolution to arrest the slide in personal grooming. Parting her lips, she applies a coral lipstick and slaps moisturiser on both cheeks. A stroll will do her good. 'I need the exercise, now that we've let our gym membership lapse,' she chats to the cat, using the collective 'we' for solidarity. 'You could do with an aerobic outing yourself,' she continues, pulling a face at Pugsley. 'Anyway, I want to check on the renovations being done to the Thompsons' old house on the corner. How anybody could afford extensions after spending $6.5 million at auction is beyond me,' she tuts. Slipping her bare feet into leather sandals, she leaves the house, empty handed. Her front door key lives under the pot plant by the rockery, one less thing to lose.

In the street two men are unloading water tanks from a truck parked outside the house opposite. Rosie's front yard speaks to her belief that rain, like hope, will arrive eventually. As she nears the Thompsons' she meets Grant Pendlebury, a neighbour who lives nearer the Kremmers, pushing a stroller.

'On Grandpa duty?' she asks him when they meet.

'For a week,' he says. 'Two of them. The five-year-old is at school. This one was up half the night.' Rosie smiles at the dozing toddler and she bends down to remove a juice cup from the child's loosened fingers before the drink tumbles to the ground. 'She got woken by an ambulance at some ungodly hour and she wouldn't settle.' Pendlebury's grand-daughter stirs, disturbed by the voices and the lull in the soporific rhythm of wheels bumping over cracks in the pavement. 'You better be off or she'll wake,' Rosie prods him, keen to get moving herself. 'Give Nance my love,' she sings out over her shoulder. Rounding the corner, she passes a cluster of silver birch trees, their papery white trunks gnarled with elephants' eyes.

George's black car is where it was last night, blocking Leith's sedan inside the driveway. On her way up the path Rosie scoops up the scrolled newspaper for hand delivery. Leith must be lying in, she thinks. Ascending the sweep of front steps to the veranda she glances through the tall sash windows into the living room. Two champagne bottles stand on the coffee table beside the last wedge of Leith's orange-and-almond cake fringed with crumbs, a sticky serving knife on the side of the silver platter. Yellow tape is webbed around behind the backs of the chairs where they'd gathered for book club. A burglary – Rosie jumps to conclusions, writing a script on the run. The cars, the unanswered phone, everything clicks. She looks forward to hearing Leith's account over a strong pot of coffee.

Two quick knocks as she listens to birdsong and the distant rumble of traffic on the city's arterial network. A door closes somewhere inside the house. She raps again, louder this time. Footsteps sound on the tiles, advancing towards her.

'Leith,' she calls impatiently. 'It's me.'

The door opens but George greets her silently. He's wearing casual clothes, his hair's ruffled.

'Oh. George. I wasn't expecting you. I mean, I know the car's here, but I'm so used to Leith being around and you off at court.

What's with the yellow tape?' she squawks excitedly, pointing past
him to a loose sash of plastic that flaps gently in the breeze blowing through the door. He says nothing, his blue eyes bloodshot.
She stands there uncertainly. 'Come in,' he says at last, stepping
aside for her to enter. She follows him down the hallway. A label
protrudes from the back of his crew-neck jumper and she resists
the urge to tuck it in. She'd never dare touch George. At the top
of the stairs she notices more yellow tape woven around the balustrade. Otherwise, everything is as it was when she left here barely
10 hours ago. In the kitchen, dirty plates are stacked beside the
sink and champagne flutes smeared with lipstick confirm disrup-
tion to the natural order Leith maintains. George stops in front of
the sink. He lifts his fingers to his temples, his eyes are closed, and
Rosie senses the depths of his dishevelment. She's unsure where
to put herself. He fills a tumbler of water at the tap and drinks it
down so thirstily he chokes and starts to cough – a hacking, gasping noise – and she thinks she should give him a bang on his back
but he collects himself and the pause between them is disconcerting. He slides a chair back and sits down at the kitchen table.
Instinct guides Rosie towards him. It's as though both of them
are in a car that has blown a tyre and swerved off course. On the
crimson tablemat in front of her a fine silver fork engraved with a
capital 'L' points to George.

'Where's Leith?' she asks him. A tennis ball bounces either side
of the net on the court next door before George opens his mouth

in a noiseless scream, the sinews in his neck taut like the strings of
a harp. 'She's dead,' he whispers. 'Last night.' His voice is hoarse.
His bows his head to hide and then he tells her in stilted phrases
his incredible tale.

Never at her sharpest this early, Marion loses precious minutes
watering parched tubs of lavender on the balcony. Below, the city's
neon looks tacky against the skyline's dawn glow. Hurrying back
inside, her feet damp, she finishes packing for Broome, wishing
she had a severe dose of thrush to keep Phillip away. If only she
could stuff him into a plastic bag of recycled clothes and dump him
on the pavement outside a charity store. Take the advice of those
consultants in the magazines full of tips for getting rid of clutter:
'Put what you can't bear to throw away in a box and if you haven't
needed any of the contents a year later, toss the lot'. These are the
kinds of commandments that creep into our lives. *If you don't miss
it, chuck it*. No wonder she gets so confused over right and wrong.
She envies Bernadette's clear-sighted Catholicism. 'Right' is such
a relative term in Marion's book. *Do unto others* leaves her a lot
of wriggle room, opening the door to unprincipled, sleazy behaviour that won't kill her. Lying is, for her, an everyday occurrence.
Everybody lies, surely. Except for Bernadette. And what about
Leith? Anyone who goes to that much trouble in presenting a plate
of food must be disguising shortcomings of deeper significance.
Perhaps that's why Leith loved being let in on Marion's secret.

She'd cornered Marion in the powder room last night. 'You look so happy I could eat you,' Leith had said.

'I can't keep this up,' Marion had replied, drying her hands on an embroidered linen towel. 'Two days alone with Phillip at a remote beach resort,' she'd groaned, 'and I might be driven to home truths.'

'Wait till you get back,' Leith had pleaded, 'for his sake.'

Straight out of Leith's style book, her advice to avoid a scene comes from a lifetime of putting yourself last, a selflessness typical of the homemakers Marion knows – clients who can't help themselves cleaning up after the party even though they've paid for staff. There's a lovely old-fashioned grace to these women. They conduct themselves socially without the hard-edged intrusion of market economics, competitive advantage, opportunities, networking. Marion hasn't got the patience to fluff around massaging egos unless she's billing them for the service.

She flings clothes indiscriminately into her suitcase, guided by necessity, temperature, practicality, with barely a thought for seduction or flattery; Phillip's desires are irrelevant now. If only she owned a chador, although the lure of disrobing a woman covered from head to toe apparently sharpens anticipation. The shorts, sandals and T-shirts she chooses for this brief sojourn are her version of fatigues, camouflage gear.

Her phone beeps as she packs her cosmetics: a text message from Phillip. He's on his way from work where he's been since dawn, putting in a full day before Tuesday's even begun. '4got swimmers. Pack them for me.' She grabs hers from the drawer, a one-piece, then her phone squeaks again. It's from 'W', as she's tagged him in her contacts directory.

'If you see a croc, give Phillip a kiss from me.'

'A kiss or a push?' she fires back.

'Found an old photo of you today. Surrounded by mermaids. Guess where?' She can't remember the name of the fountain where they'd immersed first a toe, then a foot, then she'd pushed him in and he'd grabbed her, dunking her under the water, slimy underfoot.

She thought the wet would never come again but it has and she's thinking of sex in a way she hasn't done for years.

She locks the glass doors to her balcony, twenty floors high, waving to the wizened fellow in a rocking chair made by their son, Matthew, out of scrap metal for his final-year art portfolio. She hasn't told him they're going away. Their daughter Lily knows. Eight months pregnant, she's ripe for the throne being abdicated by her mother. A grandchild will heal Phillip's wounds and distract Lily from her mother's childishness. She's a rebel. She's scotched Marion's model as a juggler of family and business, taking indefinite leave from the law firm where she works to mother full-time.

Downstairs Marion steps out of the lift, pulling her wheelie bag behind her as Phillip arrives in the taxi. Sitting in the back seat, he reaches for her hand and she lets him caress her fingers for a moment before she pulls back to shield a yawn, tired from her late night at Leith's, relieved for the absence of a headache.

'How was book club?' Phillip had been asleep when she got home.

'George is getting weirder. He was playing golf upstairs. He didn't come down to spread goodwill. They live in different countries.'

'Don't we all.' His lament reminds her of a cat preening for attention, rubbing back and forth against her until she gives him a pat. 'I've booked us a four-wheel drive in Broome,' he tells her. 'Did you get my swimmers?'

'Oh God.' She'd forgotten. 'We can buy you a pair at the airport.'

'We won't have time.' He's annoyed.

'There'll be surf shops up north.'

'I asked you, I sent you a text barely ten minutes ago.'

'Phillip . . .' His childish pout maddens her.

'Hey,' he springs, his innocence eminently reasonable. 'What have I done? I bet you packed yours.'

She gazes out the window at the wharves below the bridge, warehouses converted into cavernous function rooms where last week she'd organised a fundraiser for patrons of an overseas aid organisation. Banners printed with the faces of malnourished Burmese children fluttered above guests served Thai noodle salad, beef fillets and chocolate tart. He bristles at her phone chiming the arrival of a message. She fishes it out of her pocket, colouring as she reads the text. 'Work,' she fibs, tapping in her memory of the fountain dip, decades ago.

'You should turn it off while we're away,' he suggests.

Reprimanded, she gives him her attention. When they met he had shoulder-length sandy hair and the strong arms of a rower. But, deskbound for decades, he's grown into a fat man who combs back his lengthening fringe to hide his baldness, a sleight of vanity she dislikes. Shave it off, she tells him, preferring the shiny pate young men wear, but he won't hear of it.

At the airport she gets out to retrieve their cases. Phillip pays the fare. While the driver slides an imprint of his credit card he looks at his wife fondling her phone, a whimsical, faraway smile on her lips, and it's as if he's eavesdropping, excluded. This observation unnerves him.

'But we were only there last night,' Eva tells herself, slumped on the bed where she took Rosie's call in her bra and pantyhose, the last of the group to find out. The suddenness of Leith's death strikes it out of bounds. 'I can still smell her on me. I remember kissing her goodbye and feeling her hug me close.' Her voice trembles as she struggles to comprehend how Leith can be flesh and warmth one minute, then gone.

Eva's always thought of Leith as an extension of herself. One summer the two girls toured Europe, working as au pairs in Paris with their schoolgirl French. George was studying at Oxford and they visited him there, serving ploughman's lunches in a tourist pub by the Thames. Leith wanted to stay, in love with the spires, the punts on the river, the laneways, the cane baskets on bicycles. 'You can't stay,' Eva urged the night before their train to London. 'We're travelling together.'

'You're the one who says follow your heart.'

Eva turned away and went on stuffing her backpack, Leith's excuses filling the small room of the youth hostel. Guilt got the better of her, Eva thought the next morning when Leith swept on to the platform. But it was George who'd persuaded her to join Eva 'because promises should be kept'.

Once both of them married they'd turned away from overseas capitals to motherhood, still trading stories and comparing notes even as they journeyed along parallel paths.

Restoring the house ate up chunks of Leith's time, with trades-men coming and going. Eva's days sped by, her career scheduled around childcare pick-ups and frantic dashes to the supermarket between meetings. Their friendship struggled during these years. Eva didn't want to hear about the handmade birthday party invita-tions or Leith's quest for aniseed colouring to make grey icing for Jesse's shark cake. Leith closed her ears whenever Eva let drop names of newsmakers that she'd shared a panel with at a Sydney conference. Once in a while they'd attend literary luncheons in the city, Eva up and down from the table to network, introducing Leith to women with name tags and punchy acronyms underscoring their importance. Both of them avoided judgement of the other's trade-offs. Leith's maternal urges pricked Eva's guilt; Eva's strong sense of self-preservation, her conversational larder stocked with publishing gossip and workplace jargon, undermined Leith's confidence. Their time together was rationed. Eva was forever cancelling catch-up dates, shifting coffee from this week to next month, playing phone tag – until the book club was formed. This was Eva's idea, her way of adding value to social occasions that might otherwise be written off as a sunk cost. The certainty of catching up once a month had kept the two women close. They shared names, memories, the smells of an era, a cultural backdrop of plays, films, music and books. If one of them forgot, the other would be sure to remember.

Eva hears Vince's key turn in the front door, home earlier than usual. They're meant to be attending a book launch tonight, an invitation she'd accepted for the purpose of advertising her availability. She'd spent the day with a recruitment firm, gilding her curriculum vitae, completing psychological assessments, her ego pulverised by the smooth young executives grooming her for disappointment. She wipes her eyes with the bedspread and rises to pluck tissues from the box on the mantel so that she can recover herself enough to tell Vince what's happened because she knows he'll be upset. He's always enjoyed Leith's company.

He doesn't look at her when he walks into the room, unbuckling his watch as he readies for his shower, every gesture loud with resentment at having to socialise tonight on his wife's behalf. She didn't show this much mercy when he was retrenched from a job that he loved, running the research arm of a large philanthropic foundation. When the sum of his professional life was packed into four cartons ready to be couriered home, she was too busy feathering her own prospects to minister his flagging spirit. She told him to 'move on' as if he was a rogue cow, mouthing the jargon she's come to despise on the receiving end of corporate pragmatism.

These days they often talk to each other in tones of voice she wouldn't use to address a stranger. Trivial things irritate her: the way he slices cheese, too thickly; his habit of fondling his balls, one hand down his pants, while he watches television; and the sound of him crunching dry biscuits in between meals. If guests begin to smell after a few days, like fish, it follows that bedmates of twenty-plus years must reek. She's seen couples like her and Vince, walking without touching, one three steps in front of the other. They smile for the camera, arms around each other. An eighth of a second is all it takes to tell a lifetime's lie.

Vince opens his wardrobe. He slips off his shoes, his back turned to her. If he's sensed her desolation, he's ignoring her, disengaged from her upkeep.

'Leith's dead.' She spears him with the news. He swivels around to face her, stunned by her words.

'What?' He's incredulous.

'She died last night.' She stumbles over the words she has only just heard from Rosie, sobs interrupting her flow. 'Rosie rang to tell me. She says Leith went upstairs to talk . . . to . . . to George after we . . . after we . . . after we left. He was swinging his golf club and . . . and he . . . and he . . . he didn't hear her footsteps and she . . . she . . . she came in and he struck her on the neck . . . she died in the ambulance and she . . . ' Eva sits on the bed blubbering like a child while Vince lets out a cry that arrests her. 'Rosie's been interviewed . . . by the police, she says that . . . she says that we'll all have . . . to make a statement . . .'

Vince's legs buckle from under him and he swoons to his knees, his head in the crook of one elbow as though in prayer. The strangeness of his posture unnerves Eva. But Leith is *my* friend, she almost says, fighting back a proprietorial anger that gives her grief right of way. He gets up slowly from the floor and walks into their ensuite, splashing his face with water over and over and blowing his nose in a swatch of toilet paper torn from the roll on the wall. Eva holds herself, exhaling slowly. The idea of murder competes with the fact of Leith's death, doubts surfacing, George's story dissolving, a police inquiry probing the circumstances that precipitated this killing. Vince stands trancelike in the doorframe, observing her dark eyes, swollen, puffy. His thinning dark-grey curls are slicked messily. The cuffs of his shirt hang below the tips of his long delicate fingers as if the world's swamping him — a vulnerability that first attracted her to his olive skin and angular face. No middle-age flab, for all the sitting around feeling sorry for himself.

He mumbles, rocking slightly on the balls of his feet, as he takes off his finely framed glasses, stylishly modern in metallic blue. She'd bought them for him. Now that she's job-hunting, she's hyper-conscious of appearance.

Something about Vince's tentative manner arouses her interest and she leashes the testiness that often corrupts her responses to him. He plunges his hands into his pockets forcefully, tugging the cotton twill into tiny darts that split a seam, and she starts to point this out when he speaks.

'Leith and I had an affair,' he reveals in the sparest of phrases because there is no way of delivering a bomb other than dropping it swiftly out of the sky. When it explodes in Eva's consciousness she's unprepared for the aftershock. A suffocating cloud of deceit rises up like an intoxicating gas so that she almost can't suck in breath.

'Last year,' he begins, 'we bumped into each other. We had a coffee that lasted all afternoon. Then we met again and it went from there.' His words float around the room like stringless balloons touching the furniture and the walls then lifting up and away. Her emotions somersault.

'We felt guilty, both of us. It was harder than we thought to . . . to . . . Leith was lonely. We comforted each other. The two of us.' Vince's lips quiver as if he can't believe his admission. His tongue moistens the roof of his mouth.

How many times has Eva flirted with leaving Vince, summoning up memories of other men even while she's having sex with him? Never in her creative narratives has she imagined him as the betrayer.

Turning away from him she lies on the bed, bringing her knees up to her chest so that she can shut out the tormentors, mocking and stamping and shrieking in their morbid dance. Leith's treason, sweetly, sincerely, superbly executed, has no parallel in Eva's experience. There can be no comeback, no alternative explanation to make sense of Vince's confession. My husband, a man I ridiculed and you laughed at, gets the last word on your motives, your fallibility. *One is not betrayed by an enemy* . . . Eva thinks of a line from a Graham Greene novel that she and Leith both studied at university. Why has he told her this now? Were they planning to move in together? Is that why Leith went upstairs last night, to tell George their marriage was a sick joke?

Darkness falls with no reason for Eva to get dressed or undressed, and she is barely aware of going without a meal or her mobile ringing, barely able to slip between the sheets still wearing her bra and sheer black tights. Vince disappears. She hears him leave the way he came, the click of the door his parting shot.

WEDNESDAY

Bernadette slips bare-footed into her laundry, a twenty-year ritual she finds impossible to quit even though there are no school shirts and uniforms to fold and stash in the plastic pods she kept for each child. Customs are comforting when trouble tramps through uninvited. If there was a mass on she'd attend. As there's not, the cloister under the stairs brings some peace before she leaves for her early-morning walk with Clara, who lives across the lane-way separating their back gates. Her lightly freckled face is long and wan as she moves about unsteadily. Monty's suspicion of George's guilt flares like a spider bite, swollen, itchy. The grief that had quietened while she lay during the night uncoils to the tips of her fingers. Overcome by the need to tidy, she squats down beside the cupboard under the sink and rearranges the bottles of cleaning fluid; blue, green, cloudy white, chemicals for bleaching surfaces, stain removal, polishing windows, disinfectants. Leith once dubbed her 'Agent Orange' for her carrot-coloured curls and well-stocked armoury of germ blasters; mostly, though, she called her 'B'.

'Leith, I'm so sorry,' Bernadette repents over and over. The questions she and Monty had batted back and forth until late in the night bother her as she kneels in her linoleum pew, reordering the bottles of poison as methodically as she counts the rosary beads under her pillow.

'There must have been an argument,' Monty said. 'They must have fought. How could he not have heard her come into the room?'

'He was making an incredibly loud noise. We could hear him from downstairs. We were laughing at him murdering mammoths,' Bernadette countered, her voice fading as she remembered the sound of George's club hitting the floor above.

'Was Leith drunk?' His wife had arrived home tipsy on Monday night, heavy footed; he'd found her keys hanging in the front-door lock when he'd left for work yesterday morning.

'There was something funny about her. She was on a high, sort of floaty. She made a toast to us, thanking us for being her friend. I had a flash that maybe she was sick, I mean really sick, with cancer or something. A week ago she told me she was having a check-up and I forgot to ask if she was okay. Surely she would have told me if she'd had bad news. She must have gone upstairs after we left. That's what I can't understand.'

Monty's rare encounters with George were prickly, superficial. 'He went for her. He must have. He's murdered her,' he declared.

'Why? What could have provoked him? He's not violent. He's the most deliberate, considered man I know.'

Why would George have lost control? Drink? Loathing? She knows a nitpicking complaint can flare in a marriage just as an ember sets fires to layers of debris, but she can't picture this decorous couple at each others' throats. During the night she'd combed through every hypothesis to find a credible motive that could solve the mystery of Leith's death. Accidental, how so? Someone or something is always at fault, the invisible strings of design revealing themselves later. A balcony collapses. A road disintegrates into a swollen river. A jumbo crashes into a paddy field. Balance is lost and a body tumbles on to the rocks below. But where did the violence of George's swing come from? Monty's certitude chills her, the notion of wilful aggression increasingly plausible as she scrutinises the character of a man who makes her edgy too.

She turns on the iron and chooses pillowslips and tea towels from the basket of clean clothes as thoughts of Leith churn and tumble. A lover of crime fiction, she searches for clues, freezing every moment she and Leith had been alone together on Monday night in case she's missed something.

Why did Leith go upstairs? She used to joke about 'George's den', as she'd dubbed his haunt, invoking the separation of church and state. Rosie's account of dirty glasses and plates in the kitchen also jars. What was so important that it couldn't wait until she'd cleaned up? Leith likes spick and span, Bernadette debates with herself, as she presses the creases out of a pink striped pillowslip she would never have ironed in the days when five lunch boxes were lined up on the kitchen table waiting to be filled. George's golf club whacking the floor upstairs in the big house reaches a frightening pitch in her head, the gruesome circumstance grizzlier for the presumption of guilt. Rosie's been interviewed by the police. They'll all be called in to make a statement. She puts the neatly folded linen into the cupboard, unplugs the iron, and then tiptoes back into the bedroom to get her runners.

Monty rolls over at her rustling and steals her pillow to prop himself up in bed.

'Do you think we should contact George?' she whispers.

'He killed her, B. He lost it. I'm sure he gave her one. He's strong and she's a midget beside him. She didn't stand a chance. I don't know what we should do.' He swings his legs on to the floor, sitting on the edge of their bed. 'I feel like going over there to drive a truck through his flimsy explanation. We owe it to Leith. Otherwise he'll get away with this. No one's going to hang a judge.'

She sighs as though she aches, then looks at her watch. 'I'm going to be late for Clara,' and she's out the back door, laces undone, to meet her neighbour, who's waiting for her under a flickering street lamp in the laneway.

'I can't believe it,' Clara says, reaching out to give her friend a hug. 'I saw it on the news last night.'

Bernadette bites the inside of her cheek because the sympathy of another friend just as dear makes her teary. 'Shocking,' she says as she bends to tie her shoes and wipe her nose before they stride over the uneven bluestones to the smooth bitumen of the street.

'I can't believe it,' Clara says again. 'What was he doing with a golf club inside the house?'

'They have a huge house,' Bernadette begins as they cross over at the milk bar like a pair of carriages on a track, sticking to their daily route. 'George has this room upstairs that used to be the children's rumpus area. That's where he practises when he's at home. He's got a sort of putting green set up there. He was play-ing the other night. We were all laughing at him, Clara.' Bernadette stops walking to make her confession. 'Every time I think of it I feel sick.'

The day's imminent arrival begins to draw shapes out of the blackness. Bernadette sees Clara's eyes glistening with eagerness, anticipating details of a drama that will transfix the city. They pick up pace around the park, past the perimeter of the childcare centre. Bernadette looks at her friend then straight ahead, her steps slowing. 'How could he not have seen her?' She locks eyes with Clara again, stooping to pick up an empty bottle lying on the path near a park bench. She flings it into the garbage bin with the confident aim of a veteran netballer.

'Whichever way you look at it, he killed her?' Clara ventures. 'Why haven't they locked him up already?'

'There's an investigation.'

Their steps shorten and their breath quickens as they climb up the steepest hill, Clara's commentary making Bernadette anxious at the prospect of strangers poking into Leith's affairs, presuming things.

Clara waits until they're done nodding to the dog walker they meet every morning. 'There's no way a man could strike his wife with a golf club across the head by mistake.' This logic blurs Bernadette's vision of the city's skyline as they crest the highest point on their walk, neither of them talking while their imaginations explore the violence of a metal club travelling at 100 kph. Clara knows that blind rage floods the capacity for thought. She's seen her father this mad: the memory of him going for her mother with a dinner plate, daisies patterning its rim, is vivid even now. They reach the top of the hill, a place where most mornings they pause to enjoy the view, a gentle sloping patchwork of orange-tiled rooves and industrial warehouses, autumn's turn on the coppery treetops circling a church spire.

'I think you're right.' She blinks her tears.

'He snapped. He must have.'

'Change of subject.' Bernadette signals a code they have used for years to avoid argument or if one or the other's been hogging the conversational concourse. 'I wanted to talk about nothing else this morning in the laundry but now I just need to let it settle in here,' and she touches her breast with a balled first.

'Are you working today?' Clara complies.

'Yeah, but it's a short day. I've got my African women. I've told you about them. From the Sudan. Terrible stories of the war, they're so grateful for things we take as given. Peace, for one.'

The sudden bark of a dog behind a picket fence startles Bernadette. They continue in silence. Turning the corner for the last leg of the loop that brings them back to the milk bar, Clara can't help herself.

'Was Leith having an affair?'

'No,' Bernadette says but as the word leaves her mouth doubt gives her pause. She sees George's face on the newspaper poster in a wire frame leaning against the shop window. An electronic buzz announces their custom and Ning emerges from the back to sell Bernadette the paper. Clara buys a litre of milk. The two women part company at Bernadette's front door.

'See you tomorrow.' Clara gives her a hug, with a bonus squeeze for support.

The smell of burnt toast greets Bernadette as she enters the kitchen that Monty has been promising to upgrade. That's the problem with marrying a builder: her handyman's always fixing up other people's places. They met thirty-three years ago in the alpine town of Merrijig. Monty was invited by his mate to a working bee at a ski lodge where Bernadette's parents were members. They were all smiles while Monty was repairing the antiquated boiler in the drying room but when he took to squiring their daughter around town in his green Holden panel van the bonhomie wavered because her father had his eye on the doctor son of a family from the parish. In the back of that van, on an old sleeping bag, Bernadette found how gentle Monty's roughened hands could be and they made love wherever they could find a place to park and whenever the mood took them, which was deliciously often – and still is, although Monty's truck, for all its accessories, isn't a mobile love nest any longer, and bouts of lower-back pain diminish the spontaneity. When they went around the circle at book club one month, Bernadette had to swear on the Bible that she was not making up the fact that she and Monty have sex at least six times a week.

She screws the lid on his thermos of coffee as he sweeps through to collect it on his way out, dressed in his fawn King Gee shorts and a tartan lumberjack shirt that hangs loosely, hiding the paunch she airbrushes out of sight when she pictures him: tanned, hale and hers. He bends to kiss her, burying his mouth into the soft folds of her neck beneath her cascading frizz. Leith's death moves him to grab at her. However it happened, it's reminded them of the things you don't see coming, but he purges this thought before it trips him. The ends of his soft brown curls are licked together, wet from the shower, and he smells sweet.

'Love you, honey,' he says.

'Same,' she replies. She pours herself a coffee as she hears his ute roar off, and flattening out the paper, she turns to the death notices. There are three for Leith Millicent Kremmer. The first is from George.

'Event perverse!
Thou never from that hour in Paradise
Found'st either sweet repast, or sound repose;

John Milton

Suddenly, as the result of a tragic accident at home. Loving mother of Art and Jesse and everything to George.'

Leith's brother's brief, bare tribute is next.

Leith. All my tomorrows will be paler without you. I would die to bring you back. Cameron.

She's surprised there's no mention of his partner, but it's nothing like the disconcerting shiver she feels on reading the third, unsigned farewell immediately below.

My beautiful Leith. The odds for us were never good. I love you.

The blue eyes staring at Sam Dunlop from the digital screen above the escalator skittle him just as they did in court. 'Judge's wife in fatal accident', he reads before the headline is refreshed. As the moving metal stairway ferries him down to the ground floor of the mall he stays where he is by walking backwards, in case the news flash is repeated. 'Watch out, mate,' a man with a backpack shouts, swinging past Sam, who is leaning over the black rubber handrail to watch the captioned images constantly changing. Plane crash in Vietnam, blink, suicide bomber strikes mosque, blink, cheap home loans, blink, then the judge's wife – this time she's pictured, dark, small, pale, blink, and she's gone.

He sprints across the tiled forecourt, dodging jelly-hipped shoppers, their gait encumbered by rolls of flesh, no match for the light-footed 'Spring', as his mates used to call him at school. Too fast, their mothers warned. He activates the automatic doors and exits to the street. A tram's waiting for the lights to change. He dashes in front of a minibus, leaping up the tram steps just as the light changes to green. No sign of the grey-suited inspectors in peaked caps who are cracking down on fare avoidance. There's a spare seat beside a pregnant woman who's reading a newspaper and as he parks himself on the moulded plastic he casts his eye over her shoulder, searching for a story on the judge.

For once someone else is in trouble and a perverse sense of gratitude that misery gets shared around bucks him up. A screech of brakes jerks the tram to a sudden halt and passengers slide forward and back in the snarl of traffic. The woman next to him gets up and pulls the cord for the stop ahead. She leaves the paper behind and Sam claims it before somebody else does. He wrestles with the broadsheet pages, scanning up and down columns once and then twice. Below the fold of a page he spies a brief paragraph in bold type. 'Leith Kremmer, the wife of Family Court judge,

George Kremmer, died early Tuesday morning after sustaining a blow to the neck at the couple's Melbourne home. Police said that Mrs Kremmer, 56, suffered a fatal haemorrhage after rupturing a vertebral artery. Police are investigating.'

He's killed her, Sam's sure, smelling foul play in the early hour of her death. For an instant he sees the fire-cracker explosions of red and blue lights that glued him rigid the night his mother died. Looking up, he reads the cream clock tower out the tram window. He's got fifteen minutes left to catch sight of Mags in the outdoor playground of the childcare centre. Like a visitor to the zoo, he goes to watch her through the red railing, only sometimes he's the caged beast, pacing its length while Mags is on the inside, oblivious.

Rising to his feet, he tugs the bell cord and the tram rides to a halt. The doors concertina open and Sam's off, passing two portly women with identification tags who are hopping on to check for tickets. This small piece of fortune is his first bit of luck in weeks. Maybe things will start going his way. You've got to practise being optimistic, according to Angie.

He cuts a diagonal path through the cars to save time. On the footpath a girl in ugg boots and tracksuit pants holds a banner advertising discounted fashion in one of the outlet stores along the strip. In her free hand she holds a thick paperback so she doesn't have to read pity in the eyes of passing motorists. Sam got the same looks wiping windscreens. He hangs a left, then right down a cobbled bluestone laneway that leads into the grassy reserve next to the childcare centre and the local library. There's a man conked out on the bench where Sam sometimes sits. His hair's shaggy and his skin's red and cracked from exposure. Sam could tell anyone who asks how you get from here to there without trying.

Slower now, so as not to attract the attention of the lady in the floral skirt who's on duty, he scans the sandpit where Mags often plays. He sweeps the yard carefully, from the cubby house and the huddle around the dress-ups box to the two boys with their noses to the ground under the shadecloth and the kid at the easel by the toy chest. He retraces his gaze but he can't find her. She stands out because of her dainty build – smaller, more delicate than the other kids. She's bossy too, like her mother. He spots a boy crashing a car that's minus a wheel into the sides of the sandpit. Perhaps Mags is in the bathroom or getting a bandaid for a cut. But then the lady claps her hands, calls the children inside and closes the doors, and he's whipped 'cause he can't ask where his daughter's got to and it's not right that he doesn't have a clue. Cornered, that's how he feels, shut out of everywhere, short on patience, hogtied by Family Court orders that violate the natural order, a father together with his kid. Judge Kremmer won't notice the breach, not now, not with blood on him. Sam twitches with excitement and a wicked splurge of lawlessness, because seeing his daughter is a crime he'll easily commit.

Eva needs to talk with someone. Leith is the one she thinks of first, her reflexes lagging behind the coup d'état up-ending her world.

She folds a damp facecloth against her eyes and goes from room to room seeking sanctuary. She finds Vince asleep in the spare bed, where he'd crawled under the covers in the clothes he was wearing last night. On his desk, atop a pile of papers, sits a seashell, a pair with the one she'd held in Leith's car on Sunday. She turns it over in her hand, spilling fresh tears as she remembers Leith's blithe lie ('Jesse found it'); the sting of being conned wallops her. There are no cubbyholes in this architect-designed, open-plan house. No closet under the stairs to hide in like she used to do when she was small. She doesn't have a shrink. Leith was her sounding board. At 56 she yearns like a child for her mother's comforting arms.

When Alistair came clean, Eva counselled Rosie to punish him. 'Cut his suit pants into pieces,' she'd instructed, biblical in her menu of punishments. Vandalism seems lame revenge to her now. If only she had an office to go to, a job, a deadline to devour her attention. Every corner she rounds holds an unpleasantness. She remembers arriving home one evening last summer. Leith's car was here. Vince was in-between jobs. She'd heard their laughter from the courtyard as she'd climbed the front steps. Nothing incriminating, just the sound of pleasure, Vince's voice higher in pitch than usual, as though he'd sucked a whiff of helium. As she walked through the glass doors Leith had stood and gathered up the empty teacups, quite at home. She said she'd dropped by to lend Eva a novel that they were reading for book club. Eva didn't twig to anything untoward. Vince was the one who enraged her.

He'd been on dinner duty yet the kitchen was dark, the double bed unmade. What Leith must think of this slovenliness was the thing that irked her at the time; the scenario occurring to her now was unthinkable then.

'What have you been doing all day?' she'd ripped into Vince the minute Leith had left. 'Sleeping? Window shopping? Yakking with Leith? You promised to pull your weight around here. It's not that difficult, is it? Making one bed, switching on the dishwasher, buying something for dinner? I'm not expecting you to slay a bison or pluck a pheasant. A boiled egg would do me. God, Vince, you've got no energy. I'm expected to hold down a job, keep you in clean socks, run the house, and then when I fall into bed you abuse me because I'm not interested in sex.' The dishwasher shelf slid on to the floor with the force of her anger as she pulled it out to show him how labour's done, breaking the crockery, including the last three dinner plates from the set they'd picked out together as a wedding present from his parents. 'No job, no ticker – you're just a sook on legs!' was her punchline. Still he'd held his tongue, no pejorative or profanity under his breath, as she flounced out the back for a cigarette. Now she guesses his silence was sheer gratitude at getting off so lightly.

A week later she and Leith had joined Marion for a girls' night out. They went to see a comedy on menopause that was prosaic and humourless so they'd left at interval to salvage the evening. All of book club had been invited but Rosie couldn't come because she'd had her aunt's eightieth birthday party. Bernadette was babysitting grandchildren. They'd had dinner afterwards at a restaurant overlooking the river, sitting on the balcony so Eva could smoke. Marion had fed them stories of her extramarital adventures online, preparing each segment as if it was the juicy flesh of a ripe orange. Her new love is an old flame, a man with whom she'd had a fling thirty years ago. 'We met in Venice. Four days together, mostly in bed. Didn't get to ride a gondola under that bridge, what's it called?'

'The Bridge of Sighs,' Eva and Leith spoke in concert because they'd done that together.

'He went off to Asia and I came home. I was too young to realise that what we felt might never happen again. He emailed me out of the blue. I was going through my inbox deleting, deleting, deleting. Then I saw his name and it was like touching an electric fence. I replied. He wrote back. We started comparing notes, playing memory games, talking about our spouses, people we know in common, anything and everything, our marriages. He was happy enough in his, then one day his wife announced she was leaving. She'd found a job after years of being at home and she'd fallen in love with her boss – a woman.' No one had expected this qualification.

'People hide their sexuality under the skirts of marriage,' Leith had said, before Marion reeled them back to her electronic foreplay. 'I was flattered by the attention. I couldn't wait to open my inbox. There's something about rediscovering an old lover. You don't have to bother with the history because you share a piece of past.

Maybe it's because you can sort of pick up where you left off, or maybe because you feel like you're twenty all over again, you shed the baggage, the mistakes you've made, the parts of yourself you don't like. Don't you ever wonder what would have happened if you'd married different partners? I know I do.'

'That saying that clumsy people are all thumbs is on its way out,' Leith had joked as they watched Marion tap out a flirtatious reply to her latest SMS.

'Do you remember Mark from uni?' Eva had asked Leith. 'Tall and lanky. He came from Gippsland – a vet, I think. He always wore crumpled moleskins and R. M. Williams boots. I often think of him. We sort of drifted apart and I never really gave much thought to what I was letting go. I just couldn't get my head around living out in the sticks. So shortsighted, so stupid. But then again, maybe I was right, maybe I would have gone mad with cows and sheep for company.'

'Well, I could never picture you in the dairy, birthing a calf. I remember you two together. You wouldn't recognise him now. There was a picture of him in the alumni magazine – George gets it – I meant to tell you. I've saved it. He's aged handsomely,' she'd winked, 'except he's a bit stocky. He does something odd – it was an article about the drought and how he's been helping locals find water on their property, telling them where to sink bores. There's a name for it. They call themselves water diviners, I think.'

Eva had called for another bottle of wine. 'I made a mistake,' she'd owned. 'I made a mistake marrying Vince.' Eva reddens now as she remembers what she went on to divulge. 'On our wedding night when you'd all left the hotel drunk and singing I wished I could have come with you. That night, in bed, I lay there looking at the ceiling while we made love, staring at an abstract painting of red and yellow rectangles on the wall.'

'I think a lot of couples have bad sex on their wedding night,' Leith had ventured.

'Did you?'

'We were saved from humiliation by my ridiculous dress, remember? It had one hundred and fifty tiny pearl buttons from the neck to the bottom of my spine. I think George fell asleep undoing the ninety third,' she'd laughed. 'According to Rosie's daughter, newlyweds don't have sex. They live together before they marry, *if* they marry, and there's so much fussing on the big day that they collapse into bed greedy for sleep or else sit up watching a DVD eating hamburgers and chips because they didn't touch a morsel at the banquet.'

Marion had looked up quizzically from her phone. 'You know, I can't remember whether Phillip and I had sex or not. That's terrible,' she admitted. 'Forgetting what happened on your wedding night! Psychologists would feast on that. Thank God I don't believe in therapy.'

'Companionship' was Eva's mother's salient advice on how to

choose a husband. Find someone you won't outgrow. Vince was a student politician: scruffy, busy, aligned to her causes. They caucused together, campaigned for each other, attended rallies arm in arm, and one night fell asleep side by side in Vince's tiny upstairs bedroom, tuckered out after pasting posters for a demonstration against domestic violence on every pillar around the campus. Sex happened eventually because it came with the meal, like a side order. She'd checked him over and ticked all the boxes, selecting a mate, not a lover, opting for compatibility over a mythical, unreliable thing called love. 'I never liked kissing Vince,' her truth jagged and ugly, so she'd recovered a scrap of dignity by adding, 'but the sex was good.' Leith had smiled, why? Perhaps because she knew better. Then they'd been diverted by a crew of eight rowing past along the river in front of the restaurant, their oars breaking the surface of the black water as they stroked forward.

'You should chase up the water diviner,' Marion had counselled, her eyes on her screen as she sent off another SMS. 'You might decide your grass is greener with Vince. But if you ask me, we weren't meant to live this long with the same person.'

'What about you and George?' Eva had asked Leith, hoping for revelations to confirm that couples stay together for crazy reasons, most of them habit-forming.

'I think Marion's right,' Leith said.

'Do you ever wish you'd married someone else?'

'Sometimes,' she'd wavered, her watery hazel eyes flitting from side to side, uneasy with the conversation's turn. 'But it's point-less, all this wondering, because every decision you make there's a reason why at the time and, yes, with hindsight it might prove to be wrong or selfish or shallow but you can't go back, you can't, no matter how much you try.'

'Who do you think about?' Eva's intensity started to annoy Leith.

'God, Eva, I just told you that I try not to fall into that trap.'

'I was just wondering,' she'd said, her voice shrinking. 'What about Miles Noonan?'

'Well,' Leith let a smile kiss her lips, 'I googled him a couple of months ago out of pure curiosity, just for fun, to see how he turned out. Popular name, Miles Noonan – you wouldn't believe how many I discovered, including a taxidermist who lives in Connecticut,' she'd laughed.

'Don't you ever imagine what your life might have been like if you'd married him?'

'Not really,' Leith shrugged. Then the waitress swept by and Marion ordered coffees, and somehow the conversation jumped a track. Eva hadn't taken Marion's advice. She'd renewed her interest in Vince, conscious of the sanity in Leith's argument. But she'd felt as if she was inflating a rubber mattress with a pinhole of a leak.

This morning it is all she can do to digest the news of Leith's death. She is mauled by interest in their affair. Grief comes upon her in lurches. First her brain shut down as it absorbed what she had learnt. Now she wants to talk and examine carefully all she knows. Questions pummel her. How often did Leith and Vince have sex? Was it exciting? Where did they hide? Who made the first move? Did they laugh at Eva? Did they talk about George? Were there phone calls or letters? She'd never thought to look for evidence, too pressed for time to unfurl crunched-up receipts in Vince's pockets, too prosperous to bother with a line-by-line scrutiny of who's spending what, too careless to care.

As she towels herself dry she wonders whether George had an inkling of what Leith was up to. Did she lie to him or did she simply censor their conversations so there was no need for dishonesty, just as Eva edits unpalatable truths for Vince's consumption, skipping sustenance as dieters do, learning to live hungrily, only ever partly satisfied. She can't imagine lust anaesthetising certain loyalties, can't imagine abandoning her oldest friend while still meeting her gaze. If Leith had held a gun to her temple, Eva would have trusted her to pull the trigger and fire a blank. She mourns a friendship. This is the harder to bear, losing the very thing which can't be taken even when the body decomposes. 'Wasn't I a good enough friend? I tried to be,' she whispers. 'I truly did.' She can't fault her allegiance to Leith in the way that she can own her lapses of loyalty to Vince. This gives Leith's betrayal its venomous sting.

From her wardrobe she selects a suit, the pin-striped navy, and a pale-blue shirt, because you never know who you might meet. Carrying her blue suede heels she creeps past the room where

Vince is camped, slipping the shoes on her feet once she's outside. The newspaper is on the pavement out the front. She can't bring herself to read it so she hurls it back up the steps; it lands with a thump near the front door. A police paddy wagon pulls into the driveway of the apartment block opposite. For a second she thinks it's her they've come to visit. But a young uniformed cop gets out and walks down the driveway to the rear of the building, leaving his partner in the car.

In her thirties, Eva worked as a researcher for the national broadcaster, extracting information and insights, kneading the dough of stories, slanting facts this way and that. She knows that what she carries around with her now, pinching her sharply planed face, could sink George Kremmer. Leith's affair with her husband, however brief, however unsuccessful, seeds suspicion that George found out and flew into a jealous rage. That's what people would swear, if they knew. Poor George, Eva sympathises; he's suffered Leith's disloyalty too and their common grievance rescinds momentarily the question of his guilt.

She crosses her arms for warmth. The women who signpost the street at dusk dispensing sex for a flat rate are somewhere else this morning. Their faces are more familiar than her neighbours' – renters mostly. She buttons her coat, scattering a clump of leaves on the pavement as she walks to her car, one foot in front of the other, retreating from a panoramic view of George's guilt to the acute angled problem of where to go next on a day unlike any other she has known.

Outside their local café a man in a scarlet beret perches on a plastic crate reading the tabloid press, a glass of coffee to his lips. A young couple tuck into plates of scrambled eggs at a large communal table messy with newspapers that skirt a tall glass vase of purple irises. Behind the counter a barista in a white T-shirt and a chequered bandana is bantering with a guy in jeans and a white collared shirt. The girl bangs the jug on the bench to settle the froth. 'Of course he murdered her,' she says, lightly swiping the stainless-steel nozzle clean. 'He just boiled over.' She moves swiftly, swirling milk into takeaway cups set out on the bench. 'She was having an affair and he found out.'

'Nah,' says the man, lifting his sunglasses, his oily hair clinging to the furrows left by a comb. 'Accidents happen, you know.'

'Yeah, if you let them.' She pops lids on and pockets the cups in a cardboard tray. 'Can I help you?' she asks Eva, who has picked up a newspaper from a stool by the bench, surprised by the photograph of George in his wig and gown, his blue eyes fixed sternly on the camera. 'Hello?' The girl waves a delicate brown hand in front of Eva's face.

'Oh,' Eva says. 'A skinny flat white, thanks.'

'So what do you think about that judge?' the girl asks. 'Did he go crazy or not?'

Leith's death has swamped Eva in waves of emotion that keep shifting the sand beneath her just as a storm surge rearranges the shore. 'I don't know,' she answers truthfully. 'I don't know.' The girl's attention is diverted by the machine's hissing and spitting.

Eva's mobile rings. The number's withheld.

'Hello?'

'Eva Myer?'

'Yes.'

'Detective Inspector Dan Sinclair. I'm from Victorian Homicide. I'm investigating Leith Kremmer's death. Rosie Hayes gave me your number.'

'I was expecting your call,' Eva says, cradling the phone with her shoulder as she pays for her coffee, mouthing a thank-you to the girl, who would be tickled if she knew of her random brush with this true crime. 'Do we have to do this right now?' Eva says.

'I was hoping you could come in some time today,' he bargains.

'I only found out about this last night.'

Sinclair's never verballed a confession in his life. Eva took longer to learn the power of silence in loosening another's lips. She doesn't speak as she leaves the café, stopping in the street where she buckles inexplicably. 'How long will this take?'

'It all depends what you can tell us.'

'Okay.' She might as well get this over with; besides, she has nowhere more pressing to go.

As she starts the car, her phone rings again.

'Have you read the paper?' Rosie's breathless. 'Leith was having an affair.'

'Who with?' Eva switches off the engine, calm in her panic.

'It doesn't say who but it's in the paper. There's a death notice from a lover. Unsigned. '

'Read it to me,' Eva orders her. 'What does it say?'

'My beautiful Leith. The odds for us were never good. I love you.' Bernadette copies the anonymous death notice over and over as if committing a commandment to heart, filling an entire page of her lined exercise book instead of preparing for today's class. Straight out of Monty's phrasebook, this reckoning of fate. Now that she lets her mind ferret for clues, she sees what a gamble she took allowing his Saturday outings with Leith. The two of them, waltzing off to Caulfield race track last weekend. Leith had won a motzer while Monty's bets emptied his wallet and he'd arrived home hours later than he'd promised.

'Leith's good, you know,' he'd said admiringly of her friend, his student for the better part of a year as he'd flung the jacket of his grey suit on the back of their couch. Beneath his pride in having schooled Leith well was envy at her success, which Bernadette reinterprets as attraction as she replays events, alert to possibilities she'd never contemplated before this morning.

'I thought we were going to need an armed guard to escort us back to the Kremmers,' he'd joked. Enquiries about the net balance of gains and losses are off limits but his bragging invited questions.

'How much did Leith win?'

'Guess,' he'd said, opening the way for her to stumble because she really had no idea what they risked aside from reckoning that Monty stuck with a modest kitty because they'd never had to sell their home.

'Two hundred dollars?' Her estimate was greeted by mirth as he opened the fridge for a beer he didn't need.

He'd shaken his head, reinforcing her outsider status as he'd ripped the ring-pull off the can and swigged thirstily. She liked him in a suit, his purple and green striped tie sloppily strung around his neck, brown eyes smiling.

'Give up?' Bernadette had nodded. 'Sixty-five thousand!' he'd said, staggering them both. Bernadette repeated the figure, struck not so much by Leith earning in a matter of minutes what average wage earners collected at the end of a year's hard slog, as by the guts a bet like that takes.

'How much money did she risk?'

'A lot.'

Disapproval kicked in later when she thought of her Cape of Horn women and how they stretched every dollar. She hadn't been sure whether her dampening view of Leith's booty was green-eyed.

Why would Monty be unfaithful? They adore each other. All last night he'd held her and stroked her, both of them thrown by Leith's death, comforting each other as they speculated, theory upon theory. They'd rocked each other to sleep.

I'm being paranoid, she tells herself, hoisting a bag of lemons she's picked from her tree over her shoulder on her way out the door. This year the harvest of citrus fruit has stocked a basket which sits on the counter at the shopfront office where she works, alongside a sign saying, 'Take one. They're free.'

She drives through the side streets, one-way lengths barely the width of two cars, her radio on. A lawyer is talking about the family court. When she hears George's name, she turns up the volume, and then the breakfast show host interrupts. 'We've just been advised that the Judge at the centre of this inquiry has this morning informed the Chief Justice of the Family Court that he will stand aside from hearing any further matters pending the outcome of police investigations which are underway as we speak . . .' Bernadette brakes behind the car up ahead that has stopped for a dark-haired young man darting across the road, clutching a small child in his arms – a little girl, anguish in her eyes, a red ribbon askew on her mousy hair. The child twists in his arms to keep sight of a skinny woman with streaked blonde hair swept up in a ponytail screaming for help, losing ground, stumbling in her high-heeled boots, an upturned stroller sprawled in the gutter.

Car horns sound from behind, irritated by the hold-up. The driver in front accelerates, unwilling to stop and broker peace. Upset, Bernadette pauses, then, determined he'll see reason if she can get to him, turns her steering wheel hard right as she reverses just enough to swing around into the laneway after him (she knows these alleys from her morning prowls with Clara). He's fast in his crepe-soled grey shoes but Bernadette keeps him in sight until he darts across an intervening road, ducking easily between cars, disappearing into the alley beyond. She jerks to a halt as a cyclist cruises past. At the next gap in the traffic, she tears across the road, her white station wagon scraping its underbelly as it bounces over the dip into the lane. She's lost the man and the girl. She accelerates at the instant a large black cat flashes across her path, low to the ground. Bernadette slams her foot down, catapulting lemons from the back seat on to the dashboard and floor, where they roll under her heels. In her rear-view mirror she sees a splotch of crimson on cobbled bluestone. She's killed the cat. Ill in the pit of her stomach, she checks to make sure. The swollen nipples mean there's a litter all alone under a house or in a box somewhere nearby, mouthing hungrily for their mother. She gets back into her car. Everything is coming unstuck. Regretting her intervention, she says a quick prayer to steady herself. 'I was only trying to help,' she pleads.

'I don't know,' George Kremmer mutters despairingly and Detective Inspector Dan Sinclair is quiet for a spell. They sit across the table from each other in an interview room on the seventh floor of police headquarters, a camera mounted high in the corner. Dan consults his notes and George picks at a scab of dried milk on his navy flannel trousers. He'd soiled them in the kitchen this morning while fixing himself a bowl of cornflakes, the first meal he'd eaten since dining with Leith two nights ago.

'You and Leith were married for how many years?' Dan resumes, establishing a fact beyond dispute.

'Thirty-three years, five months, three days,' George says witheringly because he's exhausted what little patience and courtesy he has. His descent into the smog of suspicion means he must study a single frame from their life together as if the magnification of its elements will uncover a motive for what he's done. For the past hour he's recounted for Sinclair the events of Monday evening: details of his dinner with Leith, their conversation, his disappearance upstairs, his absorption in the movement of his club through the gate, inside-to-out, explaining James Douglas Edgar's philosophy with the aid of pen and paper to prove his level of engagement, deaf to her progress up the stairs after midnight into a room she did not visit as a rule, proving beyond reasonable doubt that he was mildly inebriated and unprepared for her arrival. With an eye to the transcript of their conversation, he relies on the law, on the nature of admissible evidence, because the truth is a wily slip of prey neither Dan nor he could wrestle to the ground even if Leith were here to help them.

'Was it a happy marriage?' Dan asks, stepping back to take a grander sweep of history.

George strives for civility. Uncrossing his long legs he repositions himself on the lightweight plastic chair so that he no longer faces his uniformed interrogator, a man whose treacle eyes are fringed by bushy brows.

In all the years of his marriage, George assiduously avoided questions that gauged contentment. Leith blamed her husband's exposure to domestic warfare for his aversion to the psychology of relationships. Early on she had fretted over his emotional withdrawal. 'Do you love me?' she would beg of him. 'Are you happy?' Like an autistic child who is taught how to interpret tears and smiles, George learnt responses to satisfy her, until eventually she stopped questioning. He thought he loved Leith. He at least loved her sufficiently to shield her from the truth about himself, although this concealment served him too, because then he didn't have to shed his skin.

He turns to address Dan directly. 'We were happy enough,' he replies. 'It wasn't perfect. I doubt there is such a thing as a perfect marriage but it was a perfectly ordinary marriage in that we got along together most of the time pretty well.'

Dan waits for him to continue, because a bevy of questions fired at a suspect is likely to elicit nothing more than, 'I can't recall.' The trick is to give them space, allow them to talk. Sometimes the sound of nothing unsettles people, lubricating their tongue, luring them into complicity.

'You must know from attending traffic accidents that every bystander tells it differently,' George begins, 'the chronology out of sync, so that sometimes you have to wonder whether they've observed the same events. In marriages, accidents happen on long stretches of road. Your eye wanders, or you go to sleep at the wheel, or you collide with something you didn't see until too late.

There's usually only one other witness. Sometimes the survivors walk out without a scratch. Sometimes they're handicapped for life, write-offs like wrecked cars, piled one on top of each other, sandwiched sheets of crushed metal, rusted carcasses. Some wrecks get peeled off electricity poles, killing every one of the passengers trapped inside. Others are simply abandoned, dumped by the side of a road for a newer model. I've seen more dead marriages than most people experience in a lifetime. Perhaps that's why my own marriage seemed to be roadworthy.'

Dan doesn't reply, sure he's about to hear an unravelling, but George is holding back tears, a feat requiring every muscle and nerve. His musings have affected Sinclair, who remembers the songlines of his own marriage: the sweet beginnings, the souring end. Sniping became situation normal – that's what he remembers of its disintegration. The less he communicated with his wife, the more trivial their disputes became and in that last year together he would lie masturbating beside his wife as she feigned sleep.

'Did you and Leith argue much?'

George takes a sip from a glass of water on the table. Conscious of the stillness, it's as if he's entertaining in the formal front rooms of a house.

'We argued whenever we disagreed. We argued about sex.' He's sure Dan will misinterpret this to mean George wanted more than he could get, and the twitch of the policeman's lips confirms it. 'There were sources of aggravation between us,' he continues.

'Leith loved entertaining, I couldn't be bothered. I leave lights on, she switched them off. She wanted to rent our spare room to foreign students, I refused. She clipped her toenails in the bedroom, the sound got on my nerves. She loathes clutter, I hoard things. I voted for the government at the last election, she hates the Prime Minister. People who live in close proximity police their territorial borders. We had come to an arrangement in a home that was big enough to operate as a federation of states.' He thinks of their residence, disturbed at night by the sound of Leith turning the pages of her book as she sat reading, ears plugged against the thud of his club upstairs.

'Did you suspect your wife was having an affair?'

He'd wept this morning when he read the anonymous death notice for Leith. His hollow reliance on Milton seemed pompous, heartless, beside the sweeter, simpler declaration of love. How he'd sweated over the tribute, unable to say what he felt so that he'd fallen as he always does to second-guessing, imagining his words being sieved for meaning by fellow judges, Leith's friends, their neighbours, the world. He looks a fool.

'No.'

'How often did your wife go to the races?' George tries not to curl his lip, telegraphing intolerance of a pasttime he can't fathom, because where's the self-improvement in a game of chance? You get better at losing? Their respective absorption in worlds far apart gave them something to talk about. As her interest grew, he'd felt more comfortable about the prospect of a future that had begun to tempt and taunt him at once. He'd creep out on Saturday mornings for a day on the green without kissing the shiny black hair and pale brow under the covers of their king-size bed, and he'd return with just enough time to shower and change if they were going out together, which they seldom did.

'Do you know who she went with or who she met when she got there?'

'She went with a friend.' George hesitated in naming Monty; the scent of red-blooded maleness will divert Dan Sinclair down a cul-de-sac. 'Monty.' He meets Dan's gaze. 'Monty O'Neill. He's married to one of Leith's friends.'

'I met your wife once,' Sinclair says, desperate to prise another droplet from the basalt of a man opposite.

George gives him nothing more. He focuses on a scuff mark on the wall, disengaging as he'd learnt to do in anger management, lighting upon a silver hair that has caught on the dark cloth of his pants. He wraps the strand around his index finger until it snaps.

They part, not for the last time.

Back at his desk, Sinclair resists the wafting invitation to cadge a hot chip from the beaker in his colleague's hand because one French fry is never enough and before he knows it he'll be buying his own bucket of fat from the fast-food counter in the canteen. Lunch is top of his mind and he's happy to let this imperative elbow Kremmer aside. His phone rings. Reception's on the line.

'Eva Myer's here to see you.'

He's relying on Leith Kremmer's book club. Women notice the small details, expressions, haircuts, changes to the atmospheric pressure in an interior, the shadows of emotion, nails bitten to the quick. Even though they'd left before things got violent, Leith might have confided in one or two of them, or one or two of them might be expert at reading the calligraphy of domestic disarray.

Sam hides behind a car on the other side of the street, watching Gabe drag Mags' stroller through the tall security gate that her parents installed. She keeps the gate ajar with her foot, calling over her shoulder to their daughter as she shakes crumbs loose from the seat, impatience in her sharpness. She doesn't notice him walking towards her between the morning traffic as Mags emerges, holding up a red ribbony thing. 'Do it for me, Mummy.'

'Hurry,' Gabe urges and she squats down, working her fingers through her daughter's scalp to draw hair back from her face into a ponytail, expertly winding the red elastic around twice, snapping it tight. 'There you go,' and she steps back through the gate to lock the front door.

Sam pounces, grabbing Mags, who's light as a puppy. He starts to jog as she squirms in his arms. He crosses the street in front of a car he doesn't see with his head turned towards Gabe, who's screaming as she chases after them. Mags clings to him, crying out for her mother.

He ducks down the laneway, on the brink of turning back as he hears Angie's steadying voice in his head. Then he sees a white station wagon on his heels and he runs until his chest hurts. Desperate and unsure where to go he pushes up against a back gate that swings open into a yard, untidy with loose bricks and planks of wood; a builder's sign against the fence falls face-down as the gate flaps shut. 'We're going to see Angie,' he lies to Mags, breathless, sweaty, 'and we have to hurry because otherwise we might miss her.'

'I want Mum,' Mags whimpers, unimpressed by the promise of an aunty she can barely remember. 'Mummy,' she throws back her head and wails. Sam panics.

Flipping out in his head at the mess he can cause in five minutes flat, he hears the mewing of newborn kittens close by. He puts a finger to his lips to hush Mags while they listen. Still snuffling, she tilts her head at the sound of other, smaller animals in distress, and a tremor shivers her tiny diaphragm. A siren in the distance transfixes him as Mags takes his hand, concentrating on the squeaky peeps coming from the back veranda where a striped canvas awning has come adrift, faded, frayed and torn. On a strip of fabric bunched beside a dusty box of white bathroom tiles are three kittens – two tabbies, one black – their bodies entangled as they search blindly for their mother's smell. Sam bends down and gently lifts one, holding it in the palm of his hand for Mags to stroke. The kitten's eyes are slit, hair matted, skin stretched over fine bones. Mags' face dissolves into wondrous disbelief.

'Can we keep her?' she asks him and he smiles assent on a morning when impetuosity prevails. 'Where's its Mummy?'

Sam casts his eyes around the yard before feeling the depression in the fabric still warm from the body of a cat. The mother's not far away. He hears a car screech to a stop.

'Shush,' he tells his daughter. 'Don't make a sound. We mustn't frighten the kittens. I'll go look for the Mummy.' Around the side of the house rusty paint tins caked in dribbles of white are stacked near a ladder on its side. He peers through the window. The linoleum has been torn up and the chimney grate in the furthest corner of the room is stuffed with paint-stained rags, fast-food bags, newspapers. A car revs in the laneway and he hears it driving off to join the distant hum. Quiet, then the soft caress of his daughter's words soothing the kitten on her lap.

'Hello little kitty. Good girl. You can stay with me. At my house. I make a bed for you, all for you,' she assures confidently.

'Daddy?' she calls to him and he melts to be needed, willing to do whatever she commands. If she asked to go home, well, he'd take her. 'What'll we call kitty?' she says to him when he reappears from around the corner of the house and squats beside her.

'You pick a name,' he suggests.

'Umm,' Mags thinks hard.

'We better check whether it's a girl or a boy first.' He takes the kitten from her lap.

'Careful,' she chides as he holds it up by the scruff to discover she's a he. 'Do you mind if it's a boy? We could swap him . . .'

'Nup. I like him,' Mags says as he returns the tiny bundle to her lap. 'I think I'll call him Paddy.'

'Patty?' He's misheard her. 'That's a girl's name.'

'No it's not. Paddy's a man. He's Mum's friend.'

Rocked by her words, he wants details, he's desperate for details but reluctant to ask so he waits, hoping she'll chatter on, colouring in this stranger. She's enraptured by the kitten.

'What's this Paddy like then?'

She screws up her face as she looks at her father. 'Old. Like you.'

He squeezes her out a smile, wishing they could stay in this limbo forever. He imagines Paddy as a doctor, someone with money, reliable, good car, fussing over Gabe, who's as beautiful as their daughter, and he hankers for what he's lost. He takes out his mobile and when he turns it on the phone seizures like an epileptic. Thirty missed calls. 'Shit,' he leers at the caper he's unleashed. He taps out a message to Gabe. 'I'll drop Mags off at 3. Cross my heart.'

The sun is rising, warming the veranda where they sit while the kittens nap just as Mags did for the first weeks of her life. How rich they'd felt with happiness, he and Gabe tucked up tight, him working to earn money that, spread carefully, saw them through, with rent taken care of by Gabe's brassy parents who'd forked out for a three-room semi where their daughter still lives.

Her pregnancy was an accident. Taking a contraceptive pill, daily, didn't fit easily into a schedule hijacked by the hunt to score – an almost twenty-four-hour occupation. She didn't know when her period was due so she couldn't remember when it was late. The swelling soreness of her breasts got her thinking but by then an abortion was impossible.

Gabe got a nine-month jump on him. Feeling Mags squirm and grow inside her got her clean. His recovery took longer. He's not sure really what he did to piss her off although his guess is he just wasn't the kind of provider, in a longer term down-the-road sort of way that Gabe and her parents were looking for. Mags they could shape from scratch: send her to a decent school, get her a toffy accent, nice clothes, perhaps a pony . . . He laughs at this dream and tousles her hair.

'What's so funny?'

'You riding a horse.' She looks at him as if he's crazy, like her mother says.

'Can we take Paddy with us when we go to Angie's?' He'd forgotten his sister. 'Why don't we get Angie to visit us here? That way she can see the kittens.' She returns to the creature curled on her knees and his relief, his pleasure in this moment, is marred by what he's done to get this close to what he craves.

'My full name is Eva Ruth Myers. I live at 14 Seaton Street, St Kilda and I'm a freelance editor. On the night of Monday, March 22

I arrived at the Kremmers' house at 25 Calypso Avenue, South Yarra at around 8 p.m. Bernadette and I went in together.'

'Bernadette who?'

'Bernadette O'Neill. She and Leith were student teachers together at a high school out west. Bernadette says Leith tamed her Year 10 monsters with morning teas, plates of sugar-dusted madeleine cakes.' Dan doesn't know a brioche from a croissant and he shreds this extraneous fact before it lodges in his brain.

'Is Bernadette married to Monty O'Neill?' he asks.

'Yes.'

'Was Leith having an affair with Monty?'

'I don't think so.' But her ignorance of Leith's affair with Vince encourages amendment. 'I don't know for sure, but I doubt it. Monty adores Bernadette. They have the perfect marriage – at least, that's what it seems from the outside.' Every impression is up for re-evaluation now.

'Can you tell a perfect marriage?' Dan asks the question on her mind, genuinely intrigued.

She thinks before answering. 'By the very smallest of gestures,' she says. 'I remember Monty coming up to Bernadette while she was talking to me one day, and he caressed her hand to catch her attention. He had to tell her something – a housekeeping thing. It's the physical warmth between couples, that's how you know.'

'Why did Leith start going to the races?'

'Her father was a punter. She loved the thrill of winning, taking a gamble, and yet I wouldn't describe her as a risk-taker, exactly. This was a new thing, the races. It was *her* thing, something that she had over us, if you know what I mean. I think she liked that, and dressing up.'

'How was she when you and Bernadette arrived on Monday night, what was she doing?'

'She was in the kitchen with Rosie, preparing food. Everything had to be perfect. She put the rest of us to shame. Not intentionally, she just had this gift so that whatever she cooked tasted glorious. I offered to help her but she waved us off into the living room and Rosie opened a bottle of French champagne . . .'

'Do you always drink champagne?'

'Hardly ever. We usually drink wine.'

'What was the occasion?'

'I don't know.' Eva pauses. 'Leith was in a racy mood,' she continues, unsure how to describe the buoyancy that's gained gravitas as she remembers her friend fussing around them, fixing drinks, flaunting her supplementary reading of Plath's letters to her mother, attending to every need. 'She seemed hyper. She'd gone to a lot of trouble and I thought she was just excited to see everyone. She loved entertaining. Then at the end of the night she made a toast, out of the blue, before we left. We'd all had a bit to drink. She thanked us for our friendship.' Eva flips back and forth through a chart of murky emotions, close to tears. 'Which was really odd,' she adds, her voice beginning to quaver, 'when you think about it, because why would she have wanted to thank us?' She turns away from him to find a tissue in the leather shoulder bag at her feet. Dan notices her shapely calves and her blue suede heels.

'Where was George during the evening?'

'He was upstairs. I didn't actually see him but we could hear him practising. It sounded like he was chopping wood – great violent blows that came one after another.'

'So he didn't come down to say hello?'

'That's not unusual. You've spoken to George, haven't you?' Dan nods. 'Well, he's not a gregarious man. Vince always says that whenever I phone the Kremmers he can tell if George answers because my voice hushes and I become obsequious. It's the judge thing. I think that's been hard for him. Husbands don't come to book club. We get glimpses of them through the eyes of their wives. Anyway, to answer your question, he didn't show his face on Monday night.'

'Have you seen this morning's paper, the death notices?'

Eva's eyes water. 'That's what hurts.' She hadn't meant to blurt her exclusion. 'I can't believe Leith kept it hidden. We went shopping together on Sunday. Vince used to say she grew taller in a shop.'

Dan lets her roll.

'Leith helped me buy his new glasses,' she says to herself more than to Dan, who's disappeared in her fog, remembering moments that have changed their spots. 'She said the blue frames went with his olive skin.' Eva's gabbling to keep from crying.

Baffled by this scattergun recital of personal vignettes, Dan feels as if he's watching a home video. 'Do you know who Leith was seeing?'

Eva shakes her head, wary of perjuring herself, unwilling to advance Vince's role in this saga until she's grasped the dimensions. Silence stretches. Dan looks down at his notes 'You mentioned Vince before. Is that your husband?'

Eva nods.

'How were George and Leith as a couple?'

'She was lonely, dissatisfied, but she wanted to keep the family together. I think we both kept up a façade for each other. She'd given everything to the children and to George, so she could never let me see that she felt short-changed. We wore brave faces in each other's company. But she seemed happier lately.' Eva's voice quietens. 'On Monday night she was ecstatic.

'What time did you leave?'

'Around midnight. We all left together.'

'Was Leith intoxicated?'

Eva shrugs, not sure whether alcohol or lust or fear was gingering her friend as she stood at the door waving them goodbye, and not willing to prejudice George's innocence with all she now knows of his wife.

After seeing Eva out, Dan buys a plastic tub of caesar salad from the canteen, wolfing it down in the car on his way to the city, impressed by Leith Kremmer's black belt in the art of discretion.

He parks in a no-standing zone outside the city's broadsheet newspaper, a low-rise brown brick barn, frumpy beside the undulating red swell and metallic shine of the rail terminal. Smokers congregate near the entrance. Inside the foyer he announces himself to the man behind the glass screen at reception then steps aside, his hands in his pockets, facing a mural that portrays the paper's history: clean-scrubbed delivery boys on pushbikes, nothing like the motley mob Dan remembers from his pre-dawn round thirty years ago. These days it's grown men short of dough chucking newspapers at houses from the windows of their clapped-out bombs.

The lift doors open and a woman with short auburn hair, wearing tight grey pants and a striped shirt, steps forward and extends her manicured hand as she walks across the carpet.

'Sorry I'm late but the girl who handled this is off today.' She sits down with him on the couch beneath the mural. 'I've done the best I could but there's no record of sale for this ad. It was a cash transaction.'

'I see,' Dan grimaces. 'What if she was shown the security footage?'

She lifts her shoulders in an exaggerated shrug.

'I'll get a subpoena for it because you never know. Worth a try.' Her crimson talons remind him of his ex-wife's nails that would leave scratch marks on his skin in the early days of their courtship. On her left hand he notices a single-diamond engagement ring.

Put a bean in a jar for every time you have sex before you get married, take one out every time you have sex after you get married, and you'll never empty the jar, his uncle had whispered to him dryly on the morning of his wedding.

Inside her car Eva turns on the radio to hear reports of extra troop commitments and the threat of further water restrictions. She waits for a cyclist to pass before pulling out from the curb. The clipped voice of the newsreader announces a homicide investigation into the death of a judge's wife in her Melbourne home on Monday night. Eva's promised to debrief Rosie and on her way there curiosity leads her past the Kremmers' house, little expecting the crush of camera crews and outdoor broadcasting vans in the street. The tall wrought-iron gates are closed. Leith's car is in the driveway. Reporters on the nature strip turn to stare as Eva slows to rubberneck and she's overcome by an inappropriate awed giggle because Leith would be mortified by this indignity. For a moment Eva imagines Leith's here, beside her, drinking in all the weirdness, that laugh of hers setting them both off. The aftertaste of this hallucination is bitter for it reminds her of what she'll miss.

At Rosie's she greeted by a fruity whiff of liquor as they embrace on the doorstep, unfamiliar with meeting mid-afternoon, mid-week, their personal schedules shot by Leith's departure from their lives less than forty-eight hours ago. She was their lynchpin.

'I still can't believe it,' Rosie says, teary again, glad for Eva's arms to ease her loneliness. 'Did you know Leith was having an affair?'

'No.' Eva's succinct denial is insufficient. Technically correct, yet grossly inadequate, just like her answers to the detective's interrogation. Neglecting pleasantries she drops her handbag on a stool beside the marble bench and reaches for the newspaper nailed to the counter by a coffee mug and the cordless phone. Her tailored skirt, stockings and heels appear over-groomed beside Rosie's sweatpants and loose T-shirt. The work ethic is in repose here.

Eva finds the death notices. George's poetry seems arch, phoney beside Cameron's spare epitaph; his mourning seeps through her layers of anger, hurt and humiliation. The anonymous tribute sits underneath, clumsily compact. No wordsmith, that's for sure. It couldn't have been written by Vince, she reasons hastily, unless he'd rung or emailed the paper last night when he left the house. What time was that? She checks the copy deadlines printed in a box across the top of the classified section: 8 p.m. She remembers checking her watch at 7.15 while he was in the bathroom. Reading it over, the language ropes Monty into question with its bookies' reference to a relationship against the odds. 'Have you spoken to Bernadette yet?'

'Her phone switches through to message bank. She must be teaching. And Marion's gone to Broome with Phillip, remember, at some corporate thing.' A nervous blush reddens Rosie's neckline in reaction to the excitement. 'Leith can't have been having an affair.

She would have told me. She used to sit right there where you are now, just me and her.'

Eva takes her bag from the stool and searches for the cigarettes kept in a red enamel case that hides pictures of clotted arteries, green teeth and gristly tumours plastered over every packet. 'Do you mind if I smoke?' she asks.

'I'll join you,' Rosie demurs, walking behind the bench to the sink where she reaches underneath for an ashtray. She slides it across to Eva, whose scratchiness is a surprise. Rosie had expected that Leith's oldest friend would be more unhinged. Why isn't everyone behaving as they should?

'I can't remember the last time I smoked in someone's kitchen,' Eva says, lighting up.

'I need a drink,' Rosie declares. 'We really should have a brandy,' – almost as if stiff liquor is prescribed twice daily for times like these – 'but I'm having a wine. What about you?'

'Just one,' Eva says. Just this once, she thinks, because it's not often, thank God, that she has so many reasons to wipe herself out early in the afternoon.

Rosie twists the cork by hand and it pops with a melancholic echo. 'Do you remember on Monday night before we left Leith's place, she made that speech about how much we meant to her?' She takes two chunky goblets from her cupboard. 'I keep thinking she must have had a sixth sense about her death, a sort of déjà vu in reverse. Otherwise why would she have wanted to thank us?'

I lent her my husband, Eva thinks, taking a slug of alcohol.

'George seemed surreal when he met me at the front door on Tuesday morning. If it'd been me, I'd need sedation. I'd be sick with guilt, grief, remorse. Can you imagine?' she asks Eva. 'I'd want to kill myself. I couldn't live with it.'

'That's his manner,' says Eva dismissively, her own mask fixed, conscious of how trauma dishevels people in peculiar ways.

'Why doesn't he behave as if his world's fallen apart?'

'He's in shock. He keeps his emotions under wraps. Just because he didn't break down . . .' Eva begins but her thoughts deliver her to Vince's collapse on hearing the news. That's the textbook reaction to losing your nearest kin. 'Everybody deals with it differently.'

'He'd been drinking.'

Eva grimaces at Rosie's temerity.

'The police told me.' She squints at a business card propped on the windowsill. 'Detective Inspector Dan Sinclair. He wanted to know how much Leith had drunk. He'd counted our empties. Five bottles of Moet. We must have had one each, more or less.'

'He didn't say anything about that to me. He just wanted to know why we had champagne. Why did we?'

'I still don't know. Leith fobbed me off when I spoke to her on Monday morning – said it was a surprise. I know she was flush with money because Bernadette told me at book club that she'd won sixty-five thousand at Caulfield on Saturday.'

'Dan Sinclair wanted to know whether Leith was having an affair with Monty.'

'She'd never dare do that to B.'

Eva stiffens. She thought she'd enjoyed the same immunity.

'You know George has had trouble keeping staff at court.' Rosie builds her case against George.

'He's got a short fuse. That doesn't make you capable of murder. It just culls your friendship group,' Eva says, trying for balance. She runs a hand through her hair, fanning the white stripe across her dark curls. 'How do you know about the staff? Did Leith ever mention it?'

'No, she didn't.' Rosie's eyes skitter nervously. 'Someone told me,' she says, taking the ashtray and emptying the butts in the bin. 'That's why she made him play golf. Don't you remember?'

Eva's forgotten. 'More than any of us George has achieved everything he set out to do and yet he can't relax. When you raise anything personal with him it's as if his forehead is signed like a freeway ramp: Wrong way, go back. Except when he talks about Jesse – then his face opens up.'

'Well, I've never really warmed to him,' Rosie says, the alcohol starting to take the edge off this strangest of days. 'The funny thing is,' she pouts at the paradox, 'Leith always reckoned George couldn't kill a fly. She said he'd baulked at disposing of the dead possum on their lawn last week. He's meant to have a weak stomach. Don't you remember how he refused to change the boys' nappies? Even Alistair did that!'

Rosie's habit of hopscotching from one square to another usually annoys Eva, but today she jumps off on her own tangents. She thinks of Vince, who pushed the boundaries of tradition, pioneering a gentler fatherhood than the one he'd experienced. He'd been the first in his circle to take paternity leave. 'You're more of a mother than your wife,' Eva's mother-in-law had told Vince, ruffling her compliment with disapproval of a daughter-in-law who didn't worship her son with sufficient conviction.

'Imagination fails some people,' Eva pronounces. She'd often wondered whether there's another George, whimpering in the cellar of his soul. Leith told her once that his mother had crushed his adolescent desire for the stage. Thirty-five years she's known him but she can't remember him surrendering his guard. She's familiar with his CV, his love of photography, his favourite poets, the cars he's driven, his preference for meat done rare – a biographer's stew of offcuts, enough for an obituary – but she couldn't tell what chilled him to his bones or whether he loved his wife with all his heart. He hadn't strayed from Leith as far as she knows but Eva had never seen his fingers linger on her skin. They were an odd fit, not just because of the geography between his height and hers. For all of her interior design skills, Leith hadn't found the right throw-rug or limestone wash to cosy her granite statue.

'I always assumed Leith was happy.'

'They were resigned to each other,' Eva snorts.

'That's what I meant, I guess.' Rosie frowns because it's not what she meant at all. 'Companionable,' she offers up as a meagre substitute for mutual adoration.

Eva considers how outsiders would interpret her and Vince's relationship. They often bicker in public, their arguments gangrenous. Eva heard another couple snitching at each other in a restaurant last year and for several months she tried harder not to slice Vince's conversational hypotheses with her sharp tongue. And whenever he begins a story that she's heard, she simply tunes out. Last Saturday morning they'd sat at the kitchen table. He buried himself in the newspaper; she was trying to finish Ted Hughes. He rose to make a pot of tea. Eva ground coffee beans, leaving rings of brown powder on the bench. Waiting for her brew she heard him bang cupboards as he cleaned up, the air sharp with disinfectant as he sprayed the stainless-steel island, wiping vigorously, and it strikes her now that his recently acquired fetish for keeping the kitchen spotless was his way of covering up this dirty part of himself.

'I can't believe Leith had a lover.' Rosie's still stuck at this jump.

'Why?'

'Because we're friends, because we tell each other all kinds of things that we don't let on to anyone else.'

'Do we?'

Eva's contrariness rattles Rosie. She tops up their glasses and helps herself to another cigarette. 'We do, or at least I do.'

'No we don't. We preserve our friendships by fibbing. We tell the truth when it suits us.' Eva's itching to dump her bundle. 'Or when we get caught lying and the truth might rescue us. I don't think any of us know each other's darkest selves. We pretend to. We make assumptions based on the flimsiest proof.'

'Leith didn't lie. She wasn't a sneaky person. She didn't slight you or Bernadette or Marion behind your backs.'

Eva suggests Rosie opens another bottle because the last was only half full. Her phone rings. Vince. Let him think she's parked in a lonely dangerous place, which is half true.

'Who was that?' Rosie asks, disappearing into the pantry for dry biscuits and nuts that she assembles on a white china platter.

'No one important.' A mote of loyalty floats in her heart. She determines to keep his affair secret from her friends, happy to sprinkle Leith's pyre with lies of her own.

Sam had warned Angie that parking was tight around here and for once he's right, she thinks, as she completes another slow lap of the inner-city block, relieved when the police car behind overtakes her in case it's searching for the very same wrongdoer she's come to tackle. A girl in gym shoes and sweats crosses to a car on the other side of the street. Up ahead is the laneway. She turns in and backs out quickly to snatch the parking space, her blinker staking claim as she waits for the girl to buckle up and depart. Half an hour is all that's left of her lunch break. Grabbing a plastic bag of sandwiches and drinks from the back seat, she goes looking for a gate on the left-hand side, draped in ivy.

There's a dead cat on the cobblestones, flies buzzing around. Checking to make sure she's alone, she pushes the gate inwards.

'Sis,' her brother's voice hisses from around the corner of the house, and he emerges, towing Mags behind him. 'Look what we found,' the little girl sings out. Angie picks a path through bottles and knee-high weeds, delighted by the welcome. She hasn't seen Mags for seven months and she bends down to hug her tight.

'Look at you,' she says to her niece, but Mags won't be still. She leads Angie to the veranda where the smell of cats triggers Angie's allergies and she sneezes three times in quick succession.

'That one's mine.' Mags points to a black burr of fluff interwoven with two tabby kittens.

'She's gorgeous,' Angie says, wondering if its mother is the cat mown down outside.

'It's a him,' Mags corrects her, 'an' his name's Paddy.'

'We used to live next door to a dog called Paddy. Do you remember, Sam?' He's glad for Angie's way of fattening up his past so that Mags has a sense of him belonging, and therefore her too.

Angie sits on the veranda. 'Let's have a picnic,' she says to Mags, spreading paper napkins on the wooden slats and arranging the sandwiches on top. 'There's chicken, ham or peanut butter. And fruit salad for later.'

'You pick first,' he offers his sister, who takes the chicken.

Mags peels the triangles of bread apart and licks off the peanut butter. Sam eats ravenously.

'You've done it this time,' Angie says quietly to her brother. 'I'm not going to ask why but you'd better come up with a good reason otherwise the court will do whatever Gabe asks and you can kiss Mags goodbye.'

'The kittens are hungry too,' Mags instructs. Angie nods as she swallows a mouthful of food and opens a small carton of milk that Sam asked her to bring.

'See if you can find a dish or a lid to put the milk in,' Angie says, and the little girl wanders off to search.

Angie screws her napkin into a tight wad. 'Gabe's already got the police on your tail. You've had it this time. I thought you said you were learning from me but it's in one ear and out the other with you.'

'I'm taking her back at three. I've told Gabe. I sent her a message.'

'Let me take Mags back. Please. That way there's less chance of you being nabbed. I'll try and talk to Gabe. She's frightened of you.'

'That's crazy,' Sam drawls, leaning back until he's lying flat.

'It's not, you know,' Angie says. 'I'm frightened of you too. Frightened of what you might do because you never think about the consequences of anything. You only think of yourself. You don't even think. You just do, then you think. You're 28, Sam. You're too old to change. But if you could just think about the people you say you care about. Me, Mags. That's all I'm asking you.'

He hates the mantle of loser, the feeling that he's no good and never will be.

His remorse comes and goes like a headache. She doesn't know whether to scream at him, disown him, try a touch of cruelty or empty another flagon of love down his throat knowing it'll never touch the sides. She looks around for Mags. 'One more thing,' she whispers. 'There's a dead cat in the lane. She looks like the mother of this lot. Bury her in the yard when we've gone. It's the least you can do.'

'Can you lend me some money?' he pleads. 'I get a cheque tomorrow. I had to buy clothes for court.'

She opens her purse, wishing she had something smaller than a $50 note.

'Thanks sis.' He gives her a kiss before taking the money, pulling his wallet from the pocket of his jeans.

'You've dropped something.' She reaches for a scrap of paper on the ground.

'Oh yeah,' he says, smoothing out the crumpled column of print for Angie to read. 'Judge Kremmer's up for murder,' he tells her.

She cringes at his stupid grin.

For two days the media bustle outside the Kremmers' house entices drivers from the city-bound boulevards to crawl past a murder scene that is attracting notice because of Leith's poise and George's status. Speculation's become a parlour game. Everyone has an opinion: the man in the ATM queue, passengers in taxis, shop assistants making small talk while customers fumble for a credit card. Any time there's a gap in proceedings, theories are expounded vehemently. 'She had a lover', 'She taunted him', 'They had a blue', 'Why else would he strike her?', 'A drunken brawl', 'She was a lush', 'There were empty bottles everywhere', 'He's got a violent streak', 'His eyes are creepy'.

One particular colour photograph feeds their excitement. Dug out of an electronic file, it was taken for a Sunday paper at an opening night. The portrait flatters Leith. Striking in a pea-green dress with her grandmother's fake ruby necklace, her smile tipping into laughter as she faces the camera, she almost obscures George, who stands two steps behind her, his head turned slightly, his gaze sombre. They rarely attended these occasions. George always feigned tiredness, but he'd buckled under pressure from Leith to grace the premiere of a play written by one of Cameron's friends from student theatre.

She looks flirtatious. Her helmet of dark hair is tidily clipped against her creamy skin. George is in her shadow, his eyes holding her on an invisible string. It's an image that nurtures popular assumptions of a marriage thought to be stiflingly close, jealousies easily inflamed. Leith's elegance is a magnet but his profession is the sexier drawcard. The judiciary is an exclusive club, with membership contingent on propriety and a reputation that is starched, spotless, as well as a mind like a Swiss clock. These attributes were first articulated by his father as if the law was a family grocery business that George would inherit one day if he sharpened up and drew quarter from his father's example. Prudence engulfed him, marshalling his instincts, trussing his wings, so that every utterance and gesture was released only after incubation. That he'll be tried for murder is an improbable end for someone who's done everything expected of him to conform.

From his observation tower in one of the spare bedrooms upstairs, George parts the curtains a fraction of an inch to spy on the media stalkers. Some leave messages on the home phone, polite at first but impatient now that the spectre of murder dangles over him. He counts two vans marked with the logos of rival networks parked in the street. The passenger door of one swings open and a girl flicks her cigarette butt out then stands to dust crumbs off her short black-and-white houndstooth skirt before resuming her seat. She opens a laptop on her knees and sits tapping, lifting a hand to wave at a middle-aged man with a beard and horn-rimmed glasses who saunters along the pavement towards her, his shirt tail flapping. They talk, glancing up at the house as if they see him hiding, and he steps back, pinching the curtains closed. The pathway gate, rarely used, whines on its hinges. Footsteps crunch along the gravel path towards the front door. George prepares for the dull knocking that he refuses to acknowledge in a drawn-out game of bluff, stuffing his ears with plugs fashioned from cotton wool, face down on the bed, pressing the corners of a down pillow around his head.

He can't bring himself to read the salivating coverage of the investigation into Leith's death, their marriage, his personality, his reputation as idiosyncratic and impossible to predict. Imprisoned in the house, he avoids performing routines as if his life is continuing as normal. Instead of holding himself hostage to the codes of behaviour befitting a judge, he must abide by other rules. Grief should be a licence for eccentricity, an indemnity that gets you off every hook, but he knows there's no latitude for composure. He's observing protocols. He hasn't picked up a golf club since Leith's death. If he finds himself positioning his feet out of habit to practise his swing, just as the mother of a newborn sways instinctively even when the babe's out of her arms, he feels the heat of shame. This morning he fingered the remote control of the television – day one of the US Masters – but he couldn't find it in himself to depress the button. He's not a new arrival in hell, its sulphurous fumes familiar to a man who's spent most of his adult life papering over his cracks to preserve the family name. East George tightens control of his public persona, a regimented state of being that crushes the yearnings he dubs West George, for they are decadent fantasies.

As a student he'd been captivated by the bronze sunbaker in a photograph he'd seen in an exhibition at the gallery. He'd bought a framed print for his room at college. The image aroused him at night, his subconscious eloping with the man on the sand, swimming or lying, skin to skin, and he awoke with an erection, sweaty, his heart galloping. So he took the picture down from the wall. Leith had held these dreams at bay.

The first night they slept together, relief was the primary colour he felt. Not only had he performed satisfactorily but he'd enjoyed the sex, his eyes closed. Leith seemed content, shy of her nakedness, and her reserve suited him. During their early years he'd felt secure, snug, at peace with his compromise, one arm cuddling him to her like a soft toy as they'd drifted off to sleep, both of them knackered by the arrival of children: the broken nights, toddlers' tears and sticky chaos. Two children were not enough for Leith and her rapacious desire for pregnancy gained a manipulative intent that repelled him. They haven't kissed for the longest time or touched each other intimately. When she tried to lead him, desperate for his seed, the sunbaker crept back into his sleep. By then Art and Jesse were underfoot. At first his sexual urges stayed within the boundaries of night's realm. But the stalker escaped, rearing up at him in a doctor's waiting room where he'd gone for a sperm count at Leith's request. He was supposed to be coveting a Playboy bunny, her shapely legs wide open in a full-colour centrefold, but what brought him to a climax was the face of a man in an aftershave advertisement. At the very time Leith wanted sex he didn't desire her body so he superimposed the razor man, pale like Leith, on the sunbaker's bronze body. Sometimes, Cameron would roll into the weightless arms of his dreams.

The ascent of East George was a way of managing his con-flicted lust. Self-discipline helped him deny the sunbaker entry. This deprivation both made him and undid him. Like the climber who saws off a limb to free himself from a crevasse, George ampu-tated a part of himself to survive. His years on the bench watching families disintegrate had made him determined to keep his own house in order.

Loyal to his wife, his sons, too afraid of risking everything, he couldn't renounce them. And now, in a second's miscalculation, he has done just that.

Leith's death has bankrupted him. On Monday he was wigged up, looking down upon Sam Dunlop – an ominous beginning to the week that might bury him yet. This morning the Chief Justice appeared almost pleased to cut him loose. 'I have no choice,' he'd said from behind his expansive desk. George had fixed his eyes on the public gardens beyond the window where the elm trees are distressed from lack of rain.

'I don't pretend to know what happened between you and Leith on Monday night. I know it would be easier in some ways to continue with your routines but the court is bigger than us both and we have to protect public confidence in the system. You should make use of the counsellors here. You have a lot to work through. The media's the least of it, really, but for your sake I hope the police guillotine this in a speedy fashion. I've spoken with the commissioner to this end.' He looks up at George for gratitude. 'When's the funeral?'

'Next week.'

'Well, we'll be in touch before then. Good luck.'

George didn't object as he rose to shake hands. He didn't haggle over the press release announcing his drop down the chute until further notice of any charges that might be laid. He departed noiselessly, leaving behind his putters, his wig, his books, his papers for collection another day, on the presumption, however slight, of a reprieve. The *Sunbaker* was all he took, tucking the print under one arm as he rode alone in the lift.

He'd returned to the house an hour ago, braving the media picket line, car windows tight, a pair of aviator sunglasses obscuring his face, thankful for the remote control of the driveway entrance. Once inside his cool dark prison he tries Jesse's mobile for the umpteenth time but the phone rings out, not even a message bank. He understands why their youngest boy chooses the solitude of copses, fern-carpeted groves, forests where the mighty thighs of trunks punch the sky. Yesterday George wrote him an email that took hours to compose, fiddling with how best to break the news. 'Your mother died on Monday night,' was what he settled for after countless false starts. 'She loved you dearly,' came next because she had, and in the middle of nowhere, alone with his horror, George had wanted to wrap his son in every comfort he could provide. He'd intended to stop there, saving the details for when they talk, but he'd rushed on in a confessional tone, apologising for his absences, his stand-offishness, his wretched insecurity, and then he'd deleted his efforts and begun again with a bald statement of death. Logging on this morning George had found his email acknowledged by auto reply.

Art had answered his phone on the second ring when George called early on Tuesday morning. Abrupt, busy, a television in the background, he'd listened to George describing the accident, explaining the lateness of the hour, succinct so as not to sound panicked, rounding off with a declaration of remorse and love for his wife.

'An accident.' Art had repeated George's phrase as if searching for sense in its syllables. The white noise in his office ceased, all distractions muted by remote. In the silence George heard sobs. The sound of Art's distress unlocked his. 'I'm sorry, boy,' he managed gruffly through his tears.

'Where's Jesse?' Art asked but George couldn't respond even if he'd known the answer.

'I want to see Mum,' he said, 'to say goodbye.' George nodded his consent, desperate to placate him. 'I'll come as soon as I can, as soon as I can get organised.'

'I'll pick you up at the airport,' George offered.

He stumbled through the timetable of these next few days: the police, the coroner, Cameron's return to Australia, the likelihood of a service next week.

'Did Mum suffer?' Art had swung back to his mother's fate but the intensity of her pain couldn't be quarantined to the hour of her death.

177

Leith lived for her boys. George had been less prepared for the joys of parenting. He's watched young male associates around court immerse themselves in the magic from the start, carting strollers and bags and bottles of milk that they warm in the microwave on his floor. When Leith brought Art home from hospital George was terrified of dropping him, happier to throw balls with the boys when they could walk and run, and in his element as the story-teller, introducing them to A. A. Milne, R. L. Stevenson, J. R. R. Tolkein. His fondest memories are of their perfectly formed pink lips open, their eyes devouring his impersonations of Long John Silver or Gandalf – chin extended, sword raised – because he loved acting until his mother skewered his dream. As teenagers they'd wriggled free from him and he'd let them drift away, slipping into the authoritarian mould of his own father, hearing the dictum to study and strive tumble forth like some strange incantation.

George had gone to see his mother on Tuesday morning at the aged-care facility next to the golf course. He'd ended up shouting his news at her with exaggerated lip movements so that she might read the words she couldn't hear clearly. 'Oh God,' was all she said, closing her eyes as she's always done under duress until she sub-dues whatever's upsetting her by force of will. She'd schooled him in this art. He'd sat for a while holding her jewelled fingers, the purple veins protruding from hands almost transparent. She didn't ask him for further details. 'I'll come to the funeral,' she'd croaked as if her attendance was even in question.

Not a soul has visited the house, except for Rosie. If Leith had killed him – well, he is sure the benefit of doubt would win her presumptions of innocence. Baskets of flowers and food and sympathy would be sweeping up the drive, passed from hand to hand along a human chain of her friends.

He's been surviving on cereal, boiled eggs and cans of tuna until last night when he opened the freezer for the vodka and discovered shelves of meals – small Tupperware containers labelled and dated and stacked one on top of the other as if Leith was preparing for the siege he's enduring. Chicken cacciatore, beef daube, pesto sauce, all his favourites. Even desserts: sticky date pudding with caramel sauce, a lemon tart cut into eight single wedges.

He showers upstairs where the bathroom's laid out to accommodate a visitor's every whim. Opening the door of the cabinet under the sink, he finds toilet paper to last the length of a nuclear winter. Why was Leith keeping this house stocked for the apocalypse? The phone rings. As he stands waiting for the interruption to cease, he looks down the hallway to her study beside the kitchen, its door ajar. He's drawn by a sense of discovery. Above her desk is the wall calendar with dates circled in her hand. He fetches his glasses and examines what she had lined up for this week. 'Book club' is scrawled under Monday 22nd March. Tuesday has a gold star posted in the square and three large exclamation marks in black felt-tipped pen, drawn so vigorously that they seem to quiver.

* * *

Leith jiggled in and out of Marion's thoughts as she and Phillip drove north from Broome. Ambushed by Bernadette's phone call last night in the Sunset Bar at Cable Beach, they'd found news of Leith's death unreal from where they sat amidst a table of raucous holidaymakers, frangipani perfume sweetening the dusk. Marion wanted to turn home so she could be with the others. He'd persuaded her to stay – 'It's only two days, there's nothing that you could do back there that can't wait'. With Marion's head on his shoulder while she wept, he couldn't help but be glad, in a grim way, for a drama to bring them closer.

This morning they'd left early, conversation subdued by the heavy metal grind of the four-wheel drive as they shook over the corrugated bumps on this red dirt road. She's as relieved as Phillip when at last they see the arrow pointing left to Cape Leveque, a remote resort that had appealed to Phillip's firm for its links to the indigenous community trying to make a living from their land. They pick up their keys from a flat-roofed, army-green office beside a strip of runway where a fluorescent orange fishtail dances in the light wind. 'Another 200 metres and we're there,' says Phillip, turning the jeep on to a sandy track that winds into the bush overlooking the beach. As he navigates the very last turn up a slight incline towards their pavilion, the car sticks. The harder he revs, the deeper they sink, wheels spinning a shower of sand.

'I'll push.' Marion gets out of the car and her flat patent-leather slippers fill with sand. Trying not to soil her white shirt, she leverages all her strength as Phillip accelerates, spraying her with grit. He swears. Sweat splotches his polo shirt as he joins her at the rear of the vehicle, unsure of a remedy, barking at her to help him find a plank of wood or some stones to give them traction. He seethes at being a minute away from a cold drink and a soft bed with an uninterrupted view. What if one of his partners comes upon them stuck, stupidly adrift? He orders Marion behind the controls so that he can push when a white jeep pulls up. The receptionist, wearing boots and shorts, olive-skinned, sprightly, gets out to lend a hand. A smile soon washes over his face.

'The wheels are locked.' He points to a dial on the dashboard. 'It's not in four-wheel drive.' He bends down inside the hub and twists a silver disc. 'You should have unlocked it before you left Broome.' The car edges forward effortlessly. They wave sheepishly, grateful for an easy exit as they park in the streaky shade of a gum beside an A-frame hut built from wood and canvas, the last in a line of five on a ridge overlooking the bay.

'How humiliating,' Phillip had groaned as they unpacked. 'An idiot, that rental car guy. He should have told us when he gave us the keys.'

'Probably thought we knew what we were doing,' she chipped.

'We could have been killed.'

Marion watched him change his clothes for the barbecue and cocktails. 'I can't get Leith out of my head. Do you mind if I stay here instead?'

'Okay,' Phillip smiled and, placing his hands on either side of her neck, he stroked her cheeks with his thumbs. Usually she obliges. Get it over with is a rule she applies as effectively in business to BAS statements and sacking staff. Her mother was always refusing her father. Marion would hear their mutterings turn nasty at night from her room next door.

'I've got to show my face. You understand, don't you?' She'd nodded. 'I won't stay long.' He drew close, pressing his groin against her so that if she'd given him the merest encouragement he would've rolled her on to the bed. He'd been yearning for these few carefree days.

Once he's gone she pokes around, unpacking. She likes the mix of roughness and comfort. No television or radio but there's a bathroom with a shower and an indoor toilet. Enticed by the whip of birdsong outside, she unzips the netting and steps onto the wooden deck facing the sea in this sheltered cove, the water calm and grey in the dying day. A light twinkles at the top of a tall-masted catamaran. Along the crescent of sand a couple stroll close together. Voices from the reception in the kiosk below drift upwards, noisily. She sits on a low-slung chair, her bare feet on the wooden balustrade of the deck, displaced by their swift transferral to Arcadia, sliding from electronic foreplay to being corralled with Phillip. Monday night's memories remain vivid: the sound of George's club louder than Marion remembers, the laughter, the menacing thud, the idea of an accidental murder.

Once, during Christmas drinks at the Kremmers', Marion had surprised Leith and George in the kitchen. George held Leith's arm behind her back; their jaws were tight. They awoke to Marion as she stood there and George asked, with a Basil Fawlty click of his heels, whether he could help her with anything. They'd all laughed and she'd never asked Leith to explain, passing the incident off as a piddling scrap under the pressure of entertaining.

Five years ago Phillip had spotted George emerging from the toilets on the edge of the public gardens, a meeting place for gay men. The circumstantial evidence fed his scrutiny of George's aloofness: the way he once snatched a restaurant napkin to buff the dust from his shoes, an attention to grooming that could just as easily speak of fastidiousness – a trait clients pay for in their lawyers. He hasn't mentioned his sighting to Marion. She's mulled over George's psychology for different reasons.

One night, as they'd idled in Leith's front room after book club, Marion had picked up a framed photograph of Cameron and Leith from the sideboard and put it down above the fireplace. 'George hates things out of place,' Leith had remarked, returning the frame to its position equidistant from two black-and-white portraits in silver frames. 'George's parents,' she said. 'Father's dead. His mother Margaret's in a nursing home. Guess where?' Marion had shrugged. 'Next to the golf course!' Leith had squealed so that Marion laughed too, unprepared for the profundity that followed.

'He can't wait for her to die.'

'Why?' Marion was taken aback.

'Because then he can be himself.'

She'd never really understood why Leith held back whenever book club turned into a grudge session against the men in their circle, as if whatever bugged Leith about George must not be petty. Just a hunch.

The smallest of vibrations in her hand alerts her to mail. It's W, as she calls this old love. He's a writer of young-adult fiction; separated from his wife, estranged from their son, his fingers rarely at rest. Cheeky squirts of text dragging her under. At first she'd responded tentatively, playing along for the lark of it. But his humour weakened her core, disconnecting her from Phillip, who's unaware of her wantonness even as he senses her slipping away. The longer she continues this dalliance the bolder she gets, seduced by the ease of their push-button chat, back and forth, hot and quick.

She opens the tiny yellow envelope in her inbox. W has heard the news. 'A golf club???!!! Sleep with a gun beside your swag.'

She writes back. 'I can't believe she's dead. Makes me want to leave/live in a hurry.'

This prospect scares and exhilarates her.

Earth shifts in a marriage, opening fissures in its rooms, cracks in the walls. Since the children left home she's found excuses to be somewhere else, boredom browning the edges of companionship. This is a cost of living together for as long as they have. She became easy prey when W sent his electronic flare. After hours she's often messaging staff with last-minute catering details or guest lists, so Phillip's deaf to the work tool's buzzing. Once, when the two of them were watching television, she answered thirty text messages from W, relaying Phillip's conversation to the outsider in their midst. She's not proud of her duplicity, but you do what you must to survive. Some people drink. A friend of Phillip's takes anti-depressants. There are couples who sleep in separate rooms.

The peppery aroma of barbecued meat suddenly makes her hungry and, swinging back inside, she changes into a brightly patterned sleeveless shift that flatters her height and figure (she's fitter than she's been for years). She applies lipstick, darkens her blonde lashes, brushes her hair then checks her phone before leaving, the torch guiding her along the sandy path towards the wooden stairway.

'Where are you heading?' Phillip is surprised to see her. He's carrying a tray with enough supper for a tribe. They go back to the tent. He opens a bottle of chilled white wine. She sniffs cautiously at the thin strips of kangaroo fillet then wraps a hunk of damper around the meat. They sit on stools either side of a wooden chest, Marion's appetite ebbing after several mouthfuls.

'I'm glad you didn't come tonight,' Phillip says.

'Why?' She looks at him yawn, no hand to screen a mouthful of amalgam.

'There was speculation about George and Leith. Some story on the web quotes a neighbour – I can't remember her name – who claimed that George always has a golf club in his hand. George told her husband one day that he used it to keep his wife in line.'

'George would have been joking.'

'These things get twisted. If there's a void people fill it. In a public court there are no rules of evidence. Hearsay is gospel. An online opinion poll has sentenced him already, guilty of murder. And there's a report she had an affair. People love this stuff.'

'She's never dropped a hint in my hearing and she's had plenty of opportunities to talk.' There's an edge to her voice.

'I thought you were good friends.'

'We are, but she's reserved, like George. We don't share everything.'

He leans over to take her hand; her skin nettles with irritation. She drinks a generous gulp of wine, enduring his advances as she might a gym workout, counting paces on the treadmill, every step closer towards the end of the session. His fingers slide up her bare arm. After she'd had children she no longer liked sharing her breasts with him. Since they'd suckled her babies, their erotic purpose had been superseded. She hated him touching them. He sneaks across from her shoulder to her nipple.

'Wait,' she bargains, disentangling herself. 'I've got to take a leak.' This is true enough but her base excuse is avoidance and she closes the bathroom door. She washes her hands, girding herself for duty. He'll want to luxuriate in arousal tonight, no chance of quick relief.

Mildly inebriated, Phillip undoes his snakeskin belt, tantalised by the idea of Marion's underwear around her ankles. Her phone beeps receipt of a message and he picks it up off the end of the bed, casually glancing at the screen in case there's a catering emergency, but what he sees compels him to read on in a breach of privacy he's incapable of registering or camouflaging. He scrolls through screen after screen of her inbox, stopping to retrieve a text that begins, 'Tell Phillip that he . . .' He doesn't hear Marion emerge from the bathroom. She swipes the phone from his hand as he rises from the chair. He backs away from her as though he's afraid of what might happen next to trump the obliteration of his trust. She doesn't check the message; no need to verify the charge of treason in his eyes. Denial would demean her. She's unprepared, with no credible explanation for the illicit fun she's been enjoying.

Noise seeps in from outside: glasses tinkling, tables scraping, laughter, farewells shouted as groups of stragglers retire to sleep. A fly buzzes inside the tent, circling them before landing on the food that is wilting in the warmth.

Phillip's silhouette shadows the canvas walls like a puppet. Then he turns and exits, the clatter of his feet down the wooden steps stopping as he hits the talcum-soft sand. She hesitates for a minute before she follows him, sprinting to catch up as he strides through the saltbush away from their pavilion. She grabs his hand, but he throws her off and starts to run. Her bare legs are scratched from the sharp dry shrubs in their path. She's out of breath, frightened of snakes. He's gasping, unfamiliar muscles fuelled by adrenalin, his chest tight from holding back tears. 'Stop,' she screams. 'Please, Phillip.' His footsteps pick up speed until he runs down a dune towards the still water silvered by the moon.

'Who is he?' he bellows, turning to face her.

'Does it matter? You don't know him. We go back a long time. Before you and I met. He contacted me. He wanted to catch up.' She stops where her innocence ends. 'He googled me. He found the business web site and emailed me. I didn't go looking for this.'

The sexual inflections in the message on her phone sear him.

'How far has this gone?'

She turns away and looks into the pitted black crater of sky.

'Nowhere.' She hears the tinny rattle of denial in her voice. 'We haven't slept together.'

'That's crap.' He slams his arms so hard on his thighs it must hurt, then brings his face close to hers, repeating his conclusion vituperatively but quieter now to make his point. How could she describe to him the thrill of being preserved in a special part of someone's memory? The blankness, the boredom, had lifted the moment she saw his name on her screen. Enticing, mood altering, it'd started as a gambol.

'Why have you done this?'

'Let's go back,' she urges him gently, coaxing.

'You go back. Go back and text your old pal. He's waiting for a horny reply. Tell him your husband doesn't think much of his poetry given how many months you've been at it. Now I know why you've been behaving so neurotically when your phone goes missing. How dumb am I? I was so looking forward to coming here, for a few days of being away, just us.' She barely catches his whimper before a shout slaps her. 'And now this!' He throws his head back despairingly, 'This tatty bit of dirty phone sex . . .' Now, pleadingly, 'I want you to talk that way to me.' The carousel of emotions is spinning her dizzy. Then he's gone, back up the dune the way he came, panting with exertion into the black. She doesn't chase. Her fingers wrap around the phone in her pocket, glad for its presence. He's right. The messages back and forth are like a fix and she gets sweaty without the warm promise of the phone in her palm. She has some deleting to do. The air feels chilly on her bare arms. Clouds veil the moon.

An eddy lifts her hair and she feels insignificant, cold. The strangeness surrounding her is stranger for the speed of her undoing, tripped up by the very technology that facilitated her liaison. She looks at the screen's tiny square of blue light. Marion imagines Leith on the stairs of her house, turning the handle of the door to George's room. Did she see death coming out of the corner of her eye as they flung mocking taunts at each other, rancid accusations drenched from the stinking gully trap of their marriage? Do accidents happen or is the rottenness underfoot to blame for the fatal blow of a swinging club, or a deceit laid bare?

*　　*　　*

'Bernadette,' Monty hollers, switching on the porch light as he opens the door, puzzled by the darkness, since her white station wagon is parked out front. Usually he arrives home to the aroma of dinner and the television's hum: a welcome that has been the pattern inside their house every evening for as long as he can remember.

'I'm here,' Bernadette answers weakly from the chair where she'd sunk after work. She'd dropped her bag of groceries on the floor by her feet, unfussed about peeling potatoes or opening the clutch of envelopes that she'd collected from the mailbox hopeful of finding an itemised telephone bill for Monty's mobile that might tell her a thing or two. A private weep had lanced her misery as she'd sat twisting the interlaced gold bands on her ring finger, turning events over in her mind, not conscious of the street lamps flickering as the neighbours brought their wheelie bins in, locking down for the night.

'What's going on?' Monty kicks off his paint-spattered boots and clomps down the hallway in his thick socks, flicking switches as he goes. He's been out of sorts since lunchtime when he got the call from the homicide detective investigating Leith's death. For the rest of the afternoon he'd worked six metres up on a rooftop, as high as he could go, staying there until poor light forced him to ground, the last of the crew to leave the site.

'I've had a day from hell,' she says, glad for his clatter.

'Me too.' He opens the fridge for a beer and comes to join her in the family room. Comfortable chairs and a three-seater couch form a circle on the deep crimson and blue Persian rug. This is where they've always gathered with the kids to solve deadlocks over holiday destinations or bedroom allocations. 'The police want to interview me about Leith.'

'Rosie says they're talking to everyone from book club. Have you seen the death notice in this morning's paper?'

'The copper told me about it. Give us a look.'

She hands him the paper, softened by the creases and folds of her worrying. 'Everyone thinks you two were having an affair.'

Monty's silence is what she'd least expected. She doesn't rush him. She sits slumped, waiting for him to speak.

'We weren't having an affair,' he says so quietly she knows he hasn't finished unloading all of his mental freight. She'd rather he just stop where he is because she's happier with that simple, clean denial. But he continues. 'We've always been honest with each other, right?' He pauses, leaning towards her with his elbows on his knees to look her in the eyes, urging agreement which she confers weakly, doubts welling inside her. 'I've been thinking how best to put this because you know I'm not good with words, but I have to tell you that I really looked forward to those outings with Leith. And I'm not blaming you because I never expected you to come with me to the track. But it's funny how she grew on me. I just feel I owe it to you to tell you that because . . . ,' and he stalls as he perceives the hurt his words are causing.

His declaration rings truer, she supposes, since he is

acknowledging the stirrings he'd felt; still, she'd have preferred a blunt disclaimer.

She thinks she believes him. They have always levelled with each other. For her part she has nothing to confess, no jerks of restlessness pulling her away from him. She hasn't gone looking for outside interests of the kind Leith found time to pursue. This chance is upon her now that her youngest has left home. Self-sacrifice is a habit that's hard to break when your religion consigns you to the welfare of others. She hasn't allowed herself the indulgence of dissatisfaction. At parties she doesn't look over a shoulder for a more interesting catch, too conscious of others' needs and insecurities.

'Was it you who put the death notice in this morning's paper?' she asks, wishing that she could just shut up.

'I didn't write that. As if I would. You know me. I sign my name on a card but you always write the greeting. I've been wondering all day whether it's for real or not. Perhaps someone's made it look like me.'

'Why would anyone do that?'

'To deflect attention from themselves. I even wondered if George did it – you know, to make it look as if he was provoked.' He checks to see what she thinks of such a mad proposition but she's verifying his assertion of innocence, kneading the firmness of his account.

Monty gets up and kneels beside her chair, taking both of her hands in his own, palms pressing together, their fingers enmeshed. Then he rises to his feet and pulls her up beside him and he bends enough to scoop her in his arms and carry her down the hallway to their bedroom, where they always go to make peace. Even when her heart hasn't been in it his hands have persuaded her to enjoy their intimacy so that she forgets the ironing or the watering or the shopping or whatever else presses in on her for the pleasure of being with him. Tonight, though, she's unable to relax into the rhythm of lovemaking. Monty's erection is fleeting, their failure to connect dispiriting. They lie close, far from sleep, Bernadette restless with inquisition that she can't contain any longer.

'What did you two talk about?' Bernadette asks.

'I should have seen this coming,' he says.

She freezes. 'What do you mean?'

'She sometimes asked about us.'

'What kind of things?'

'How we met, whether I'd ever been attracted to anyone else, did I know as soon as I saw you that we'd end up together, was there an instant connection. To be honest I felt embarrassed in the beginning, but I'd try and answer in a broad-brush kind of way and then she'd always go quiet so I'd change the subject, make her laugh.'

'What else did she want to know?'

'How often we have sex.'

'But I've told her that, we discussed that at book club. I came home and told you, remember, because you and I wiped the floor.'

'Well, maybe she wanted to make sure you weren't inflating the score.'

'What else?'

'She wanted to know whether I'd marry you again, knowing how our life has turned out. Did I get things I hadn't bargained on? Plenty, I said, and I made things up. I had to in the end because I thought we were beginning to sound like a fiction.'

'Go on.'

'Um, she wanted to know whether we had sex on our wedding night.'

'Did she use the word "sex" or "make love"?' she giggles. 'We did both.' That first night together they couldn't wait until they got to the hotel. They'd left the mock Tudor reception hall and he'd pulled over to cut the empty cans tied to his truck's bumper bar. When he got back into the cabin she'd taken off her wedding dress because she couldn't stand the corsetry another minute and they'd climbed into each other on the side of the main street, oblivious to the codger walking his dog.

'You didn't tell her all the details?' Bernadette blanches.

'Of course not. It was a sad thing, her questions.'

'We're lucky.' She pulls him closer, sorry for Leith.

'Did she ever talk about George?'

'Not really.'

'Why didn't you ask her? Maybe she would have found it easier to tell you these things.'

'We weren't in therapy. This was just chat. Chitchat in between the car park and the track or over lunch. Most of the time we talked horses, honest.' He strokes the hair from her face. 'George wasn't a hot topic. The only time she talked about him was the day she backed a horse that was never going to win. A grey mare, five years old, plenty of starts and very few places, trained on the Peninsula, sired by Mr Big and Alaska. It was called Ice Block. We argued because she promised when she started coming with me that she wasn't one of those girls,' Monty spat the phrase out like a pip, 'who back a horse because she likes the colours of the jockey's silks, or because the name means something special. To be fair to L —'

'Who's Elle?'

Monty goes quiet. 'L is what I called Leith. It's nothing secret,' he pleads, 'it's just the first letter of her name.'

'Oh.' Bernadette curls as small as she can. 'So what did Ice Block have to do with George?'

'Well, she said that she and George had different thermostats. She likes the heating on high, whereas he's the opposite. He likes a chill. Leith said she thought he liked to be numb so that he didn't have to feel.'

Last Saturday, Monty remembers, Leith had worn a French hat, maroon crushed velvet, her dark hair peeping out below like a fur trim. She'd drawn attention their way, her way – people loved to stare at her. He didn't know whether it was her clothes or her size or what. Small enough to be a jockey herself, she'd stand and listen to the strappers and the stable hands talk around the mounting yard: which horse was cranky, who hadn't run well in morning track work, why blinkers would be needed on the front runner. Last Saturday she'd sidled up to him with gossip on a change of rider in race six for a horse that had won two out of five country starts.

'I feel lucky today,' she'd said. 'Do you ever get that sense?'

'Yeah. Is it luck or hope?' he'd asked her.

'I guess one feeds the other. If things go your way it's as though anything's possible.'

Then the horses began prancing into the yard, the clink of bits and bridles, a snorting of breath, and they had moved into the rails for a closer look.

Monty turns over and rubs his nose into the small of Bernadette's back, sad for the loss of his Saturday escapades and the lightness of Leith's company.

The death of his sister has orphaned Cameron in a country still foreign to him. He's adopted the lingo – he speaks of zeros instead of noughts, zee instead of zed, sidewalks not footpaths, soda not soft drink – and has swapped his broad vowels for American twang. Leith told him he'd gone native, and it's true that he's rezoned himself to fit the landscape. Being in Boston, the modifications have been nowhere near the stretch that would have been required down south or Midwest.

In a post-Leith world the distance from home tyrannises him.

This morning in the supermarket he'd knocked a packet of flour into his trolley amidst the muesli and pulses. As a boy he'd once made cupcakes with his sister to take to school for his birthday. Kids had teased him. He smarts now, decades distant from the hurt. Although younger than him, she'd be the one he'd go looking for at lunchtime if he was bullied. She was the one who'd poke your stuffing back. He'd kept boxes of her letters which he'd taken out and read last night.

His friends are fussing around him with phone calls and flowers. There's an industrial-sized chocolate mud cake from a surrogate sister who teaches drama with him at the performing arts college. He's already passed it next door – Frank's allergic to cocoa. A bunch of sweet-scented oriental lilies arrived moments ago from the head of department. Cameron arranges them in a blue perspex vase while Frank slices carrots and ginger for a stirfry.

'You know, I've been feeling kind of placeless all day,' Cameron tells him.

'Placeless?' Frank pinches a tissue from the box and wipes the tears elicited by the onion he's slicing.

'Neither here nor there, sort of lost in fright. I had this moment at the store today, thinking of Leith, and when I snapped out of it I thought, Where in the hell am I? Because there's nothing distinctive, nothing local on the shelves to say, 'You're here in Boston'. You could be anywhere – Moscow or London or . . .' Cameron shrugs.

'Or home,' Frank suggests gently. 'Here with me.'

'Home.' Cameron repeats the word as if aiming a dart at a continent on a spinning globe.

Frank hadn't been prepared for Cameron's emotional plunge. The siblings were close, he knew that from their correspondence over the years, but vast oceans had kept Leith remote, a speck on the shore in a far southern land. Hers was not amongst the numbers recorded on their list of emergency contacts if the flat caught fire or one of them blacked out in class. Frank's loud family of opinionated intellectuals dominated the cycle of holiday gatherings. He and Cameron travelled to his brother's family in Phoenix every year for Thanksgiving, while his elderly mother hogged the rights to host Christmas in her New York apartment. Australia was too far away even if George had been deducted from the equation.

'Have you booked our return flight yet? Because I need to tell them at school how long I'll be gone.'

'I'll do it tonight,' Cameron says, rubbing his eyes. He doesn't tell Frank how he's been wishing that he'd stayed in Melbourne, closer to Leith, sad to have spent half their lives apart. He and Leith had been hatching the idea of a six-month sabbatical together in Tuscany or Greece. He'd glanced over ads for cottages to rent in the back of a *Gourmet Traveller* magazine that Frank brought home one night.

'Are you okay about coming?' Cameron asks of Frank's promise to accompany him tomorrow night for the marathon across the

Pacific. Frank is big-hearted and broad-minded but confines himself to a small corner of the universe. He hates long flights.

Frank puts down his knife and wipes his hands on the faded butcher's apron that is his chef's uniform. 'Of course.' He takes Cameron in his muscular arms. He's the taller of the two, and leaner for the exercise and weightlifting which he does religiously. His small grey eyes, gold-rimmed spectacles and his Rip Van Winkle beard create an endearing impression of wisdom and mischief.

'This afternoon I danced myself crazy. I put on Leith's favourite Motown CDs.'

'Ain't no mountain high enough,' Frank sings quiet and low as the two men swing slowly, hips together. Mack gets up from his beanbag and stretches, then walks over and sits watching them.

'I felt lonely today,' Cameron says. 'Lonelier even than I was before I met you.'

They'd encountered each other at an exhibition of the sprawling AIDS quilt, its squares embroidered by the hands of sisters, mothers and lovers honouring lives stolen from them. Frank was sitting cross-legged in front of an orange velour panel he'd helped decorate with tiny brass bells for a musician friend. Cameron was the one with the big arms that day. Losing Leith makes him fear for Frank's safety, anxious at the riskiness of a childless coupling where there's no margin for tragedy, no next of kin as proof of their love.

The two of them hadn't considered starting a family from scratch. Godfather to six children at last count, Cameron also has his nephews; Frank is uncle to his sister's two kids. But sometimes he's envious of younger gay couples who are adopting children or fathering their own using donated eggs, rented wombs. Ever the optimist, even he underestimated the breadth of change in his lifetime. Merely living together was a feat of courage when he and Frank met. Plenty of men couldn't own up to themselves let alone confide in parents whose love was conditional upon taking a wife and producing a child. The Statue of Liberty didn't promise shelter for gays but he left Australia to free himself from decisions he might have rued if he'd stayed. One of his former boyfriends had taken a wife. Cameron was invited to their wedding. I guess you can change your mind, he'd told Frank, who'd agreed that of course you could because sexuality is fluid. His friend had risen to become CEO of a chain of furniture stores, collecting a number of philanthropic roles and a chair on the board of a football team. Not so long ago he committed suicide, alone in a hotel room. He'd been caught by a security camera in the men's toilet of a railway station, soliciting sex. What had hounded him most? Cameron wondered. The humiliation and shame? Conning his wife? Public scuttlebutt? Probably the lot. It had taken him a while to accept, this idea of hiding yourself, one ear always listening for the goosestep of discovery because homosexuality isn't like addiction – you can't put yourself through rehab. Frank believes that for all the enlightenment, prejudice haunts people, sometimes with lethal consequences.

'You would have made a good father,' Cameron says, freeing himself from Frank's arms.

'Maybe,' Frank shrugs, turning back to the kitchen where he lights a burner on the stove and tips sesame oil into the wok, which he tilts and swivels, painting the sides of the blackened pan with a glistening film that soon begins to bubble. He doesn't stew over this lack in their lives like Cameron does. You make choices, he reasons, whenever Cameron brings it up. 'My Dad was such a hideous role model it's kind of a wonder that I have any empathy at all. But then again, maybe that's just the kind of upbringing you need to raise a softie,' Frank says. He tosses a bowl of bite-sized chicken pieces into the wok. They pop and hiss and he flicks on the convection fan. Cameron sets the table, Mack trotting at his heels.

'Has George answered your email yet?' Frank almost shouts to be heard.

'I rang him this afternoon,' Cameron replies.

Frank looks up.

'He didn't answer,' Cameron says. 'I was going to hang up and then there was a click and I heard Leith's voice on the answering machine. I put the phone down and then I rang back so I could hear her again. I think I listened to the tape fifteen or twenty times. She sounded as though she was down the street picking up the dry-cleaning. Remember after 9/11 there was that woman who kept her husband's phone account open so she could hear his voice when she rang his mobile? I can understand why.'

They stand on either side of the island bench, their dinner preparations abandoned.

'Eventually I plucked up the courage to leave a message.'

Frank hovers expectantly. 'And?'

'I told him that we were coming home for the funeral. I said we'd be arriving on Saturday and that once we'd settled ourselves he and I could talk.' Mack whimpers at Cameron, his ears pricked, his whiskery face quizzical.

Night falls as Eva leaves Rosie's place. Inside the car she folds down her visor and squints into the mirror, the orange light of its miniature globe puffing the bags under her eyes, lines etched into her brow, her brown curls limp (the white streak seems to be spreading: less punk, more senior citizen). This, she decides emphatically, is the lowest point in her fifty-six years. The upside of the work–life balance is that they rarely go bust simultaneously, one usually bailing out the other.

She starts the car, pondering where to head next, when Vince rings again and she takes his call, tired of running.

'Thank God,' he says. 'Where have you been?'

'Rosie's,' which is hardly the clifftop she would like him to imagine.

'Come home, please.' She has nowhere else to go. 'I've cooked dinner,' he adds and she's tempted to enquire whether he's expecting a medal, but she's chastened by snatches of reflection on her role in his affair. The hours she's whiled away at Rosie's have cooled her leap to the moral high ground, Rosie's loneliness giving chase to her righteousness. Why wouldn't Vince be tempted by Leith? Eva can't remember the last time she'd been pleased to see him. No wonder he'd gone looking for welcoming eyes.

Personal history is a messy, contradictory source of comfort, within these pages the legend of icons, the key to you. She likes that Vince knew her mother, her father, her shortcomings, her anxieties, her strengths, her knocks, her habit of sucking her thumb when she's tired. He's watched her breastfeed their daughter. It's a familiarity that's hard-won, testifying to a longevity that joins them together even as the creeping sameness of these shared years prises them apart.

Hanging a u-turn, she makes for home via the Kremmers' house, where she's surprised that the media have deserted their post for the night. She parks, now that they've gone, deciding on the spur of this moment to pay George a visit. Surveying the street to make sure it's emptied of cameras, she hops out and opens the gate, treading lightly on the gravel path. She raps on the stained-glass panels of crimson, blue and green, peering into the dim hall for a shadow of movement. At this hour a house that looks foreboding even floodlit for a party is positively creepy; its blinds shut like eyelids, the pall of murder creeps over mortar just as lichen blankets slate.

Vince's admission seesaws Eva's perspective on what happened here on Monday night. Who knows what goes on in another couple's marriage? She had no idea what was happening in her own, and she's been living it.

Inside, George listens to her rapping in the inattentive way he hears possums scratching in the ceiling at night. He stays where he is, berthed in the fine Georgian chair at Leith's antique writing desk where he's been sitting for hours. The gold star and exclamation marks on Leith's calendar led him on a labyrinthine search for a meaning but he's wound up where he began, empty-handed, more determined than ever to decode the exhilaration that had winged her flight to his door.

Since her death he's been so dizzied by the speed of his descent into suspicion, so barbecued by slander, so busy arranging his story and answering Dan Sinclair's questions about their marriage, that he'd not thought to conduct his own investigation into her alibis.

The diary he knows she kept is missing. When he'd withdraw upstairs after dinner, she'd sit here, filling pages in free hand like a heartsick girl, cramming ruminations into a thin-spined book. She'd begun keeping these journals when they first moved into this house, with a mortgage that gave him nightmares. Barely habitable because of the damp and the leaks, Leith's enthusiasm for its transformation was infectious. Her first efforts thickened into scrapbooks, the pages puckered with squares of fabric, daubs of paint, pictures from magazines of colour schemes and furnishings, recipes, the law list from the newspaper mentioning George's first divorce cases, their children's squiggles. Once the renovation was complete and the boys were grown, there was more space for self-discovery. Increasingly Leith wrote about herself, becoming secretive so that he wasn't invited to share the pages of memoir. He'd been grateful that she had a place to pour sentiments he was deaf to.

This afternoon he'd turned the house upside down and in the course of looking for her keepsakes he'd identified other vanishings. One missing object linked to another so that he's uncovered traces of Leith through the absence of things in a perverse game of hide-and-seek. This exercise had required him to think first of what was precious to his wife beyond her inventory of valuables for household insurance. The silver's in its box on a cushion of velvet. Her pearls had been collected by the police from the floor where she fell. A team of investigators poured over his room on Tuesday morning, fingerprinting every surface, photographing his golf clubs, Edgar's Gate, the stairs, the door. George's detective work steals through different territory. He had to conjure up the special things that are worth nothing but meant everything to her. He hadn't thought of Leith in this way since their courtship.

She'd been his only girlfriend. As a handsome schoolboy he'd had dates for formals and balls, corsages in pink and white that he'd pinned to each breast. He'd closed his eyes, just as his mother does, when he'd found their lips for the obligatory goodnight kiss, a father's husky cough in the porch shadow music to his ears. Leith had held him like a butterfly on her open palm. That was what he'd loved about her.

Looking yesterday at the measurement of Jesse and Art in increments up one side of the pantry wall – Art in red ink, Jesse in green, every inch marked excitedly, no cheating, heels on the floor, eyes straight ahead – he sees where the years went. The expansive trunk of the magnolia tree he planted as a sapling under Leith's instruction is another mark of their lifespan. After years of luxuriating in the distance they kept he wants to locate her, except he doesn't really know what he's looking for.

He'd found a key to her safe on a ring of spares they'd had made for every lock in the house. Her wedding ring was here in an apricot satin bag – not on her hand, which he hadn't thought to examine and couldn't remember holding in the ambulance or the hospital where he'd made amends and bade adieu. Sifting through the bangles, earrings and brooches he was unable to recall whether any of this gold and sparkle mattered to her. He had marked their anniversaries with flowers from the florist near the court, ordered by whoever was managing his office. He'd never bought her jewellery apart from her onyx and diamond engagement ring that she'd designed herself, and the pearls that he'd presented to her on their tenth anniversary. Like the challenge of choosing what to take if the house catches fire, he has to ignore the obvious, conscious as he combs her drawers and cupboards that Leith's loves are everywhere, from the magnolia's blooms and the rooms of this house where style and comfort join cheerfully, to the boys, good citizens both of them, and even to himself.

He'd gone in pursuit of her grandfather's tobacco tin on a chase that took him to the kitchen where he was certain he'd last seen it, high up beside the china teapots. On the sideboard in the front room he'd found the carved frame where she'd kept the photograph of her and Cameron taken in her last year at school, Cameron's hair fashionably long over his collar, but the photograph's gone. In its place was a studio portrait of George aged four, his expression as stiff as the short pants and checked shirt chosen by his mother for this formal sitting.

The day had got away from him in the same manner as this odd collection of artefacts had departed from under his nose. He'd returned to Leith's desk to fish for letters, lists, anything that might reveal her intentions, but there was nothing here. The policeman who'd confiscated the hard drive of the home computer had been just as disappointed by the thoroughness of her purging. Her secrets were sealing his execution, today's unsigned death notice suggesting motives based on the falsest of assumptions about their marriage. She'd stitched him up so that to secure his freedom, to extricate himself from being charged, he'd have to tell the truth about his love and where it lay.

The girls are out on the street whistling for customers when Eva pulls into the twenty-four-hour petrol station a block from home. Heidi's the only regular she recognises for her bibbed black dress barely covering the top of her lush thighs, her bleached hair worn in a single plait as she takes a cigarette from another younger, thinner newcomer, leaning in towards the flame from a plastic lighter. Both women suck in their cheeks then exhale a jet of smoke from glossed lips. A middle-aged man at the pump in front of Eva's samples the shape of their breasts and the length of their legs while filling the tank of his van. The idea of Vince enjoying another woman's flesh is a genie that's now loose. He's become interesting again as his secret washes through Eva's body. When she imagines him hustling for sex, undressing in front of Leith, she moistens between her legs, softening like butter in a warm pan.

The pimply cashier offers her discount chocolate bars when she pays for the fuel and she examines herself on the small security screen in his booth. After years of comfortable monotony she hasn't a clue what life holds and if she flipped a coin couldn't choose between heads or tails.

As she turns into her street she sees a space on the residents' permit side smack opposite the house. For the first time in weeks she doesn't have to drive around the block muttering because she hadn't wanted to live in this urban wedge, blaming Vince for inconveniences that appeal to him – like the lime and aqua graffiti on their rendered concrete fence – because they lend his life a slash of unpredictability. They've had to install bars on every window to keep the junkies out. Once, she'd stepped over a body hunched up against the front gate, getting safely inside before she rang an ambulance. She was too late. The young man, somebody's son, couldn't be revived. Sirens burn through these streets constantly so that locals grumble at having to make way for them. Pawn shops are tucked in between the cafes and secondhand book stores. Leith used to say she envied Eva her lairy neighbourhood.

Vince opens the front door, positioning himself for a hug that she resists, stale tobacco clinging to her hair. Her arms hang limply. On the hall table there's a bunch of pink peonies with vermillion rims, her favourite flowers; a tray of roasted vegetables scented with garlic on the stove; a giftwrapped box beside her place setting on the table. He seems to think they'll start again as if they are playing a board game that can be cleared of tokens and dice and cards, then reset for a new round with a fresh scoresheet.

He follows her into the kitchen where a bottle of wine, uncorked, is ready for pouring.

'A drink?' he asks. She shakes her head, tanked enough, the alcohol she'd drunk at Rosie's spreading thick as an oil slick over her anger.

'How did the affair with Leith end?' she bites.

'I was hoping we could light the fireworks later.'

'This isn't New Year's Eve, Vince.'

He pinches his nose near the bridge. After wanting to placate her, he slumps, unprepared for a fight. He has scripted a number of alternative endings, middles and beginnings, liberated by Leith's death to make up any version he prefers. Lying was easier when Eva didn't think he would.

'You're right, as usual,' he says, standing up as if to attend to the dinner, which he now realises was conceived in naivety, making him doubt also the sense of the story he has strung together for her benefit. He turns off the oven rather than burn the veal, resigned to arguing on empty stomachs.

'I'm ravenous,' she volunteers. He turns the temperature dial back to where it was, at her beck and call.

'Before we even start to talk,' he says in a steady voice that he's determined to keep civil, 'we need to decide whether there's any point. I mean, if you're leaving then what happened between Leith and me is academic, nobody's business but mine.'

'I'm betwixt and between,' she sighs. 'This morning I was ready to call the removalists. Tonight on my way home I felt like I wanted to go to bed with you for the first time in ages. I walk in the door to this,' she gestures at the sweeteners, 'and I want to storm out again. I'm furious with both of you.' The mention of their trickery whisks her rage. 'While I was at work, was it? Is that when you met? Here? Here in our bed, or did you go to the big house, the king-size bed in the big house? Or did you book into a boutique hotel or a bed-and-breakfast in the hills where no one would call you adulterers because that's the only clientele they get.' She hadn't wanted to dwell on the sex but she's drawn to the stained sheets, to the site of their own disappointments.

'Leith had an apartment.'

'I don't believe you. Where?'

'In the city.'

'Whereabouts?'

'Near Victoria Market.'

Eva searches for her cigarettes in her bag while her mind scouts for corroboration. When Marion's daughter bought an apartment in a new development on the fringe of Carlton, Leith had spoken like a realtor as she calculated its north-facing advantages, body corporate fees and underground parking spot. Vince sits at attention. He reminds her of a contestant in a television quiz show. He's sweaty, nervous of what subject he might be asked to tackle next.

'Why did she buy an apartment?' she asks in amazement. 'Was it just for you and her or did she see this as a long-term investment?' Sarcasm swirls to the surface. 'When was I going to get my turn?' she shouts at him. 'Was there a guest book for visitors to sign, adding a post-coital remark? Did you give it the thumbs up? Three-and-a-half stars? Much more savoury, I'd imagine, than a cheap motel near the airport.'

Vince lowers his eyes in case they don't convey his shame convincingly. She's left her cigarettes in the car so she bolts to get them, but then she turns back. 'Did George know?'

'No, he didn't.'

Eva wheels around and leaves.

He flinches every time he wonders whether George had, in fact, found out. Vince retreats from this line of thought, as he's

done all day, pulled between the agony of Leith's fate and Eva's
fury not long swept from the room. He hadn't wanted to tell her
that they'd come here. They first met one morning by accident, or
that's how it had seemed to him. He'd gone around the corner to the
hole-in-the-wall café, his reward after the demeaning morning ritual of job applications. Leith had been sitting there in the sun on
an upturned milk crate reading the paper, nautical in her horizon-
tal-striped sailor's shirt. Although he'd noticed her distinctive black
helmet of hair, he'd assumed this was a case of mistaken identity
until she'd turned around and smiled at him. She said she'd been
looking at an apartment, but she'd asked him not to tell, and he'd
felt anointed by her trust. Morning bled into noon, time galloping
as they each became absorbed by the other, delighting in the joy
of an undivided audience. They started to meet more regularly, by
arrangement delving into each other, engaging in the playful conversations special to the first phase of courtship. Ten years, fifteen
years, twenty years into any relationship each partner has a track
record that punctures baloney and ties possibilities on a short rope
to a stake in the ground. Actions speak loudest to the marathon
runners but the sprinters, the starters, can spin any yarn they like.
Leith talked. Vince listened. That's what Eva had liked about him
when they met.

George's persecution of Leith was subliminal. They hadn't
fucked for ten years. Like some freakish couple on Jerry Springer's
show. She said George never wanted to look at her. When she kissed

him he said she was stealing his air. One day when she put her lips around his penis he said her nose was cold. How could his pleasure be spoiled by a patch of cool skin? She never tried again. For years she thought he must be having an affair.

He became pedantic. If there was lint on his black socks he complained. He gave up their theatre subscription. He refused invitations which came through his chambers. He hated entertaining. Book club was the exception to his rule that the house was his hideaway. Leith did everything for him. He doesn't even know how to work an ATM.

Vince had kept her confidences. He'd asked his wife once about Leith and George, wondering how she perceived their relationship. 'Stuck in a rut,' she'd said. 'But it's a comfortable rut. She'll never leave him.'

'Do you ever talk to her about us?' he'd asked Eva. 'I wouldn't risk boring her to death,' she'd replied wickedly. The night after Leith's death Vince told Eva that the affair had gone cold, which was a self-preserving fib he plans to build on. There is no other satisfactory exit.

The front gate bangs. Vince opens the oven door and the smell of roasted meat fills the house. He turns towards her. 'Can we declare a ceasefire for twenty minutes or as long as it takes us to eat?'

She shrugs and slides open the glass screen facing the courtyard, where she paces back and forth the cell-block length. She drags on her cigarette while Vince tosses a salad and watches

her. Neither one of them is hobbled. He could leave tonight.
Maybe she will. Life's precarious, he says in a silent prayer to
Leith.

As Marion picked a path through the scrub back to their pavilion
she heard the four-wheel drive roar off and by the time she'd clam-
bered up the slope, the porch light blazing, Phillip and his bag were
missing. The bottle of wine they'd barely touched stood open on the
table, her only company a small lizard grazing on the leftovers of
her supper, small bulbous eyes brazen with entitlement. She starts
and the lizard escapes as if by magic through a glimmer of space in
the floorboards. She rings Phillip but he doesn't pick up.

Showering for longer than she should, in defiance of a polite
notice tacked to the wall, the whiskery nicks on her ankles and
legs turn pink in the warm water. Eva was right. The nights are
cold here. She's shivery as she gets under the covers, her sleep
light and fitful. Leith visits her during the night wearing a pair of
blousy orange overalls of the kind assigned to prisoners in custody. She dreams that they are in a warehouse packing tea-chests
spilling over with clothes, CD players, saucepans, pasta-making
machines, books, stuff that multiplied faster than she was able to
tape up one box and fill the next.

It's 3 a.m. In the darkness she listens to the rustle of insects,
the snap of twigs, every sound amplified so that she imagines the
footsteps of beasts and lunatics. The faint sound of gears changing

draws her upright and she turns on the overhead light in case Phillip needs help finding his way, but then the engine cuts some distance off. Deaf to the meaning of rhythms that mark time in this place she wonders whether fishermen are coming or going to catch the tides or whether an unhinged recluse in the camping ground on the ocean side of the ridge is on the roam. There are no doors to lock and the lack of security drives her into the kitchen where she takes a bread knife from the drawer to lay by her side, for protection, in place of Phillip.

Whoever thinks through the long-term consequences of their vows? Marion took each day as it came when they first met. Just as she'd floated into her father's business she'd acquired Phillip as her husband, rivalling him for breadwinner honours. He didn't mind, so he said, because the buffer encouraged him to take up social justice causes and his actions eased her conscience. He has his legal crowd, she has her clients. Theirs is a modern marriage: a two-income unit, property jointly owned, separate surnames (they'd stopped short of hyphenating for the children). Acquaintances outnumber friendships as diaries are over-run with functions and fundraisers – Marion can't remember the last intimate dinner party they attended. Since their youngest left, they've lost the pull of gravity and yet freedom creates its own impediment by removing the incentive to go. Staying is easier, or it was whilst she was able to contain her wanderlust in electronic corridors. He's done her a favour, burgling her messages, bringing on a confrontation she's avoided because life jangles enough without separating from a man she's held close for half her life.

Phillip's a good citizen. Always the one to pitch in, enlisting his firm's support for causes like the inaugural indigenous scholarship he set up ten years ago. 'He should've married you,' Marion often tells Bernadette. She respects him. They are cocooned in a shared life, with familiarity that anchors them even as she yearns for novelty, though she's wise enough to understand that if you live long enough with any person under the same roof, boredom and disappointment will settle like dust on the rafters.

What would friends say of their marriage if she died here overnight, her body stiff and cold in this bed? No one heard them fight. Nobody saw her at the barbecue. Would Phillip be fingered, guilty for abandoning her? How would the two of them stand up to magnification? Would their external blemishes encourage diagnoses of deeper dysfunction in the same way Leith and George's union could be misconstrued?

Over the years Marion had come to appreciate Leith's unhappiness, hard and monolithic. A quietness had crept over her, dulling her down so that she listened to them all undress without jostling for air time. She had faded gradually in front of their eyes, like the fabric on the back of a couch where the sun passes each day. They hadn't noticed in the way you do when a friend loses weight or appears one day wrapped in a scarf to hide a bald scalp. Beauty, intelligence, refinement and money armour plate vulnerability, and

Marion hadn't wanted to pry, to trip her up. You can tell a friend she has parsley in her teeth but how do you ask, 'Are you dying inside?' Whenever she'd enquired whether Leith was okay, emphasising the *okay* to deepen its gauge beneath the vicissitudes of everyday, Leith would laugh at her concern. Bernadette said Marion was imagining things.

She tries ringing Phillip again but the voicemail answers. The flap of canvas in a flurry of wind stirs her anxiety: the possibilities for an accident, his car rolling on a dirt track at speed, blood caked on his face, unconscious, hours until a vehicle passes, no one to haul him free. If he dies out here she'll be asked to explain his half-cocked departure after midnight without water or maps in an unfamiliar setting. His survival is all she cares for now; her guilt is a given, with only its quantity in doubt.

No hope of sleep, she drifts. She recalls sitting with Leith and Eva in the restaurant by the river, listening to their maudlin raincheck on men they might have married – purchaser's remorse, no refund possible. She doesn't regret her years with Phillip. She heard of a former philosopher who made a list of pros and cons before marrying his wife, weighing up the burden of visiting her relatives against the plus of togetherness. Love's chemistry eludes the science of prediction. Luck is a critical element deserving of inclusion in the periodic table, meriting its own symbol to describe reactions, since love is altered by poverty; wealth; the death of a child; ill health; depression; conflict; hearts worn down unevenly like the sole of a shoe; personalities disordered by the span of years in close proximity; loyalty weakened by the allure of a second chance.

Leith had raised her glass glowingly at book club, her eyes gleaming and her manner unusually plucky as she'd served them like queens. She didn't arrive wherever she was bound but Marion suspects she'd departed already; her decision made, she was steadying her friends. Marion warms to Leith's bravura. Lifted by a rush of resolutions, airborne with the wind of 'why not?', she gets up and gathers her belongings. At first light she'll seek the ranger's advice on her return to Broome, other destinations presenting themselves before the journey's begun.

THURSDAY

Bernadette hatched her plan in between dreams of screeching brakes and dead animals that reared up out of nowhere, bones crunching, the sound of Leith's head splitting, newborns mouthing for a teat. She rose without waking Monty and made a cup of tea, settling at the kitchen table to finish a funding proposal for her African Women's Group before collecting warm milk in a thermos, an old bunny-rug from the rag bin and a torch. As she leaves to meet Clara her phone beeps receipt of a text message. 'Can't walk 2day. Early staff meeting. C u 2morrow.'

'Damn,' Bernadette swears because she could do with Clara's help. Ordinarily she wouldn't continue in the darkness alone. Stepping out the back gate, she picks up her pace, practically jogging through the park.

None of the regulars they pass each morning appear to notice she's not paired with her friend. The clouds in the eastern sky are fringed in pink and orange.

In the laneway she feels for the torch in her bag, listening to a car door slam, then an engine coughing as she looks for a dark stain on the stone. She follows a smear where the cat's body's been dragged across the lane to a gate on the lean, covered in creeper.

The hinges whine when she pushes her way in, heart pounding. Amongst the weeds is a small mound, freshly covered in dirt, with an improvised cross made from broken sticks tied with a strip of rag. There's an empty milk carton on the veranda. She wields the torch like a painter's brush, up and down, side to side, illuminating the backyard to get her bearings. On the path she sees a scrunch of bright red. It's an elasticised ribbon like the one worn by that little girl yesterday. She hears footsteps scuffing in the laneway. Her heart gallops. The gate bursts open under a firm hand. There's nowhere to run. She blinds the intruder with torchlight. It's him.

He's about to turn and run for it when he hears her call, 'Stop.' And he does because she speaks calmly, like his sister. He shields his eyes from the light, which she shifts from his face to the synthetic grey shoes on his feet.

'I think this belongs to your little girl.' She hands him the red ribbon, which he accepts, wondering for a moment whether this woman's a plain-clothes cop.

'Ta,' he says, though that's not what he came back here to collect. 'I'm looking for my wallet.'

She offers him the torch and straight away he sees it by the fence where he was burying the cat late yesterday, digging a shallow hole with a rusty spade he'd found next to the paint cans. He opens it to check on his Medicare card and his licence, tucked into the clear plastic sleeve underneath the photo of Mags.

Bernadette itches to know his story.

'She's a beautiful child,' is her opener and Sam smiles.

'Yeah,' he says. 'A heartbreaker.'

'I saw you yesterday, running with her in your arms.'

Sam glares at Bernadette for assuming he's the thief when he's the one who's had his heart tricked by a woman smarter than him.

'I might be able to help.' She can't think how right this minute but an offer is the place to start for a disciple of the well-intentioned notion that a broken will can be mended like a bird's wing with food and comfort, a hand-me-down blanket and a pot of lentil soup.

'Are you a lawyer?'

'No. No I'm not but I know people who work in family law.'

'My sister's helping me out.' He dismisses her as a do-gooder and brushes past so he can check on the kittens. She follows him, touched by the way he attends to the tiniest of the litter.

'I've brought warm milk,' she says, reaching into her bag for the thermos and he's struck by how much this woman seems to know about everything that's happened. She pours the milk into the lid of a plastic takeaway tub. 'I've brought a blanket too.'

The feel of the soft flannel awakens his earliest memory, the only one he holds of his mother: the warmth of her body as they shared a blanket at night, her fingers tracing circles on his goose-pimpled skin. He lifts the three kittens in his large hands so that Bernadette can rearrange the bed for them.

'I'm Bernadette,' she introduces herself.

'Sam,' he answers because this much information can't hurt.

Dogs bark until a man's shout hushes them.

'G'day little Paddy,' Sam says, tapping the head of the smallest ball of fuzz.

'Do the kittens belong to you?' Bernadette asks.

'No,' he says. 'We hid here yesterday.' He feels like howling at his hopelessness and he rubs his eyes with his fingers hard in his sockets as he always does to hold himself in, forcing out words to stop himself cracking. 'We found the kittens. This one belongs to my daughter. She picked the name Paddy.' He settles the kittens on Bernadette's rug, turning away to wipe the rogue tear from his cheek. Standing up, he hands back her flashlight and in its beam he sees she's an older woman, creased and kindly, in an old blue tracksuit with yellow paint spots and a grey T-shirt. Bernadette notices he needs a shower and clean clothes – his jeans are grubby, probably from putting the cat to rest. She doesn't want to let him go. 'Have you got a mobile?' she asks him. He nods. She takes hers out of her pocket. 'Give me your number. I'd like to help you.'

* * *

The radio alarm wakes Vince with shouting and screams from an Israeli street where a car bomber has blown up a bus stop. He reaches over and flicks off the pandemonium on his bedside table before it disturbs Eva. They'd fallen asleep very early this morning, slipping limbs between thighs in familiar resting places, soft against each others' skin like the velvet smoothness of well-worn cotton sheets. He hasn't told her that he's rising early for a meeting with the police, worried by what they know, burning with questions of his own for the strangers constructing Leith Kremmer's epilogue.

His reconciliation with Eva is a fragile proposition secured partly by the high priority alert beside the email she opened after dinner. They'd slumped into their corners, hoarse from snarling. He'd retired to the couch. She'd turned her back to him, facing the screen of her laptop, the tapping of keys restoring a tenor of civility. 'A job!' she'd clapped at the offer of a communication position with a pharmaceutical company, relieved by the promise of a desk and a phone and an office and a title and a security tag to hang around her neck on a coloured strap as proof of her existence. He'd smiled, since he'd felt the same restoration of faith himself on joining the Institute of Public Affairs after six months of sinking confidence.

He looks at his wife, tuckered out on her back, her lips parted so that a snore sneaks out when she exhales. Her dark hair pillows her face, a wisp of white curled on her cheek. He's glad that the body's circadian rhythms force warring couples apart. How else does the heart heal? He steals the briefest of showers, then dresses. Sliding a shirt from the skein of drycleaner's plastic, he sets the hangers clinking until he stills them with his hand. On his way out he grabs a banana from the fruit bowl. The silver earrings that he'd bought for Eva lie unopened on the table. He tiptoes back into the bedroom, putting the gift next to her watch, for when she wakes.

Outside, the green bins stand in a crooked line, next door's overflowing with bags of trash. Vince locks the front gate behind him and walks up the street to catch the tram, exchanging glances with the girl working the corner. Amongst the rumpled early risers he's conscious of his polished shoes. The tram cruises to a halt. There's standing-room only, the aisles crowded with adolescent kids in purple uniforms lugging musical instruments, laptops and bags to school several stops short of his along the wide, tree-lined boulevard which leads into the city.

A television crew accompanies him into police headquarters. The multistorey brown brick tower is distinguished from the office blocks on either side by its arrhythmic pulse: accidents and tragedies beat randomly so that the building can hum in the middle of the night and fall quiet when the lifts next door yo-yo at daybreak. He observes the cops coming and going while he waits for Inspector Sinclair, who arrives promptly, younger than Vince had presumed from his weary voice. He clips a numbered visitor's pass to the pocket of his jacket. They share the lift with three uniformed women who are trading footy tips. Sinclair shows him into a windowless room where they sit across from each other at a laminated table, exchanging the obligatory question of club loyalty. Their teams are at loggerheads in the first game of the season. The detective takes a sheath of papers from his cardboard folder and stands them upright to even the edges before laying the pile flat. He switches on a micro cassette recorder, its tiny coils of tape circling slowly, a red light flickering. Horizontal stripes of pink, green and yellow highlighter pen pattern the phone records in Sinclair's grasp.

Vince supplies his full name, age, address, occupation. Then Sinclair asks him, 'How well did you know Leith Kremmer?'

'Leith was a friend of my wife. They met at university.' Vince isn't sure why he's revealed these archaic reference points other than to hint at the gross impropriety that stunted his relationship with Leith. It's pointless to deny the liaison documented in Sinclair's hands. 'We fell into bed together.'

'By accident?' Sinclair asks wryly.

'Without thinking through the consequences.'

'When was this?' Sinclair asks him, wanting to nail down dates as if the affair was a strictly limited season of Gilbert and Sullivan.

'I'm not sure exactly.' Vince wrinkles his forehead.

'You must have some idea.' Sinclair consults the pages on his desk, flicking through them to answer the question himself, emphatically. 'She was calling you regularly up until a month ago.'

Relieved that his conversation with Leith last week has gone undetected, Vince relaxes enough to unbutton his black suit jacket. He rests his forearms on the table in front of him as he considers how to minimise his role in this investigation and preserve what's left of his marriage. 'We'd stopped seeing each other before then. It was the beginning of summer, early December.' He remembers driving to the beach by the bay.

'Who called it off?' Sinclair asks because his personal experience confirms everything he's gleaned of infidelity. Affairs end because someone or another gets caught. 'Or did you decide to put things on ice for a while, to be continued . . .?'

'She couldn't bear the guilt.' Why not allow her innocence a touch-up? Eulogies edit lives just as the funeral parlour powders over a bruised jaw. 'Leith wanted it to stop.' Vince registers the absence of a gold band on Dan Sinclair's left hand, although the skin is paler where a ring might have been embedded, once.

'Was Leith scared of George finding out?' Sinclair taps the table with his ballpoint.

'Yes and no.'

Dan frowns.

'She was scared of George, scared of Eva. So was I. We had everything to gain, everything to lose – especially Leith. Sometimes I think she wanted to bring things to a head but she worried George was suicidal. She was afraid of how he'd react, what he might do to himself. She'd feel responsible. She was unnerved by his moodi-ness. It struck like a migraine only instead of light he couldn't bear the presence of other people, even Leith. He didn't show her affection and that injured her. She felt unloved.' Vince pauses. 'Not that uncommon, I suspect, in a lot of marriages.'

Dan's face flickers with accord. There were days when he loitered at work later than he needed, sat in the car out front to call his mother, anything to postpone his arrival in a home where he wasn't adored. He knew his wife would leave him the day he saw her roll her eyes at him behind his back, her contempt caught in the bathroom mirror as he shaved.

'I didn't think she'd ever leave him.' Vince lowers his guard. 'They lived a very comfortable life. You've seen their house?' Dan nods, wondering where Vince is leading. Solving gangland murders might be riskier but at least the money-trails from backyard amphetamine laboratories progress in a sensible sequence. 'She'd lost herself,' Vince continues. 'I think our affair was a part of her recovery.'

On their last day together they'd sat beside the calm grey water, alone on the beach: him with sand in his ears and between his teeth, her small and sumptuous, unshackled. She'd picked up two shells and given him one. When they went to wade in the water, feet sinking into mounds of kelp, he'd slipped, pulling her down into the slime, and they'd begun wrestling, playfully. Then she'd bitten him as he'd writhed inside of her, tattooing his arm with a ring of teeth marks. Later, in the car, he'd exploded. We live together or we give it up, he'd dared her. For weeks there was sand in the grooves of the upholstered seats and in bed that night a sprinkle of grit from between his toes. Eva had never asked how it got there.

'Did you put a death notice in the paper?'

'No. I thought about writing something.' Vince offers this as if tossing Dan a crumb for his endeavour. 'But for what?' He shrugs. 'So you don't know who did?'

'Was Leith seeing anyone else?'

'No, I don't think so. What's your theory?'

'At this stage,' Dan begins, then stops to consult the oddments he's collected to date. 'I'm not sure,' he shrugs. 'How could you not see someone come into a room that's not much bigger than this?' His head swivels around to indicate a space where you could almost complete a golf swing. 'I don't have the answer yet.' He gathers up his papers and puts them in his folder. 'Do accidents happen? Of course they do. There's an old copper – my first boss, retired now – he used to say that if there's a choice between a conspiracy and a cock-up, it'll usually be the latter.'

A convenient philosophy, Vince thinks as he shakes Sinclair's hand, keeping his conspiracy theory to himself.

The week before Leith's death he'd rung her from work.

'I've been meaning to ring you,' she said.

'I think of you every day,' he'd gushed.

'I've been thinking of you too,' she'd said. 'I wanted to thank you for roughing me up in the car that day. Gutless, you said. You were right. I'm ready to leave.'

'When?'

'Soon.'

He hadn't believed her.

A grey squirrel scampers along a knobbly branch of the cherry tree outside the apartment block where Frank waits beside two black suitcases tied with a twist of red ribbon for easy identification. Cameron had left home an hour ago, carrying the dog, his basket, bedding, bowl and a bag of dried pig's ears for treats. Mack sported a new brown leather collar. He's boarding with a teacher from Cameron's school who's recently buried a fourteen-year-old spaniel and volunteered for babysitting. The dog had known something was up as soon as the suitcases came down from the top shelf of the cupboard last night, bringing the box of Christmas decorations along with them. Angels and gold tinsel tipped all over the floor in a glittering mess. A whimper at the sight of the luggage made them laugh at Mack's aptitude. He even appeared to grasp his exclusion from the travelling party, refusing to let Cameron out of his sight, tripping him up underfoot as the men packed. Frank had stayed behind to lock up. Standing outside in the chill air with his hands thrust deep in the pockets of his camel-coloured coat he runs through the list of jobs he'd ticked off this morning before closing the door: turning off the central heating; leaving a front door key with a neighbour; emailing the school his contact details; telephoning his sister; cancelling his tutoring session with a troublesome state ward he oversees once a week; turning off the taps for the washing machine . . . damn, did he do this or not?

This is his mother's fault, the result of years spent tagging behind her as she yanked the plug from every socket and twisted every faucet so tightly that once they'd had to call the plumber in to unstick the bathroom tap when they came back from vacation. He's determined to ignore his departure anxieties. Then, throwing his hands up in hopeless surrender, he turns on his heels and takes the stairs two at a time, opening the front door, charging inside, and yes, he'd done this last thing after all.

Like a madman he rushes back the way he came, panting as he runs, worried now that he'll have a heart attack or return to find the suitcases stolen or Cameron in the cab wondering whether he's been kidnapped. But when he bursts out the front door the cases are where he left them. He takes off his coat, wiping his brow with the back of his hand, his heart rapping in a loud recriminating dig at his frenzy. The squirrel perches upright, its black peepers blinking nervously, alert to what might happen next. Frank checks the time. If you divide the world into those who like to arrive at the airport early and those who skid through the gate with a second to spare, he's in the first category, preferring a good three hours to grow accustomed to the prospect of leaving solid ground. He knows he's more likely to be killed by a bus or a malignant tumour than end up a piece of flotsam amongst charred scraps of fuselage in the sea, but his fear remains.

At the end of the street the mail lady rounds the corner in her fluorescent orange jacket. Plugged into an iPod, she goes from house to house until she gets to the apartment block and dismounts from her scooter to deliver an armful of mail. Frank steps forward to empty their box. A Barney's clothes catalogue; a subscription offer to the *New York Times*; the newsletter from the country club that he and Cameron joined last summer so that they could use the swimming pool, shaded by sturdy oak trees in a lake of green lawn. On the bottom is a fat cream envelope with a blue-and-white air-mail sticker. He studies the handwriting to be sure but her bubbly script is distinctive, a flying saucer riding atop the 'I' in Brightwater Tower. He checks the post mark for the date: Monday 22 March. The day Leith died. She'd held this in her hand four days ago. He lifts the envelope to his nose and smells for a scent of her.

Intrigued by the weirdness of a posthumous epistle, he doesn't hear the cab until it toots at him, and he jumps, as does the squirrel, which darts higher up the trunk of the tree. Cameron beckons impatiently and he decides, on a whim, to pocket the letter until they are above the Pacific Ocean. The driver opens the trunk to stow the cases. Frank stuffs the mail in his black canvas satchel and as he gets into the cab, he sees the small furry creature watching intently.

Frosted-glass doors glide open, admitting Marion to the executive lounge at Sydney Airport, far from the budget travellers and their polystyrene cups. She's been travelling since early this morning, when the ranger at Cape Leveque got her a ride on a six-seat charter plane to Broome in time to catch the only departure east all day. Her eyes sting from tiredness. She turns on her mobile phone. No missed calls but a couple of text messages: one from their daughter Lily who's unnerved by possible complications spotted during an ultrasound. Lily reassures her mother she's 'feeling up' this morning, which is a long way above Marion, who responds with sentiments becoming of a grandmother.

'Don't stress,' she types with her hyperactive thumb. 'Remember the old man who said he'd wasted his life worrying about things that never happened.'

'Did you panic before giving birth to me?' Lily asks. Marion worked right up until her waters broke. Annoyed by Lily's punctuality, she had to leave the finishing touches for the wedding of the daughter of a conservative MP, straightening napkins on her way out the door. How readily she recalls the trivia of a client's milestone and forgets the mood and mystery of preparing for her firstborn. Phillip's the family biographer, with his anecdotes stored and filed in his voluminous memory. He gave the speeches for Lily's twenty-first and her wedding, full of vignettes to illuminate her curiosity, her sociability. She leans back and thinks hard, summonsing up their dash through peak-hour traffic, Phillip cursing the old red Mazda as he sped to the hospital, refusing to run a red light. 'I was calm, cool and terrified,' Marion taps in response to her daughter.

As fleet as the electronic dispatch are the waves of guilt and shame because her daughter's welfare, her grandchild's wellbeing, is a complication that someone with a business built around anticipating every social grenade shouldn't have forgotten to consider. She's not thinking of anyone but herself, an adolescent again, silly with excitement. The second message in her inbox appeals to that teenager and she keys in for a conversation.

'I'm steaming up the windows here thinking of you there, hot and skimpily clad.'

'Phillip opened my mailbox. I'm at the airport – on my way home.'

She waits for W's reply. Another yellow envelope appears.

'Book us on a flight.'

'Where to?' she replies.

'Somewhere chaotic so we can lose ourselves.'

She looks up at the departures listed on a nearby monitor – Hong Kong, Dubai, Hanoi, Delhi – hallucinating their escape to an Eastern destination. Make-believe is a game she never tires of playing with him in these staccato conversations.

'Baghdad?' she taps, switching from predictive text to spell the name of a capital in ruins. 'BYO bullet-proof vest.'

'I don't look good in fatigues.'

She smiles as she taps her reply. 'You won't be wearing them for long.'

'Why don't you come to Romsey tonight? If we . . .'

'If we what?'

'If we anything.'

She takes a moment to compose her reply. 'If we anything, he wonders, holding a fiery ring aloft, daring her to leap through into the arms of us.'

A delicious mood of abandonment curls her toes. If she was sitting in her office, staff buzzing around making amendments to the whiteboard behind her desk, she wouldn't entertain the crazy ideas tempting her now. She's untethered, orbiting her life. Bernadette will earth her.

'Let me guess. You're in the laundry.' Marion hears the washing machine doing a mechanical jig in the background.

'I'm so glad you rang,' Bernadette welcomes.

'You go first,' Marion instructs her, swivelling around in her chair to keep her eye on the sliding doors of the lounge in case Phillip should touch down.

'Monty's been interviewed by the police. I'm supposed to be making a statement tomorrow.'

'You're breaking up, I can't hear you,' Marion says.

Bernadette walks into her kitchen. 'Is that better?'

'Much. Now, what were you saying about Monty?'

'Monty's spoken to the police. They suspected him of having an affair with her. He swears he wasn't. But he was tempted. It's really knocked me. I didn't suspect a thing. It never occurred to me to be suspicious.'

'They were friends, B, nothing more sinister than that.'

'They were closer than you think. She was lonely.'

'She had all of us.'

'But we're all busy apart from Rosie.'

'You know, the saddest thing is her thanking us for our friendship when she never really tested its mettle.'

'Monty says she was about to start looking for a job as a cook. She told him all sorts of things which she never revealed to me.'

'What kind of things?'

'That she'd been unlucky in love. That she longed to be loved.'

'If she was unhappy, why didn't she leave?'

'You get stuck. You lose your confidence. The longer she let things drift, the harder it became to go. You know she won sixty-five thousand dollars last Saturday. She was flying high at book club. I think she was planning something but she wanted to execute it before telling us. It's like they say about people who commit suicide: the ones who talk about it never go through with it.'

'I think he turned on her.'

'So do I. There's no other explanation. How could he have swung at her by mistake? I just don't believe his story. I can't get the sound of his club out of my head.'

'I know, and us laughing at him, mocking him, winding him up.'

'I can't help thinking that if only I'd stayed behind, if only I'd offered to help clean up so that she had some company. When you unwind those hours, I see a thousand ways I might have saved her.'

'It's not your fault, B.'

'I just don't know how much to tell the police.'

'Stay with the facts,' Marion advises her. 'That's what Phillip says.'

'How's Phillip? How's the holiday?'

'It's over. I'm in Sydney.' Engulfed by exhaustion, she feels like reclining on the soft couch next to her. 'Phillip intercepted my phone. He went crazy.'

'Oh, honey.' Bernadette settles herself in an armchair for serious counselling.

'I'm leaving him. Otherwise I might end up like Leith.'

'I can tell you haven't thought this through,' Bernadette cautions.

'I didn't plan for this to happen!'

There's a pause. 'Well, you sort of did.'

'Don't Mother Superior me.'

'I'm not. It's just that this phone thing's been going on for months. It's not like you've been caught with dope that someone's planted in your bag. You have inhaled.'

'I haven't betrayed Phillip. We haven't had sex.'

'You're splitting hairs.' Bernadette's firm.

'Well, I haven't been unfaithful in the traditional, orthodox sense of the word.'

'Where does phone sex stop and adultery start? You tell me. We've gotten so good at rationalising what we want – and I include myself in that slur. What did Phillip say?'

'He begged me to flirt with him. I couldn't do it. I won't. I can't.'

'Marion, listen to me: Phillip adores you. He's done nothing to hurt you.' Try harder, is what she wants to say to her friend. Stand up to yourself, be honourable. But she's learnt not to impose her gospel on others. What does she know about chasing happiness? It's always come easily to her, a blessing she's thankful for every day of this life.

'I've been a good wife. But I hate being with him now. I can't stand it when he touches my skin.'

'Poor Phillip.' Bernadette sides with the injured party.

'I just wish I'd told him so that I could have protected him. He had no idea.' She revisits the disbelief in his face as he held her phone, his lips twitching.

'Where is he?'

'I don't know. He left me in Cape Leveque. He took the car with him. I've left messages on his phone but it's turned off.'

'You don't think he'd . . .'

'What?' Marion bites.

'Nothing.'

'I've got to go. My flight's boarding. I'll ring you later.' She gathers her jacket and bag and exits the lounge. A yellow envelope bobs up on the screen. She opens it. 'Take the first right after the bridge. I'll be waiting at the gate, fiery hoop held aloft, arms of us all yours.'

Bernadette picks up the cordless phone and dials Leith's number, determined to do what she regards as the proper thing. Chickening out at the last second, she pushes the 'end call' button, tongue-tied, her lines muddled. 'This is ridiculous,' she coaxes. It'd be easier to write a note but how can she post him condolences? She redials, listening to the ring tone, hoping that Jesse or Art will answer in their father's stead. Then, just as she's pleading for voice-mail, George's imperial tone.

'George, it's Bernadette.' A dumper of emotion knocks her because Leith's not there to take the phone and never will be again. 'I meant to ring you earlier but I . . . I just wanted you to know how distraught we are about Leith. It's a truly terrible . . . thing.' She doesn't know what to call this accidental murder. 'Monty and I can't seem to think about anything else since we heard and I know, well I imagine, this must be horrendous for you, too.' She pauses to wipe her nose and cheeks. 'Is there anything I can do? Are the boys home with you?'

'Art's coming this weekend. I can't get hold of Jesse – he's in Tasmania, on a field trip . . .' His voice falters. 'Leith's brother's on his way here from Boston.'

'Why don't I bring a meal over for the weekend?' she offers.

'There's no need, really, although that's very kind of you.' She hears him swallow. 'You see, Leith left me months of meals, labelled and dated. Do you know what she was up to?' he asks. 'I'm completely in the dark here . . .' Another silence. 'It's bizarre,' he says, 'not just the frozen dinners, but there are other things as well that suggest she was planning her absence.'

Bernadette waits for him to tell her what these are but he's waiting for her to enlighten him and an uncomfortable moment passes, broken by them both simultaneously so that they stop and George speaks first. 'You asked if you could do something and there is a favour I want to ask. I was wondering whether you could say a few words about Leith at the funeral?'

'I'd be very happy to do that. I'm honoured to be asked.'

'Thank you,' he sighs, overwhelmed by the middle distance. 'In the meantime there's the investigation.'

'I know,' she assures him. 'Monty's being interviewed by the police tonight.'

'I'm so sorry.' He sounds exhausted. 'They might charge me. They haven't a clue. They really haven't a clue. This is such a long and complicated story. I don't know how much you know of our saga,' – she thinks she hears him break – 'but it's hell here without her, unrelievedly lonely.'

She conjures up the big house – a witness to Leith's death, full of her belongings, intolerable – and reaches out instinctively. 'You can come here to us.'

'Thanks for your kindness – Leith always said you were the one who held the group together. But I'll stay here, Jesse might call. The isolation is penance for what I've done – accidentally, mistakenly, you must understand that.'

'Yes, yes,' she says, suspicious of his designs, preconceived or not, because he killed Leith. It's all about him, she thinks, swirling from one to the other, overcome by an image of Leith being belted to the floor. She thinks she hears him weeping.

'She had no idea,' he says slowly. 'I would swap places with her if I could, if only it were possible.'

'One day at a time,' she says because what else can he do? His nightmare is beyond time's healing.

They say their stilted goodbyes. The wind rattles the windows in gusts and she glances at her watch. She hears Monty's boots hit the wooden veranda as the key turns. 'You up?' he trumpets from the door.

'Yep,' she says, standing to greet him with her arms open for a hug, which he reciprocates warmly after dumping his esky and a tambourine of metal keys on the bench.

'You've been crying.' She lowers her head onto his shoulder, her hair tickling his cheeks as he massages the back of her neck, loosening muscles knuckled tight.

'How was it?' she mumbles of his visit to the police.

'I'm glad it's over with.' They move apart and he switches on the electric kettle while he considers how to convey what transpired.

'He wanted to know about our Saturdays together. I told him that Leith and I were friends, good friends.' He tilts his head with this qualification. 'He asked me about their marriage. I said I was aware of tensions, that there wasn't much warmth between them.'

'Marion thinks that Leith was going to leave George.'

'Well, she didn't flag anything to me.'

'So does George,' she says urgently. 'I rang him tonight. I had to, I couldn't leave it any longer. I suggested I bring around some food and he said he's got all these meals that Leith left for him.' She searches Monty's face.

'The police have gone through her phone records. He asked me if she was close to Vince Melogenis.'

Oh God, she thinks. The kettle clicks off as steam shoots from the spout.

'Was Leith having an affair with Vince?'

'She couldn't have been. She's too close to Eva. She's known Eva longer than she's known George. I don't believe Leith would do such a thing.' Bernadette is sure her own conscience would forbid hopping into bed with the husband of her best friend. Bernadette's phone rings and she rifles through her briefcase, its pockets bulging, a bag of figs resting on the top, contra for her lemons. She retrieves it too late. 'Marion,' she says, reading the number of the missed call. 'She's leaving Phillip. Everything's coming unstuck.'

Monty spoons tea leaves into the pot.

'It's funny,' she says, 'Leith used to laugh about wearing her best camisole in case she had to be cut out of a car crash one day – it's one of those stupid things women think of when they're getting dressed. If you know you're going to die, you get organised, I guess: you make your will, you tell the kids who's getting what, you get rid of incriminating paperwork, letters or things you don't want people reading. But if you die suddenly, out of the blue, you have no control over what you leave behind. Of course, it doesn't matter in one way because you're dead, but everyone else has to cope with discovering things they didn't know and perhaps weren't meant to find out.' She opens the cupboard and takes out two mugs.

'What's that noise?' Monty lifts his finger to hush her, his head cocked as he strains to identify the sound. Bernadette listens for a moment, then laughs. She jumps up and leads him by the hand down the hall, opening the laundry door carefully.

'Look,' she says, pointing to a plastic tub cushioned with towels where three kittens are mewing, mouths opening like hungry starlings. Monty shakes his head.

'You are unbelievable! We're not keeping them,' he says, bending down to pick up the black one.

'That one's Paddy,' she smiles.

They hadn't talked about the cat or her discovery of Sam Dunlop. He's a gulp of fresh air in the muggy haze that has settled since Leith's death.

'I've met a young man,' she tells Monty.

His gaze jerks up to look at her so that she tickles with pleasure, getting him back in the spot where he's hurt her.

'Not that kind. Sadly,' she winks at him. 'He needs a job.'

'No,' he wails. You promised me after that bloke, what's his name . . .?'

'Haili Monbessa.'

'Well, you promised you'd never ask me to do that again.' He settles the kitten gently into the tub.

'He's young and strong and desperate for the money.' She doesn't touch on the troublesome parts of Sam's résumé. 'I know it's a head-ache,' she pleads, 'but a hand up might get him on his feet. I feel as though I need to glue someone back together right now. I can't explain why. I just do.'

'You're a saint, that's all,' he says, reaching for her and reeling her in close. They kiss on the nose, lips, cheek, brow, neck.

'Not in front of the kittens,' she protests playfully.

Enduring the hours from 5 p.m. until lights out is a slog Rosie hates. She paces herself with a game of distraction, setting herself tasks such as pulling the weeds from between the flagstones in the back garden or reading twenty-five pages of fiction to fill in time between glasses of wine, not always successfully because there's no one to catch her cheating and she's good at justifying each fresh lapse. Addiction is her menace. Why, why, why, she whimpers, knowing perfectly well the sorry combination of weakness and dismay that flings her this low.

Cooking dinner is a ruse that Leith once suggested, presenting her with a recipe book for single-serve meals. The front-cover photograph of one pork chop on a large white plate garnished decoratively with stewed apple and wilted fennel looked sad. 'No more sandwiches for dinner!' Leith had written sternly inside the cover. Most nights, Rosie nibbles on dry biscuits and creamy dips which she buys from the delicatessen, yet another kind of ploy for passing the night because a meal is quickly demolished while cocktail food affords leisurely grazing with a glass in one hand.

She misses Leith. Living so close was an advantage she tried not to exploit by becoming a pest so she relied on Leith to drop by – which she did regularly, shortening this mournful span from dusk to bed. 6.47 p.m. blinks the dark screen on her microwave oven. Leith's absence will be tougher on her than Eva or Marion or Bernadette. An imperfect partner is better than none. Someone to snitch at, someone to grouse to, a lump in the bed, a place at the table – all ward off insanity. There's an army of women like her, only older, their husbands either dead or senile. Somehow she's managed to join them prematurely. She spies these ladies in the late afternoon, walking small dogs or shopping with a green bag, becalmed by inactivity apart from a weekly game of bridge or golf. They line the streets like skirting boards along the wall.

The phone rings. Chances are it's a telemarketer or a research company. She answers. There's a click and two seconds delay before a young woman with an Indian accent requests 'Mr Alee-star Hayes'.

Without so much as a 'No, thank you', she pushes the 'end call' button.

'Alistair Hayes,' she scoffs at Pugsley, who's scratching his claws on the chair where Alistair used to sit reading or watching telly. The metallic blue brocade is shredded from the arm rest to the floor. One night after sharing a pre-dinner drink with Leith, Rosie had plunged a carving fork into the back of the chair in a burst of rage. 'Our punching bag,' she confides in the cat. He stops ripping at the chair to stare at her. Reupholstering seems a pointless expenditure.

She'd take Alistair back, if he'd relent. But why would he, unless he was sick; then she can imagine him creeping back, and she'd take him, feed him, bathe him, drive him to his chemotherapy. Pathetic as it sounds, she would look after him because he's family, her children's father; she couldn't reject him in need, for poorer, for worse. She's tempted by an urge to ring him. 'I can't stand being alone,' she mourns, stroking the cat now curled in her lap. 6.52 p.m. flickers at her from the kitchen. Sometimes she does a lap of the neighbourhood, half hoping the heavy stale breath of an assailant would at least give her a heart-starter and welcome attention once word of her encounter spread up and over the high fences.

The phone rings again. She lets it wail, glaring at the impudence of these corporate raiders. Then she cracks and decides to blast them. Pugsley howls at his undignified slide to the floor as she launches herself out of the chair, twisting her ankle as she dives for the handset on the bench. There's a second's delay before she hears a deep voice ask: 'Rosie?'

'George? Is that you?'

'Yes.'

'How are you? I've been meaning to come around and check that you're okay,' she lies, voluble, on fast-forward, nervous.

'As well as can be expected,' he says.

She flounders. 'You must come around here for dinner.' Realising that her invitation could be taken as now, this minute, she adds, 'Not tonight, because I'm going out, but another time in the near future,' inadvertently mimicking his formality.

More silence that she can't help rushing to occupy. 'Of course, I'm not a patch on Leith. In the fancy food department, I mean,' she blunders on, hoping he'll say something so that she can collect herself before she upsets him, but her tongue runs ahead of her thoughts.

'That's generous of you,' he says, touched by the offer. 'The kitchen here is silent as a shrine.' He hears in his voice the horror he harbours.

'I miss her terribly.' Rosie's defences disintegrate.

He can't tell her where his own thoughts and emotions have tossed him.

'Were you very close to Leith?'

Now that Rosie's got hold of his tempo she walks across the

room to get her empty glass of wine. 'Yes, I was,' she says eventually, 'particularly after Alistair left.' She checks her speech as a witness being cross-examined is taught to do. 'I mean, Leith held me together,' she says. Taking a bottle of wine from the sideboard, she applies her corkscrew, which hooks its catch silently like a fine angler. She hears a clink of glass from his end. 'Leith must have frittered away half her life listening to me and that's a rare quality these days, in a world where everyone's so busy, so self-centred, engrossed in themselves. With Leith you could talk your heart out and know that it wouldn't get around.'

'And what did she tell you?' George crunches her testimony like the bones of a small quail and she startles, flighty again because he has touched upon the sorest point of these exchanges.

'Nothing,' she blurts, immediately taking it back. 'Well, that's not true. I mean, she told me all sorts of things but she never . . . she didn't . . . I mean, I had no idea that . . .' The intellectual effort of answering George without losing face or betraying Leith or feeding his paranoia saps her of a conclusion.

He assumes her inarticulate response is dissembling with intent. 'Was Leith having an affair?'

'I don't believe so,' she interrupts, relying solely on instinct with nothing else to prove her claim. For a moment they are both busied by their thoughts.

'Did she say anything to you or to the others to suggest that she might be leaving me?'

'No, she didn't. Nothing really,' she mumbles, reluctant to recall for him the glimmer of goodbye in Leith's final address to her friends. 'Why do you think she was going to leave you?'

'Some of her things are missing,' he says. 'I thought she might have discussed her plans with you.'

Mortified, Rosie can't understand why Leith shut her out. 'If she was going away,' her voice fades with her sense of importance in the pyramid of friendship, 'then you weren't the last to know.'

'Please don't repeat this conversation, Rosie,' George begs, because he knows how truth can be distorted to fit the available facts, and Leith always said that Rosie couldn't be relied upon to hold her tongue.

'Certainly not.' She gives her word, utterly confused now.

'Thank you,' he said as if dismissing her from the bench.

His suspicion and Leith's shadowiness crisscrossed in her head the rest of the night until the alcohol conquered completely. She woke, fully clothed, on top of the bedspread. In the kitchen the digits of the clock glowed censoriously as they clicked forward. All Rosie felt as she got under the covers was relief that the birds hadn't begun to mock.

Frank grips Cameron's hand as the jet trampolines, buckling the legs of a middle-aged woman making her way down the aisle to the toilet. She clings to Frank's steadying arms until the flight attendant arrives to help her back on her feet. The seatbelt sign lights up and through the intercom the pilot apologises for the turbulence. 'Oh God,' says Frank, closing his eyes in a silent prayer that they do not tumble into the freezing water below.

'It's Qantas,' Cameron tells him, as if he needed reminding because he refuses to fly on any other airline.

'There's a first time for everything,' Frank whispers, 'and it'll be my luck to be on board the airline's inaugural crash.'

'This is uncharacteristic, your fear of dying.'

'Are you crazy?' he opens one eye a peep. 'I've always been afraid of flying.'

'I said dying, not flying.' On the ground Frank is unassailable. He regards death with a nonchalance Cameron admires. High up in the clouds, however, he's a wreck.

'If I'm going to die I need to get accustomed to the idea,' Frank says, then wants to swallow his words because Leith bobs into his mind. He wonders whether she knew she was done for. Her letter's in his bag. He'd intended delivering it to Cameron after dinner, an hour away at least. Do they still provide paper sick bags? he wonders, feeling around in the pocket in front of him.

'What are you after?' Cameron asks.

'I'm feeling queasy,' he whispers. He finds the plastic card for what to do in case of an emergency. Gradually he relaxes, thankful for the calm of other passengers around them, plugged into music or the in-flight entertainment or reading blockbuster novels, not a whiff of alarm. The rough patch behind them, an older male steward stops beside their row of seats. 'Everything okay here?' he asks.

'The less excitement the better,' Frank manages a smile, 'so if you could just let them know in the cockpit . . .'

'Terrorists in balaclavas he can handle,' Cameron adds, 'but any sudden movement in the downward direction and he's a jelly.'

'Please don't even mention the T word,' says the steward, good humouredly. 'Don't even mime it. You'll trigger a security alert.'

Cameron's mind drifts, wondering whether there is such a thing as a golden age when life on earth, according to some kind of index or scale, was poised as close to perfect as possible. The drama of Leith has drained his optimism and, coming back to bury her, he can feel the dregs evaporating. Frank squirms next to him, trying to retrieve his satchel wedged under the seat in front. Cameron unclips his belt now that calm has returned.

'This arrived before we left,' Frank says, handing him an envelope. Cameron recognises the handwriting. He looks at Frank bewildered.

'Why didn't you tell me?'

'The mail came just before you picked me up and I made an executive decision to wait until you could read it quietly, without any distractions.'

'Hell,' Cameron says, lifting the envelope to smell for Leith's scent. Frank smiles at the echo of his own reaction. Cameron holds it in his palm as if weighing up contents that he can't begin to guess at as he gathers his courage to break the seal. Rather than read over

Cameron's shoulder Frank decides to stroll to the bathroom at the other end of the plane because the suspense is unbearable.

'Open it,' he urges, as he rises from his seat. Cameron slides his finger gently along the fold as if defusing a homemade bomb.

Monday

Hi Gorgeous. Happy Birthday! By the time you receive this letter you should have well and truly recovered from carousing. I've been putting off writing this for days, finding a million excuses as to why it can wait, and true to form – equivocating is one thing I have perfected in my life – here I am almost out of time.

Remember when we took the boys on that skiing trip to New Zealand only it didn't snow! I feel like you must have felt that day standing on the bridge outside of Queenstown all hooked up for your bungee jump, counting down to the moment when you dived headfirst into the ravine praying to God that the cord around your ankles wouldn't snap. I know how you felt because I was there watching, or not watching, actually – hands over my eyes where I was standing with the boys on the observation deck listening to your terror and then that scream of joy.

You laughed when I said I'd rather die than bungee jump and I'm not about to change my mind. But I'm about to step off a ledge.

Tonight if I can keep my heart from cardiac arrest I am going to tell George that I'm leaving. He won't have seen it coming. I'm writing to you not so much to explain why I'm going because

I suspect, deep down, you're wiser than me about why this separation was inevitable, but more in self-defence, I guess, because I want you to understand why I've stayed here in this house, this home, for as long as I have.

Cameron lifts his eyes from the page as Frank settles back into the seat beside him.

'Leith was going to leave George,' Cameron says. 'She was going to tell him on Monday night.'

Frank's not surprised. George's story of an accident seemed too fantastic for him. He hasn't wanted to unpick the mechanics of its execution. Cameron reads on, deciphering her undisciplined flow, leaping over words that have been crossed out as she refined her meaning.

Why are some of us born for the frontier, like you two? I keep wondering whether it is braver to follow your heart, as everyone exhorts us to do today, without caring too much about the fall-out and the hurt to others, or whether it's nobler to muzzle your desires and passions if the pursuit of them injures the happiness of those around you.

Honour seems a quaint, courtly notion in a world where vows are easily forgotten. We took ours seriously. George was an only child, a dutiful boy, a man who could not bring himself to disappoint his mother, so he rebelled against himself instead. I too accepted a certain responsibility within our family for delivering to Mum and Dad things that you couldn't. No one asked me to, no one insisted, but these unspoken assumptions govern to some extent the decisions I've made.

I was entranced by George from the moment I met him with you at the airport. How perfect was our meeting, I used to think. I loved telling the story, going around the table as couples do, recounting for each other the hour, the season, the circumstances of their falling for the other, because it gave me the chance to talk about you too. I've always been so proud of you. But I came to hate that conversational promenade because ten years into our marriage I realised that George couldn't love me in the way that I wanted to be loved. He'd always found physical intimacy difficult, which I'd put down to his sheltered, prudish upbringing, but I began to feel as though I repelled him. He rarely initiated sex, apologising when he brushed me off by saying he was tired – he often was, but then he'd rise and go upstairs for hours on end. I felt devastated. I chose not to leave then because the boys were at a difficult age and all the literature on divorce persuaded me they needed to grow up with their father, and he was a good father. They respected him. They loved him. He wasn't one of those knockabout dads but his absence was a presence in their lives, as it was in mine too. I knew he was ambitious. I respected his dedication, his discipline. When he was at the bar he'd rise every morning at 5 a.m., if he had a case in court. He began staying in his chambers until late so that we got used to making do with rare sightings because he stood on a pedestal.

You and I were raised by parents who maintained a charade of togetherness for the sake of us. They put us first. Blind eyes were turned in every direction. Dad's gambling. Mum's affair. The allowances I've made for George over the years prove that I was as good as Dad, perhaps even better than Dad, at the blind eye. I don't think George has a lover, but he's unhappy, we both are. Once the boys left us he became depressed, angry, and he carried this simmering with him everywhere, even to work, where it became a dirty secret amongst staff unburdened by loyalty like me. In order to protect him I made excuses when the Chief Justice rang me, confidentially. I stopped trying to encourage George to seek help because he hated discussing his emotions. He's hidden them for so long they've disfigured him.

About a year ago I was poking around in stuff that he's always promising to sort through – old school magazines, ribbons for races he'd run, class photographs, a review in the student newspaper of the skit which you and he did for the law revue. I found a diary George had kept at college. I started to read through the pages, his descriptions of rehearsing with you – very funny – and then a letter fell out, which I shouldn't have read, only it was a letter addressed to you. I don't know why George didn't send it to you. I'm going to ask him about it tonight. I'm sending it to you now so that we . . .

Cameron leaps ahead over the page he's holding to find George's neat, taut script, each line turned respectfully clear of wide margins on college stationery without a single amendment. No second thoughts hastily scribbled, no postscripts – such a contrast to the gush of Leith's pen.

September, 1967

My Dear Cameron,

I don't know what came over me tonight. If I gave you cause to believe that you might lead me across the Styx then I blame the drink. My sexual fantasies are strange, frightening spectres I can't embrace. There is no excuse for my reaction to your gentle advance. I am deeply sorry. Please forgive me.

Yours affectionately,

George Kremmer

Cameron leans his head back. A salty trickle rolls down his face, dropping from the bottom of his chin on to his thumb. He closes his eyes to stem the flow. Frank's hand brushes his as he folds the letters and returns them to the envelope because he's not ready for Frank to explore the dank place that his sister has uncovered, rolling back the years that concealed its entrançe.

Marion scrolls through her log of missed calls as she disembarks from the plane in Melbourne. Phillip wasn't on board. She'd walked from nose to tail just in case he'd swooped on a seat at the last minute. Two small children who'd been sitting in the row behind her hurtle past into the wide open arms of a spry, elderly couple. She's resisted child-proofing their twenty-fourth floor city apartment and decides she'll feel differently when she has a bundle of flesh nestled in the crook of her arm. She calls his mobile as she takes the escalator downstairs to the carousel but he's not answering. The grandfather arrives on her heels, lifting the youngest of his charges up in the air. His wife nags him to be careful as she keeps the other child's tiny hands clear of the black snake disgorging suitcases from its rubber-tongued mouth.

Outside the terminal taxis queue, their exhausts puffing clouds of carbon monoxide into the wintry dusk. People wheel baggage around her, everyone hurrying to get somewhere. Blasts of cool air blow in through the sliding doors. The intercom crackles with a final call for two ticket holders who have not yet boarded their flight to Brisbane. She tries the apartment but gets the recorded message.

The grandmother shakes her head firmly at the child, telling him to wait for Mummy, who is collecting a trolley for their cases. Marion's leather bag tumbles on to the carousel. As she elbows her way through the crush to claim it, her phone rings. Phillip's face flashes onto the screen like a calling card.

'Where are you?' She backs out of the crowd to a thinly populated space near a pillar so that she might hear him better.

'I'm in Broome,' – weary, stranded – 'tossing up what to do.'

She should tell him to come home.

'I was looking forward to being with you for these few days,' he pleads with her again. 'We've paid off our debts, we've raised our children, we're about to become grandparents, next it's the crematorium. The business side of us is over. I'd been hoping we might finally fall in love,' he says quietly, his desolation exhaled across a continent. 'Anyhow, I see from your phone you've made other commitments.'

A wail goes up behind her where the granddaughter has thrown herself on the ground. Marion is forced to back away from this furious tantrum into the path of a man who is dashing to catch a woman riding up the escalator. She has a shiny black helmet of hair. 'Leith!' Marion's heart leaps at the likeness but the name dies on her lips because it isn't. The woman turns around and smiles at the man as he races to catch her and Marion sees now she is plumper than Leith, younger too, her lips fuller, opening in excitement as she reaches out for him. They are new partners, she can tell. She watches the couple disappear from view, her resolve revived by this phantom, reminding her that life is short, sometimes brutal.

'What are you going to do?' Phillip asks and she parachutes out of her caution, flying as the crow does to a place she might never have got to otherwise.

'I'm going to Romsey.' Now there can be no change of heart.

'Why Romsey?' He's momentarily stumped, figuring out her

intentions too late to snatch the question back. 'You're moving out, then.'

'Yes,' she says. He hangs up. She runs, trailing her case behind her, all the way to the parking station, desperate to get on the road.

FRIDAY

Today's express post letter from the solicitor acting on behalf of Gabe strung Sam up, rattled him, because his swipe and run with Mags was dumb, even for a few hours of sunshine, kittens in her lap. He knows Angie's sick of bailing him out. She told him through the sigh of a full stop when she'd come to the end of the dot points laid out in neat black paragraphs stark on the page. They're sitting on flimsy aluminium chairs eating sushi outside the café near where she works. Angie hands him his letter.

'You're going back to court,' she tells him. 'Judge Kremmer's stood down. Your bad luck must have rubbed off on him.'

Sam's eyes narrow at her needling. 'He had it coming to him.'

Angie studies him as she wipes soy sauce from her fingers.

'Why?'

'Why what?'

'Why do you hate everyone who has it in their power to help you?'

He falls quiet. 'I don't,' he says, looking up at her, the exception to his rule. He sweeps the leftover grains of rice and sauce into a corner of his plastic tub with his finger, which he licks clean.

'I've met someone,' she blurts.

Sam's happiness for her collides with his fear of abandonment. 'Angie,' he says, reaching out and holding her hand. She clenches his in both of hers and her upper body does the quiver thing that she used to do as a kid when she was excited. 'He does stuff with computers. He lives in Hong Kong. We met in a store; he was buying a sweater for his sister, and he asked if I could hold it up against me because I was the same size, and then he bought two, one for her and one for me because he said the colour suited me.' He sees now that the tangerine top sets off her dark colouring. 'And then he insisted on shouting me a coffee.'

'Will you move there?'

She laughs and he hears hope in her excitement. 'I was in town delivering a document for the boss and I popped in to look at a dress in the window and that's how we met. I can't stop thinking about him and I just have this feeling.'

Her eyes flame with possibility, there's colour in her face, her spirits unencumbered, and all this gladdens him. 'You deserve it. Everything you've done for me, I've never thanked you properly but you know you've saved my life so many times and I'm grateful, sis, I am.'

'You've got to make your luck, kid.' She holds his gaze. 'Turn it around, go on,' she says, 'I'll race you!' She smiles because this was how they dared each other as children – she got a headstart but he always beat her by a nose once he'd started to run. 'You can change things, start walking in a straight line instead of ducking and weaving, get work, hold it, save some money, stay sober, make me proud of you, make Mags look up to you. Tell me about the job.'

'It's charity,' he shrugs. 'That woman I told you about, the one who killed the cat? Her old man's a builder. She's talked him into taking me on – nothing permanent, just a couple of weeks on a site. They're short of shitkickers. She feels guilty or something. She's all over me with clothes, food, too many questions, as if she wants to adopt me and convert me. She wears a gold cross around her neck.'

'So what did you tell her?'

'About God?'

'No, the job.'

'I said I'd think about it.'

Angie tenses. 'No more thinking. Please. Do it for me.' She puts her dirty napkin and plastic chopsticks into the receptacle, tidying up his rubbish as she goes. 'I rang Gabe yesterday.'

Sam glares at her. 'What for?'

'Just to make sure she was all right after what happened this week. There's no harm done,' she placates her brother's brooding. 'I'd like to see Mags occasionally and you going bonkers gave me the chance to reconnect with her. I'd be stupid to let it slide. This is not a blood feud.' She pinches her lips so he listens up. 'Is there a brain in your head or just so much angriness that there's no room for sense? Gabe's done nothing to me. I've only got your version of things.' Her brother's shoulders tense, itching to punch someone, something. 'I accept what you say, you know I do, but you've got to make peace with Gabe. If she trusts me, if she thinks I'm going to be around to supervise visits, she'll let you see Mags more. Do you get it or is this too complicated for you to understand?' She half expects him to toss a chair on to the road, but he sits, tilting back on his precariously, gazing at something inside himself.

'When are you supposed to start the job?' she dares to ask.

'Tomorrow,' he says.

'Well, don't be late.' She stands, gathering up her bag. 'I almost forgot. Aunty Jo rang to ask us for dinner. It's her birthday next week. She hasn't seen you since Mags was a year old.'

He shrugs and turns to the kaleidoscope of cars, red, yellow, green, flashing past them. Angie studies her brother, a thin crescent of dirt under his fingernails, a day's growth darkening his chin, his flinty eyes, hostility bristling, yet all he craves is love. 'You have to come with me,' she urges. 'She did a lot for us, without any help. She didn't get paid – she took us on because she couldn't not, because we're family.' She stops hectoring. 'By the way, she says she's found an envelope with photographs that she took of Mum with you just after you were born. Also a lock of your hair, and,' Angie screws up her face, 'your first teeth.' Sam laughs, pleased by the trove of artefacts, their treasuring a sign someone cares.

This confirmation is enough of a spur. He's going to catch Angie. He can get work. Stick fast, stay true. He eyeballs that streak of lost boy, lost self. Angie's right. This angel of mercy, Saint Bernadette, she's his start.

Cameron doesn't even peel back the tinfoil lid of the plastic tray when dinner arrives, his appetite ebbed by the vertiginous drop to a pinprick in his past, exposing him all over again to the humiliation and hurt he'd hidden from his sister when she'd won George's hand. For a year or two after leaving Australia, his foothold insecure, those first friendships porous, George had a habit of sneaking up on him, hovering in his thoughts. Frank rescued him, filling his days with excitement for the future, populating their life with faces, family, people who embraced him. Gradually George faded from prominence, his marriage to Leith filtered through her accounts of children's milestones. Frank's nurturing fostered in Cameron a desire less venal than the high-voltage lust he'd felt for George. He hears Frank requesting two brandies from the steward, glad for his guardianship as they sit, elbows touching. Frank places the stem of a plastic tumbler in between his fingers and Cameron raises his glass in a toast before tossing the fire down his throat in two gulps. He secures his tray table then curls up under the felt blanket. Why hadn't he told Leith his misgivings?

He'd kept his rejection padlocked as if secrets can be quarantined, when they never can. They never can. Someone talks. If no one tells, the lid of silence is stretched and jerked out of shape in the interests of concealment, and this effort inevitably gives the game away. George's violent fist swinging that night in his college room seemed to prove his virility so that Cameron ignored his doubt. He should've told Leith, but he didn't. He didn't. Then he couldn't. By then it was too late for second thoughts. She was besotted, remember? Even the pigeons cooed at George in the sandstone colonnades of learning, where he stood out for his brilliance, the man most likely to succeed, a catch. Cameron never suspected George was at war with himself, so frightened of prejudice he succumbed to its lynching. George's confidence made him unshakeable. He knew what he wanted. He went after his goals, his girl, his career in a galloping dash.

But why would George stop her leaving him if they were subsisting on bread and water? Why would he strike her? Unless, unless . . . and he shudders at the thought that she had threatened to out him.

Frank dozes beside him, arms folded across his chest, ready for the brace position, Cameron decides, as he lifts the lightweight blanket that has slipped to the floor up around Frank's shoulders. Bracing himself, he takes out Leith's letter and finds the place where he'd stopped and skipped to George's apology.

I'm sending George's letter to you now so we can deal with this unfinished business. I almost rang you at some ungodly hour the night I read it, then common sense kicked in and I reasoned that this curious piece of history wasn't going to alter the past. But the discovery spurred me to other reckless behaviour. I've been having an affair with the husband of a close friend who's unaware of our treachery. Incredibly risky for all the obvious reasons that I'm not proud of jettisoning, but the experience was luscious. To be desired and relished – well, you've probably never forgotten what this is like, lucky man.

I can't squander any more of life on an accident that should never have happened, for both our sakes. Such a waste, my story seems. His too. You make a wrong decision with the best motives in the world. George risks this daily in court. He'd hoped our marriage would confirm his choice of me and us. I don't hate him. He's been loyal. He's kept up appearances. I'm the one who's been playing around.

By the time you read this I'll have moved into an apartment in town. I'm going to leave tonight. Nothing dramatic, that's not my style. Over the next little while George and I can amicably disentangle ourselves from each other. We'll need to talk to the boys. I'm going to visit Jesse next week. At least they're both busy. They get that single-mindedness from their father. I hope they learn to temper it.

I wish you and Frank had been able to experience the joy of children. Frank would have made such a good father, with his gentle patience, and you would have taught them to dress up and sing.

Learning to live with your regrets, disappointments and mistakes is the hardest part of growing old.

I've got a million and one loose ends to tie. The book club's coming here tonight. George says he hates it when I have them over but really he likes nothing better than disappearing upstairs with a bottle of red to dance with his club.

Let's have Christmas together. Somewhere exotic. Istanbul! My shout! That's my birthday gift to you. I can't wait. You plan it. I'll bring the plum pudding and brandy butter.

Love always. Leith

Cameron folds the letter quietly, as if the rasp of paper might wake Frank, and replaces it in the side pocket of his bag. He wonders whether the police know how this marriage unsprung. The plane ploughs steadily on a south-western course while his thoughts travel helter-skelter in all directions.

SATURDAY

'Sam?' Monty sings out to the nose that's all he can see of the face hidden inside the tightly drawn hood of the jacket, worn originally by their oldest son before being passed along to each of his siblings, and now warming the back of Bernadette's latest lost soul. Sam nods and extracts one hand from his pockets in a casual wave of acknowledgement before hopping in to the blue utility.

'I'm Monty.' Sam shakes his hand, roughened, warm from the car's heating, as he gets into the passenger seat, his eyes and mouth still concealed by the folds of the jacket which he keeps zipped up for the moment. Monty notices the grey synthetic shoes that will fall apart after a day or two of labouring in the sticky clay covering the building site where they'll work, forty minutes drive away. This time last week he was getting dressed in his suit, ready to escort Leith – one beep and she'd fly out the door, sartorial, her smile on the verge of laughter, form guide in her hand. He doesn't normally do Saturdays but a mate of his has a sick kid and needs help to finish this contract on time. For once Bernadette's good deed suits him at the same time as assisting her passage through the Pearly Gates.

'Thanks for the lift,' Sam mumbles as he buckles his seatbelt, 'and the job,' he forces himself to add.

On the suburban fringe they pass timbered frames of two-storey houses sprouting like bamboo behind vast billboards with photographs of smiling couples strolling around duck-filled wetlands at the centre of developments with lyrical names.

'Let's hope you're thanking me at the end of the day.' Monty wants him to know in advance that he's allergic to bludgers. His wife's thrown him the odd dud, husbands of her foreign students, whose sinking shoulders forewarn him of an attitude problem that can't be fixed on the job. He sends them packing because as he said to her the other night, he's not a welfare agency, some kind of work-for-the-dole scheme, even though he knows she's keen for him to join her in heaven. They stop at lights.

'Done any labouring before?'

'Worked for a couple of weeks once pouring concrete.' Sam unfurls his hand from the sleeve of the jacket as if to count the stints of employment on his fingers. 'Otherwise kitchen jobs mostly – dishwashing, scrubbing pots, peeling carrots.'

Monty grunts. He's glad that at least the kid's earned a buck on the bottom rung of the occupational ladder. 'Ever work at any of those flash joints where they charge you $100 for a piece of marbled beef?'

'Nah,' Sam almost laughs. 'Pubs, convention centres, clubs.' Put like that it almost sounds as though the service industry's his natural habitat. Sam doesn't explain the winding track he's taken. Fruit pickers are a steadier bet than him. He doesn't let on about the in-between shifts, wiping windscreens, rounding up super-market trolleys.

On the radio the FM breakfast show jocks are making light of murder. They chat about a woman who doped her husband's egg sandwiches before she shot him dead in a housing estate some-where in Adelaide. 'Something must be in the ether.' 'Yeah, you're right.' 'Who was that judge in Melbourne?' The female presenter struggles for his name. 'You mean the one who thought his wife's head was a golf-ball?' laughs her offsider. 'There's a rumour that he's still on the green, three holes to go to complete the round, two under par.' Sam smiles at the gag and loosens the hood so that Monty can see his angular cheekbones and black hair, damp from his morning shower, combed back off his unshaven face.

Mighty one minute, manure the next. On Monday Kremmer was determining Sam's fate; by Saturday he's the butt of jokes, facing jail. Sam's usually the fall guy, the one spiralling undone, picking up speed in descent, but for once he's ending the week on an up, calm, in control.

Sam checks out Monty, who has his eyes on the traffic and scorn on his face.

'Mind?' Monty asks as he changes stations. This is what bugs him about Bernadette's big heartedness – having to accommodate strangers who sometimes forget or perhaps never learnt basic manners.

'Nah, go right ahead.' Sam knows his place. He's glad for the ride. He hasn't got his hands grubby yet but Angie's right, as usual: this feels good, this getting up early, going to work, leaving behind his unmade bed and his grotty flat. Who knows, maybe he'll go to college, do a course, get a qualification.

Monty puts on a country music CD he usually saves for the trip home. He doesn't care if Sam cringes at his choice. He'd sung along to it last Saturday coming back from the races and Leith had told him he was a softie. She'd owned up to The Supremes and he'd half promised to take her dancing.

'You been married long?' Sam asks.

'Longer than you've been on the planet, probably,' Monty says. 'Which is how long exactly?'

'Twenty-eight years.'

'There you go. Bernadette and I, we've been together for,' – he checks his rear-view mirror as if the answer's written on the road behind them – 'let me see, all up about thirty-four years.' Sam can't imagine sticking with anyone except for Mags. Sex complicates everything. 'You've been married, right?' Bernadette had told him what she knows of Sam's bid to spend more time with his daughter.

'Briefly,' Sam grunts, stingy with the details, embarrassed by the shoddy craft of their union.

'Bernadette tells me you've got a daughter?' Monty tries again to draw him into a dialogue but Sam stares out the window at the high wall along the freeway filtering noise and fumes from the families who live on the other side.

'Yeah,' he says.

'Hang in there,' Monty tells him, unsure whether the kid's listening. 'She's going to grow up one day, leave home, drive a car, get a job, and then she'll be the one who decides what she does, who she sees.'

Sam mumbles accord, hopeful this morning that things will turn out right, somehow.

They drive the rest of the journey in silence. When Monty turns off the freeway, slowing at the first set of lights, he tells his charge what's expected of him. 'I've got a spare pair of boots in the back that might fit you.'

'Thanks. These are my court shoes,' Sam says. 'Family court,' he adds in case Monty assumes he's been up on counts of armed robbery, or worse. 'I'm trying to get a bit more time with my daughter.' Monty slows down as they pull up behind a semitrailer stacked with plasterboard sheets.

A shiny black utility with tinted windows cruises by. The driver waves at Monty who salutes his mate before reaching his arm over the back seat to rummage for the work boots. Sam strips off his jacket and chucks it on the front seat. He clambers out, remembering Angie's advice to look keen. The boots are almost a perfect fit.

Monty stashes his wallet in the glove box and takes out a faded blue cap advertising a hardware chain. He slaps it on his curls then starts unloading tools from the back. Sam helps him. He lifts a heavy metal box and waits for Monty, who secures the cover of his trailer before grabbing a nail gun in one hand and, in his other, the foam esky that Bernadette had packed with four ham rolls (two each), apples, jam doughnuts and a thermos of coffee. Using the toe of his boot Monty kicks the car door closed. Sam walks beside him, ready for sweat, lifted by the prospect of chance. It's a feeling he's known before, too many times, but there's spine in his step and this is a new thing.

Turning into the dingy street that hems the public gardens George scrapes the hubs of his car against the curb, misjudging all dimensions in his twitchiness. There's scant traffic for a Saturday night and he cuts the engine to sit for a while and see what comes swaggering past. Black-and-white striped footy fans, ruddy from toasting victory, navigate the footpath, one of them stopping to relieve his bladder on a tree that's possibly grateful for the spray in this bone-dry season.

A thin, wiry greyhound of a male in tracksuit pants and a hooded windcheater crosses in front of George's car and scurries along a track worn into the grass between the pavement and the toilet block, which is set back at a distance. The hooded man stands restlessly outside the entrance, talking into a mobile phone. Another loner trapped in this nether world, where sex is had without the gentler caress of affection or attachment. George hasn't visited here for months, possessed tonight by a primal urge to get out of the house under the cover of darkness.

Cameron is coming tomorrow, bloated with the stinking wind of retribution. He leans his head back, closing his eyes. The night Cameron came to his room at college is like the stone doorstep into an ancient temple worn down, polished smooth, by his endless procession across its threshold, wondering where life might have taken him if he'd only dared. Cowardice pushed him in a direction he mistook for self-preservation. As it's turned out the reverse was true. He loathes the crimp in his character that surrendered to the shame of being gay, the shame of his lifetime's lie, an odium that pelts him like the hardest of rains. He thinks of suicide, the ultimate absolution: justice dispensed by his own hand, a chance to even the scales. He's got a length of hose at home in the garage.

He's read of couples who die within days of each other, one unable to thrive without the presence of the other. People would approve of a death for a death. Or, instead, would they condemn him for slithering free from his noose?

He opens his eyes as a large spider scuttles across the inside of the windscreen. George freezes. The spider inches towards the dashboard. He could kill it with his fist or his shoe. He hears them laughing at him. 'Take the spider outside, George,' his mother had teased. 'Don't kill it or you'll have bad luck.' Then the gravelly voice of his father, 'Come on, son,' handing him a sheet of paper for the spider to crawl onto so that George could carry it outside. 'Pick it up, go on, before it bites me!' His mother feigned fear, goading him. He sees his mother's lips painted blood-red, her big teeth; his father's piercing eyes like a raised whip. I'm scared, he'd wanted to yell, but they knew very well he was scared. So he'd fainted, sliding slowly to the floor as he'd practised swooning in his room, and that snapped their mouths shut.

The spider scampers up towards the rear-view mirror. George slips a leather loafer from his heel. His luck couldn't get any worse, surely? Eyes on the spider, he puts his shoe back on and takes a handkerchief from his pocket and before he can change his mind he captures the spider in its fold, holding his breath, until he gets out of the car where he shakes it free. He continues walking, avoiding eye contact with the hooded man under the eaves of the toilet block, on into the heart of the gardens canopied by the branches of the Dutch elms that form a guard of honour along his path.

Here, on the lowest rung of self-respect, he slithers one further and heads off the bitumen for the low boughs of a grey spruce beyond the cone of light thrown from the lamps. Holding on to its trunk, his head on his arms, he weeps hiccuping, desolate sobs, sliding down on to his hands and knees, prickled by the woodchips strewn around the roots to spare them from drought. His tears run, moistening his face, death firming in his mind as he sucks in breath, unaware of the bats circling or the dog that comes to sniff at his feet before bounding after its owner.

He can't leave the boys without talking to them, telling them his story, her story. He's never opened his heart to anybody, even Leith, who tried her best to teach him how to love. The thought of Jesse and Art calms him. He props himself up against the rough bark and listens to the clip of heel and toe as a couple stroll by, then the whoosh of someone on a bicycle. Gradually he recovers his wherewithal. As he gets back on his feet, he brushes the bark chips from his pants, looking up and out across the park to get his bearings before he makes for his car, eyes sweeping the entrance of the toilets out of habit. The hooded man's gone. George leaves too, resolving never to return.

SUNDAY

Outside the sky is clear blue but there's a nip in the breeze that cart-wheels the lid of a takeaway cup into the gutter at Cameron's feet. He turns up the collar of his Red Sox baseball jacket as he waits for a cab near the small hotel where they are staying. The kidney brick building used to be a showroom for Rolls Royce, these words still engraved into a sandstone frieze that mocks the modern penchant for re-branding. Cameron came here as a boy, breaking free from his mother's hand to stand nose to the glass and admire the silver grille of a fancy black Roller: white tyres, leather upholstery, bigger than an armoured tank, guzzling gas with no thought then for the climate change eerily present in this city so short of water.

He lifts his forehead where it's been resting against the window of the hotel, leaving a grease spot that he wipes with his sleeve. In the reflection he sees two young guys stroll past hand in hand. When he was their age, he wouldn't have dared. He follows the couple with his eyes, watching them whisper together, repressing an urge to hug them both or cast them in silver like the winged lady on the bonnet of a Roller as a symbol of progress.

A stooped man in a heavy coat turns the corner, trudging along the pavement towards him, a newspaper under his arm. Cameron looks away as he's learnt to do when he's short of coins because the poor in American cities always make a beeline for him. The man starts to cough, spitting a mouthful on to the street. Two taxis drive by with passengers in the back seat, and Cameron's wondering what's become of his. The man has stopped at his elbow. Cameron fingers his empty pocket, waiting to be asked for spare change.

'Cameron,' a gruff voice speaks his name. He swivels around to face the old man, afraid he won't recognise a face tattered by rough conditioning, but somehow between the lines of worry and dirt he knows him.

'Miles?' he says hesitantly. The man beams a gap-toothed grin and Cameron throws open his arms to embrace a friend he hasn't seen since university.

'How have you been?' Cameron asks him.

'Sick.' He shakes his head. A taxi pulls up. Cameron is relieved, guiltily, to be called away.

'I'm sorry about Leith,' Miles says. He grips Cameron with his sad eyes, his dishevelment a shock he doesn't often inflict on old friends. But he couldn't pass up this opportunity. Cameron performs masterfully, drinking in every detail of Miles' misfortune while seeming not to have noticed, the churning inside absent from his easy manner, struck all over again by the coincidences in a city where the degrees of separation are fractional.

'That's why I'm here. The funeral's next week.'

Miles nods.

'I'm on my way to see George.'

'I see George from time to time,' he smiles enigmatically. 'But it's all over now.'

'Where can I find you?' Cameron's too ashamed to leave without exchanging addresses.

'Round about.' His eyes narrow, bitterness in their glint. Cameron doesn't pry.

He kisses his old friend on the forehead. 'Take care.' The cab driver turns on the meter and takes off, the ghost of Miles on board even though he's waved goodbye. Scenes from childhood assault him wherever he looks. The salon their mother would visit to have her hair teased up in a beehive is now a pet shop with rainbow-striped fish in tanks the length of the window. When he was five or six, Renee – what a name – let Cameron and Leith play with wigs and curlers while his mother sat under the dryer. Renee had given Cameron his first job, sweeping up hair from the pink and grey harlequin-patterned floor, pulling handfuls of it from the plugholes of the matching ceramic basins. It was Renee who'd lent Cameron the blonde wig for his law revue skit with George. 'Camp as a row of tents,' his mother used to sneer of the hairdresser, out of his hearing. But his sexuality didn't blind her to Renee's superiority with a comb and scissors: pinkie cocked, lips drawn together in concentration, he would snip expertly against the nape of a powdered neck to trim an offending curl. Renee was the first gay man Cameron ever met. He played a small and fleeting part in their childhood but Cameron often thanks him silently for the example he set. If Renee could win over middle-class matrons, Cameron knew the torch of enlightenment could be passed from hand to hand, changing minds along the way.

The cab swings into the driveway of the Kremmer residence. Upstairs, a hand parts the curtains. On the nature strip in front, a woman waits for her dog to conclude his business, her plastic bag held ready to scoop. Cameron pays the fare, impressed all over again by the Victorian mansion with its slate roof and wrought-iron lattice festooning the grey masonry. A weeping willow that Leith planted trails the front lawn with its dreadlocks.

The curtains fall shut as George leaves his watch. Cameron's as George remembers him. His hair's greyer, but otherwise he looks young in his jeans and baseball jacket, blue-and-yellow striped sneakers on his small feet, finely boned, spritely like Leith. George brushes the dandruff from the shoulders of his black sweater, which has taken the place of the suit once worn every day, saving him from another inconsequential decision.

As Cameron lifts his hand to knock, the door opens a sliver. 'Come in,' George urges him softly through the merest of gaps.

In the cool hallway, so dark that Cameron's eyes take a moment to adjust, George abandons the greeting he's rehearsed, repelled by Cameron's frosty reserve.

He sees his sister everywhere he looks, from the raffia hat on the row of brass hooks fashioned like serpents' tails on either side of a mirrored stand, to her name in a windowed envelope, unopened on the mahogany hall table, and the wooden staircase where the two men stand uneasily, each of them on the very same spot where six days ago Leith had paused for a second before her ascent. George points towards the kitchen, bright from the sun's reach through the large north-facing windows.

'Tea?' he asks as Cameron sits on the chair where Leith liked to curl with a book. Cameron touches Leith's letter in his pocket. 'No thanks.' He'd stuffed it there as an afterthought, for good luck.

George comes around and sinks into the couch, crossing his ankles, his hands tucked under his knees. His eyes are as blue as Cameron remembers them but the piercing sadness of his bearing is a shock, more so than the silver hair, combed and parted. First Miles, now George; the rush of information in their carriage assaults Cameron, who holds a memory of both men starting out.

'I've been dreading this,' George begins, spreading the fingers of his large hands out as far as the webbing of skin permits. 'Saying sorry doesn't touch the sides of my shame.' He looks up at Cameron for a second then lifts his eyes to the ceiling. His fingers smooth the bright pink plaid fabric of the couch. 'There are things that I've held inside me for too long. Do you remember the night you came to my room in college . . .?'

'Here,' Cameron points to the pale white blemish on his lip. 'Here's where you left your mark.'

George bears no physical trace of his wounding. 'I wrote you a letter but I couldn't bring myself to post it. I was afraid of blackmail, afraid you might use it against me. I think of that night almost every day, of the road not taken. I loved Leith. I tried to make her happy. I lived my lie as faithfully as I could.'

Cameron looks out the window at the rosemary bush that Leith said she'd grown from a cutting in memory of their mother. 'You didn't fool Leith,' he finally says.

'I did my best. I stayed true to the path I'd chosen.'

'And then when she was ready to fly you took aim.'

'I didn't know she was leaving me.' George gets to his feet. 'She didn't tell me. This week, alone in the house, I went looking for her. Things are missing; her diaries, the photograph of you and her when you were teenagers, your grandfather's tobacco tin. I'm presuming that's why she came upstairs, fuelled with champagne from the book club. This morning a coin from the pocket of my pants rolled under the bed. When I went after it, I found a suitcase there. She'd packed clothes, her birth certificate, passport, good-luck charms, pictures of the children, a bottle of her favourite olive oil' – this culinary detail is so Leith that they both feel a contradictory urge to laugh and weep, endearment and sorrow, bittersweet. Returning to the moment, George adds, 'There's even the photograph of her with you.'

Winded by Leith's escape from this cocked-up mess of a marriage, Cameron sits without listening to the why or wherefore.

'There was no row. There was no passion to light a blazing set-to. I didn't strike her out of anger or jealousy or fear. That's the horror of it.' He waits for Cameron's blow, his body squared for violence. When he opens his eyes Cameron is crying. George doesn't dare ask forgiveness. Instead he goes to Cameron's side and takes his hand because he has to start somewhere and solace seems a good place to grow from, to heal, his heart ruling his head, remaking a man.

MONDAY LAST

Outside George's door, Leith rides the lulls between each whack of the club, choosing her moment. Silence falls and she turns the handle to go in.

George is reading from a book open on the bench, a club in one hand, the other wrapped around the top of a wine bottle.

'George,' she raises her voice. He lifts his head from the page, bewildered by her materialising like this.

'What's up?' He's tired, impatient. The wine has compromised the movement of his swing through the Gate, inside-to-out.

'We need to talk.'

'I thought you'd be done with talking. You've been at it for hours down there.'

'It's about us.'

'Us?' He's unprepared. 'Now?' he pleads, looking at his watch. She can only mean one thing.

'Can I sit down?'

'Don't be daft, of course you can. Is that what I've reduced you to, a mouse of a woman who begs permission to sit in her own house?'

In the hub of the room he has annexed she feels an intruder, timidity draining her purpose. The light catches a photograph of Tiger Woods on the wall, his eyes below the peak of his white hat keenly tracking the ball he's just whacked. Floor-to-ceiling bookshelves are filled with titles and authors Leith's never read; *The Swing*; *Getting Back to Basics*; *The Best Golf Tips Ever*. They seem to her insufficient subjects for volumes bigger than the Old Testament.

George empties the dregs of the Grange into his glass, disappointed to be finishing the bottle just when he most wants its succour. She doesn't know whether to sit or not so she stands there with her hand on the back of a chair, watching him as he toys with his club, positioning his beautiful leather brogues on the stretch of fake turf she'd had laid at his bidding.

Histrionics aren't her style. She hadn't wanted to shout or scream, certain her arrival here would smack him to attention. Why not just up and leave without any explanation? The wild thought pilots her turn towards the door.

George is relieved by her quiet departure. One more night, one more day, won't matter. One more stroke. He concentrates on the mechanics of his shoulders and his hips and the shifting of weight from one plane to another as he takes the club back without twisting his body. Leith stops. She can't sneak out on the deadline she set herself. She turns around slowly to face him but his eyes are closed as his club completes its swing through the Gate in a perfect movement.

He sees too late the damage done.

At night George recites poetry from memory to coax sleep but in these flickering seconds between two worlds his torment deposits him cruelly at the dawn of that day. His morning duel with Sam Dunlop was a Shakespearean omen, presaging a king's downfall, so he reverses the bearer by allowing Sam to speak first, airing grievances about his daughter to hold the kite string of hope. Then, instead of visiting Sotheby's, George goes home to Leith. Over dinner they discuss their future. He tells her he's gay. She owns up to her affair in a tidy honourable ending to their marriage. But no matter how he reconfigures the truth with these inventions, it tears and scratches at him.

Thiess - eng many cos
  - Kevine sanders
    - Abdul Jarrah
      - Chevmas y wri
      Div y large
      y egineerig

ACKNOWLEDGEMENTS

If it takes a village to raise a child so a book is bound with encouragement from many quarters. In my writing I am drawn to the front line of family life and I'm grateful to every person who has shared their stories and enriched my understanding of relationships. Paul Guest is not responsible for my insights into the Family Court but he gave me a foot in the door; to the members of book clubs in Washington, Sydney and Melbourne, thank you for the privilege; to my colleagues, my friends, and my extended family for propping me up; to my literary agent, Mary Cunnane, for her wisdom; to Kirsten Abbott of Penguin for inspired editorial guidance; to Nicci Dodanwela, a goddess of small details; to my husband Gregory who keeps swinging his club in our hallway and might one day get lucky; to our sons, Jack and Tom, may love bless you.

Matt Gale
matt.gale@ntschools.net
Teaching Principal
Nganambala School
Northern Territory.